The ether wind

filled the sails immediately, and the galleon, in a smooth majestic movement, responded by swinging round to present her bottom to the sun. For a short time she oscillated to and fro, like a pendulum, but then became rock steady.

There was a long pause in which no one moved. Every man gazed about him and saw a sight that perhaps had been familiar to his grandfather. Earth shone to port, a stunningly beautiful shield. Farther off floated the moon, small and brilliant.

The sun could not be seen. It was below the hull, yet the scene on deck was far from dark. Apart from the glow of Earth and moon, there was a shimmering blue radiance cast down from the sails.

A more fanciful ship would never have made it, the captain told himself proudly. To one side of the taut sails he found a prominent red spot, and stared at it avidly and hungrily, for a long time.

Mars, angry, challenging Mars, stared back.

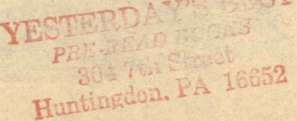

STAR WINDS

Barrington J. Bayley

DAW BOOKS, INC.
DONALD A. WOLLHEIM, PUBLISHER

1301 Avenue of the Americas
New York, N. Y. 10019

Copyright ©, 1978, by Barrington J. Bayley.

All Rights Reserved.

Cover art by David Bergen.

First printing, June 1978

1 2 3 4 5 6 7 8 9

Printed in U.S.A.

Chapter ONE

As the shrill whistling sound began to pierce the air, the customers drinking in the Pivot Inn glanced roofward and peered with interest through the engraved windows. Then, abandoning their tankards, they streamed out into the street to scan the sky for the source of the noise.

They soon saw what they were looking for. A big sailship was riding low over the tiled roofs of Olam, leaning at a perilous angle and making unsteady progress. The Pivot Inn's landlord, who had also rushed out onto the pavement, shook his fist. "She's breaking the law!" he shouted excitedly. "She's breaking the law!" No one took any notice of him; everyone knew it was illegal to spread ether silk this close to town.

As the ship approached the inn the whistling became a shriek fit to curdle the brain. Hands were clapped to ears, faces contorted, and most present squeezed shut their eyes. Rachad Caban, however, kept his gaze steadfastly on the vessel, even though the unearthly shrieking seemed to be shaking his innards to shreds. She was a galleon, square-cut at stem and stern, which were raked to allow her to cut easily through the air. Her underbooms had already been taken in to prepare for a landing on spring-mounted runners, but aloft and on the outriggers she spread a full set of bellying canvas, angled to achieve a parachute effect on the descent to the ship field. Clearly, however, she was in trouble. Somehow her master had bungled the approach to the field, and finding himself losing altitude too quickly he had—completely against regulations—run up too large ether sails whose silky blue sparkle could be seen standing out among all the white windsail. Catching the ether currents now, the ship steadied and soared over the rooftops, narrowly clearing the spire of the cathedral.

There was good reason for the ban on ether sail at such low altitude—over towns, anyway. The impedimentary waves the sails caused in the luminiferous ether, whose currents they trapped to gain momentum, rebounded against the bulking mass of the ground to set up an interference effect. The result was a high-pitched sound vibration in the atmosphere which now, ringing even louder as the galleon sailed overhead, caused all below to fall to their knees in agony.

The drill-like pain abated as the ship receded. The townsfolk came to their feet gasping. Rachad still watched the galleon. A flying sailship was always a stirring sight, with its carved and painted woodwork, its masses of sail, spars and rigging to which men clung with careless-seeming skill.

"What a goddam awful row," muttered a fat, bald man who still clutched his head.

"That's right," Rachad said lightly. "Earth and ether don't mix."

A sailor who had been drinking at the bar, wearing a hip-length crimson jacket and chunky earrings, burst out laughing. "That's Captain Zhorga's ship, the *Wandering Queen*. He'll get it in the neck from the Portmaster for this, that's sure. That old devil's always in trouble—if he can't make a landing under canvas he's about done, I reckon."

Rachad went back into the Pivot where he had left his drink. But he made a face when he tasted it: the etheric disturbance had turned the beer completely flat. After a moment's thought he decided against ordering another, since the landlord might well find his entire stock ruined.

He left the inn and made his way downhill toward the lower part of the town. Rachad was a youngish man of not unpleasing appearance whose dark eyes roved restlessly, some might have said roguishly. His disposition did not belie this impression. By nature he was adventurous, but found it a misfortune to be living in a tame and quiet world. He spent much time hanging about the ship field and drinking in the taverns frequented by sailors, and would have liked to have been a man of the air himself. In his teens he had tried to get himself taken on by various merchant ships, but already there had not been enough work for seasoned sailors, let alone untrained boys.

Sadly, the great age of flying sail was drawing to a close. The reason for this was that there were no new supplies of ether silk, the marvelous material that interacted with the ether in such a way as to be opaque to its winds and currents, deriving inertia from them as canvas does from the atmospheric wind. Earth had declined so much in its level of trade that all space-faring traffic, which had brought the silk here originally, had long fallen off. Nor could the silk be made locally—Earth was too close to the sun to allow it to crystallize properly. In consequence all ether sails now in use were at the very least a generation old, more often centuries old. Every sheet lost, every sheet torn, meant the loss of yet more irreplaceable sailing power. Rachad could not say how long had passed since the last flying ship had been built, but he had heard that down on the coast at Umbuicour they were laying the keels of seagoing ships relying entirely on wind-driven canvas and unable to take to the air at all.

But that, of course, was only to speak of Earth, a decaying backwater planet which no one from outside visited any more. What was happening on other worlds it was impossible to say. Perhaps their skies were crammed with scudding sail. Rachad had even heard of worlds where the wind blew so strong that canvas alone was enough to lift the heaviest ships, which used ether silk only for steering and tacking.

Coming to Marekama Street, he walked between gable-ended, half-timbered buildings that the weak autumn sunlight invested with a sense of nostalgia. Olam was an old town that had prospered because its geographical location in relation to the seasonal ether winds made it an ideal port nearly all the year round. Rachad had lived all his life there, and even in that time he had seen its outer suburbs begin to empty and the seedy process of decay and obsolescence begin to set in.

A movement over the rooftops caught his eye. In the distance a ship was maneuvering into its landing approach. There was a sudden flowering of white canvas and a glinting flash of blue as the ether sails were simultaneously reefed.

Sooner or later he must leave Olam, Rachad told himself for the hundredth time. He thought of cities across the world that were little more than names to him, larger than Olam and still offering a greater wealth of experience. Perhaps he would go to Umbuicour and try to get work on the new sea ships. But somehow such slow, lumbering vessels did not attract him.

Presently he came to the marketplace and wandered for a time between the stalls. He lingered beneath the awnings of merchants who had recently brought in consignments of garments from foreign lands, fingering the rich velvets and satins and admiring the gallant styles. By contrast, he glanced down at his own costume. His green woollen tunic was faded and was fastened with worn cords which left it a couple of inches open at the chest, showing a mat of curly blond hair. He could have used a new pair of breeks, too; however, all this fine garb was beyond his present means. Perhaps if Gebeth were to succeed. . . . He paused also at a nearby armorer's shop and inspected various swords and foils. This engraved blade, now, with a scabbard plated with tortoise-shell and mother-of-pearl, would lend him considerable dash. But he reflected that, even leaving aside the cost, it might advertise to others an exaggerated self-esteem and so lead to his having to use it, which was far from his desire. The short poniard he already carried was jaunty enough, with its copper pommel, and did not invite challenges.

A curious thought occurred to Rachad. When air traffic eventually dwindled into insignificance—as it must—Olam would lose its place altogether. All these goods, for which it was currently a center of distribution, would come instead through Umbuicour. In his imagination Rachad could see Olam as a tumbledown ghost town whose few inhabitants reminisced sadly about the past.

He sighed and under the armorer's watchful eye carefully replaced the slender sword. Then he left the marketplace and walked into the old part of the town where the houses were mostly of blackened timber, picturesque and ancient, until he came to the Street of the Alchemists.

In an earlier generation the street had, as its name implied, been a coterie of those who delved into the secrets of matter and labored to find the Philosopher's Stone. Those who came after them had shown only a cursory interest in such long and fruitless researches, and the street was stocked instead with practitioners of related matters—apothecaries, metalsmiths and the like. In the whole avenue there was only one proper devotee of the ancient art, and that was Gebeth, whom Rachad referred to as his mentor, in his more flamboyant moments.

As in much of this quarter the street was laid with loose sand instead of with cobbles, for such had been the custom in older times. Rachad passed by the open workshop of a maker of bronze door-knockers and, at the next house, had occasion to make use of a sample of the same man's work: a large heavy knocker fashioned in the form of Mercury, the winged messenger and symbol of quicksilver, which he pounded decisively against the thick plank door.

He had to pound a second time before there came a scraping of wood on wood from within and the door eased open. Standing in dimness, because of the shuttered windows, was the man he knew only as Gebeth the alchemist.

"Good day, sir," Rachad said brightly.

The other grunted in displeased fashion. "Oh, it's you. You'd better come in."

Rachad followed him into a small living room which, despite the bright sunshine outside, had as its only illumination a small oil lamp on a book-strewn table in the corner. Gebeth liked to shut himself away from the outside world, to ponder, study and work in quiet solitude.

The alchemist seated himself at the table, where he had evidently been reading when interrupted by Rachad. He was a man advanced in years, his face much lined by the effort of prolonged thought. His hair was white and wispy. His eyes had an introspective look, as of one given to daydreams, but when they settled on Rachad they were steady and challenging.

"And to what do I owe this unexpected visit?"

"I am here for the same reason as always, Gebeth."

"I have not seen you in three days," the older man said, disgruntled. "With such laxness you will not learn much, and why should I bother to teach you?"

"Do not be displeased with me, sir," Rachad said defensively. "I have been working to earn money. See, I have brought you a sum to help further your work."

Gebeth inspected the coins he handed over, and glanced at Rachad suspiciously. Rachad's countenance remained bland; in point of fact, the money was a part of his share in the spoils of a minor escapade—theft from a warehouse near the airfield—but he did not wish Gebeth to know that. Financing his research was a continual problem for the old man and Rachad regarded it as in his best interests to help whenever he could.

Gebeth sighed and waved a hand as if waving away the fumes of his former bad humor. In all honesty he could not regard Rachad seriously as an apprentice in the Hermetic Art. The boy was flighty and volatile, and little interested in abstract matters. Nevertheless he was useful as an assistant, which was one reason why Gebeth had kept him on. A certain amount of grumbling over his defections was an integral part of their relationship and not at all harmful. He had even managed to teach Rachad a smattering of alchemical lore.

He closed the book he had been studying, marking his place, and rose to his feet.

"Come."

With a key from the pocket of his gown he unlocked a door to a short, dark corridor leading to the rear of the house. At the end of it he unlocked a second door. Rachad's nostrils were assailed by various acrid odors, predominantly the smell of burning sulphur.

Unlike the living room, the laboratory took advantage of natural light which came through smoky glass panels in the sloping roof. It was also uncomfortably hot. Each degree of heat required a different furnace and Gebeth had half a dozen, three of which were currently stoked.

Besides the furnaces the room contained a fantastic clutter of alembics, retorts and cucurbics, crucibles and mortars, and more elaborate apparatus such as the kerotakides for performing projection, which had been used recently for it stood blackened on the workbench, and the infusorator, a cumbersome piece of equipment incorporating plates of zinc and copper bathed in acid. Gebeth crossed to the other side of the laboratory and returned with a slab of something gleaming. "This I made today by projecting mercury on sulphur."

Rachad accepted the object and inspected it. It was yellow, with a red tint; heavy and with the feel of metal. He gasped involuntarily as he turned it over, rubbing it and holding it to the light. His eyes widened with excitement and triumph.

"You have succeeded at last! You have made gold!"

With a sour smile Gebeth took back the slab. "Not gold. This is merely a form of cinnabar, which I have given some of the properties of gold. But it is not gold."

Rachad looked crestfallen, and stuck out his lower lip in a pout.

"All metals, as you know, are compounded of mercury and sulphur in various ratios," Gebeth said, "so theoretically any metal can be transformed into any other by altering those ratios. That mercury and sulphur can, by marrying, yield cinnabar, would seem to confirm this fact. Yet others besides myself have gone down this road, tinting and projecting for years on end without finding true gold at the end of it. Without preparing the tincture itself, nothing can be done."

"So?" Rachad frowned. He knew the alchemist was leading to something.

"Look at me, Rachad. I am an old man. For nearly forty years I have been on this quest, trying to turn base metal into gold. But where is my gold? Do you want to expend your life likewise, Rachad? You are not properly into the hunt yet. But once it grips your soul—" Gebeth clenched his fist convulsively. "It will not let go. My advice is to leave the great work alone."

"I have never heard you speak like this before, sir," said Rachad in a disappointed and surly tone. "You have been full of encouragement up until now."

"True, but in the past few days I have reached a momentous conclusion. Never will I make gold. Never will I have the Tincture that heals metals in my posession. Of that I am certain." The old man's voice was dry with a defeat that he had forced himself to face up to.

Rachad instantly wished that he had withheld the money he had just given Gebeth, but the thought was squashed in his general dismay. "But you have been so close," he protested weakly.

"Hundreds of others have been as close. How many have made gold?" Gebeth took out his key ring again, and moved to a wall safe which he opened with considerable squeaking and clanging of steel. Carefully, as if handling something precious, he took out a stiff, bulky book. "There are definite reasons for my decision, which means that as from today I shall probably abandon my efforts—the last in the street to do so." He paused and his eyes went dreamy, as though he remembered past colleagues and neighbors. "It is only fair that I should explain why. Four years ago this rare book came into my possession. Few copies of it exist in the whole world, and I am showing it to you now only in the belief that you can hold your tongue and speak of it to no one."

Dumbly Rachad nodded.

"Let us return to the other room," Gebeth said.

Back in the living room the alchemist laid the book on the table under the lamp. Rachad saw now that though the book was large in area it actually had few pages, but that these were thick and stiff. The binding was of beaten copper and was engraved with letters and figures in some foreign script he did not recognize.

Gebeth opened the book and began to show him some of its pages, which were closely lettered in the same strange language or else finely colored in beautiful and mysterious pictures, usually several pictures to a page, though sometimes a whole page was devoted to a single illustration. One or two of the figures had some meaning for Rachad—such as the figure of mercury, and the caduceus, a staff entwined with two serpents, which filled the seventh page—but most were completely baffling to him. Then again some of the illustrations of alchemical vessels which accompanied the text were familiar to him, but they were followed by glowing scenes which were wholly symbolic. On a high mountain grew a flower with a blue stalk, sporting white and red flowers and golden leaves, and shaken by the wind while dragons and griffins nested around it. In another picture a king and his soldiers slaughtered many young children, gathering their blood in a vessel in which the sun and the moon bathed.

Gebeth kept silent while Rachad pored over the pages.

"An interesting story accompanies this volume," he said when the younger man had closed the end cover. "The book is known to have existed nearly four thousand years ago when by chance it came into the hands of one Nicolas Flamel and his wife Perrenelle, who lived in a country then called France. For twenty-one years Flamel tried to carry out the instructions in the book, but could not decipher the symbols for the First Agents, which as you see are very cryptic, and the advice of learned men in this respect only led him astray. Finally he journeyed to another country called Spain, where he found a man able to understand the symbols and explain the text. Unfortunately this man died before explaining everything, but by now Flamel had learned enough to be able to discover the rest for himself, and after a further five years of research he completed the tincture. By projecting it onto mercury he was able to make both silver and gold better than that from the mine."

"Do you believe this story?" Rachad asked, running his fingertips lightly over the copper binding of the book.

Gebeth nodded. "For one who has studied the book it has the ring of truth. I have applied myself to it for four years now, and like Flamel know that I shall never comprehend it without help. Yet I am convinced that here is the secret of the preparation of the Tincture."

"And you are going to give up?" Rachad said incredulously.

"Yes."

"But here it is," breathed Rachad. He held the book in his hands reverently, his eyes darting here and there over the engraved surface. "All we have to do is find someone who understands it."

"That is just the point. There is no one on Earth who understands it. That I have already ascertained insofar as I am able. Yet recently I heard where the necessary explanations may be found."

"Where?" demanded Rachad, his eyes flashing. "Tell me where and I shall bring them to you—that I swear!"

"You are too rash, my friend, far too rash," Gebeth said with a smile. "Three days ago I was visited by an itinerant scholar, one of those strange people who wander about the world gathering knowledge here, there and everywhere. His conversation proved him to be knowledgeable in alchemical matters—indeed in all sciences. After some deliberation I spoke of the book to him. He already knew of it, and was greatly interested as he had never seen a copy and asked me if I could obtain this book. So eventually I showed it to him and he studied it for two hours. He then said that, to save me from further decades of fruitless toil, he would tell me a secret known to very few, which he had learned from the high priest of the Temple of the Holy Ciborium, a religious order dwelling in the city of Kalek-Tepek. This order itself sprang from alchemical origins many centuries ago, though it no longer practices the art. At any rate, it was disclosed to my visitor that there exists a second book, written by one coming long after Nicholas Flamel—something like two thousand years after. This book explains the hidden meanings in the first book, supplying the missing signs and containing much else besides. Furthermore, it is explicit enough to be deciphered by one well versed in the field. But only one copy exists, and it will never be found. It is in a secret hiding place in the Temple of Hermes Trismegistus, which is in Kars, a city in Syrtis Major."

"Syrtis Major?"

"A region of Mars."

Rachad looked stricken. "Mars!"

Gebeth nodded. "A planet at one time famous as a center of alchemical researches, even more so than Earth. Many are the tales of marvelous transmutations accomplished there. But do you see the irony? The one possibility of achieving our aim lies far, far beyond our reach."

In imparting this precious information Gebeth had a definite aim. He wished to persuade the boy once and for all of the hopelessness of seeking alchemical gold, before his ambitions gelled in that direction. Gebeth knew from personal experience what happened once that fever took hold. He thought of his past labors and fell to dreaming once more, his eyes glazed. Calcination, sublimation, solution, putrefaction, distillation, coagulation . . . he had mastered all these main operations, as well as the adjunctive ones—congelation, fixation, ceration, projection, infusoration, and so on. He had spent much money on obtaining the textbooks of this numinous work and had a library of which he was proud.

One needed to be an artist, too, to comprehend these texts. How else would one know that the silvery water, the divine water, the ever-fugitive, the seed of the dragon, the water of the moon, the milk of the black cow, were all names of mercury, or quicksilver?

A fragment of a poem from one of his manuals drifted through his mind:

... A dragon springs therefrom, which when exposed to heat,
Devours his tail till naught thereof remains.
This dragon, whom they Ouroborous or Tail-Biter call,
Is white in looks and spotted in his skin,
And has a form and shape most strange to see.

What layman, by following this poem, would be able to alloy copper and silver, heating them in the presence of mercury which bound them into a single white amalgam?

Gebeth had tried hundreds of recipes for the making of gold, generally useless and even fraudulent, which could be obtained from spurious books or from "alchemists" who were little more than tricksters. He had learned the hard way how to distinguish those works which were genuine and imparted real knowledge. Among these were *The Sophic Hydrolith* and *The Chariot of Antimony*. He well remembered how, by following these and other authenticated works, he had embarked upon a detailed procedure for preparing the Tincture. In the course of a process lasting several months he had observed with excitement the predicted color changes, first to the deep black known as the Raven's Head, then going through a reddish phase, then from the Peacock's Tail with its white, green and yellow spots, to the deep red Blood of the Dragon. Then, sealed in a transparent receptacle of rock crystal, the preparation had been subjected to the most intense heat. At last it had transformed itself into the Raven's Wing—a semi-gaseous, semi-liquid haze of glorious purple color that swirled and raved, the penultimate step, so the books said, in the creation of the Tincture. Yet try as he might Gebeth had not, after cooling and breaking open the receptacle, been able to accomplish the final stage. Several times he had started anew and repeated the whole procedure, believing that his ingredients had not been purified enough—and once wrecking his laboratory when the crystal vessel exploded —before admitting failure and immersing himself in yet more study.

On the other hand his career had not been without its joyous moments. He had, for instance, isolated the essence of animal vitality. This he had done by boiling off large quantities of urine until a residue remained. Upon his opening the vessel and exposing it to the air this residue had instantly flared up to flood the entire room with a vivid white glow eerie to behold, which had caused him much wonderment. The manual he had consulted for the experiment called this unstable substance phosphorus, explaining that it was almost unique among the compounds of earth and fire in being earth in which was mixed enormous amounts of fire in its purest state. So easily did this fire flee its corporeal prison that phosphorous constituted the natural essence for animating the body; it was responsible even for bodily warmth. Needless to say, Gebeth had been immensely impressed by this example of how subtle and variegated were the admixtures between the five elements earth, water, air, fire and ether.

Rachad was staring blankly at the tabletop. "Well, isn't that real hard luck, sir? To learn a thing like that and not be able to do anything about it."

"I imagine I would never have received the information if it had been at all possible to act on it," Gebeth said resignedly. "The high priest of the Holy Ciborium would not have disclosed the tale, nor would my itinerant visitor have disclosed it to me, were not the Temple of Hermes Trismegistus wholly inaccessible. Only worthless knowledge is gained so easily."

Gebeth smiled. Rachad's chief interest in the business was plain to see, of course. He lusted after gold. That was the reason why he had so eagerly apprenticed himself to Gebeth.

And at the beginning, Gebeth reminded himself, he too had been driven by that hunger, almost to the exclusion of everything else. But time and decades of work had somehow wrought a change. He sought the stone by this time not merely for the wealth it would bring—he was old, now, and how much good could that wealth do him? —but for the glory of succeeding in the Great Work, for the sake of verifying with his own eyes that base metal could be transmuted into gold, and for the joy of seeing the secret operations of nature laid bare in his very own vessels. He could not say just when this change had come about. It had emerged gradually over the years.

"Mars!" exclaimed Rachad in a savage tone, thumping the table with frustration.

Outside the shuttered room, the sun sank slowly in the west.

Chapter TWO

Captain Zebandar Zhorga came out of the Portmaster's office wearing a glum face. He muttered a few curses for the man, glancing back at the office's lighted windows, then padded with his lumbering gait across the beaten earth of the field.

Captain Zhorga was a man whose qualities could all be summed up in one word: bluntness. His approach to problems was always direct, often clumsily so. His weather-beaten face showed this, with its heavy-lidded, slightly bulging eyes and powerful nose that was corrugated through having been broken twice. The hairs of his beard were like stiff black wires, though fringed with gray.

He had always been an air sailor. In his time he had been a fighting man, an armed midshipman in the world's last flying navy. But that was all in the past now. As he would put it, "The world hasn't got the guts for a decent war any more." Fighting with ether sail was no longer a going proposition, all available silk having been pressed into commerce. So he had become a merchant, and in time had bought his own ship, though it had nearly broken his back paying off the installments.

The panorama of the ship-strewn field was still visible in the dusk, which was enlivened by the light of numerous lamps. From the decks of craft of all kinds—galleons, clippers, chebecs, cogs—a forest of topmasts raked the darkening sky. There was even a schooner, a relatively rare type of vessel whose highly skilled crews made use of the "ground currents" that raced along close to the Earth's surface during the hours of daylight. Over one or two hulls repairmen swarmed with much hammering and calling, while from others rose the merry sound of pipes and of singing. Most, however, were silent and dark, guarded by ground watches.

And on the margin of the vast field the rotting hulks of boomers and jammers, giant ships of bygone times, loomed against the fading sky. There was no ship owner alive who could gather together enough sail to loft one of those great hulls now. Indeed, were an air sailor of an earlier generation able to inspect some of the craft on which the world's trade depended these days, he would probably have shaken his head with dismay.

The crudest type of ether rig was the balloon jib, which was used by the comparatively primitive cogs, many of which were mastless. Consisting of a single square (or sometimes triangular) sail set before the bow, the balloon jib simply dragged its load along behind it. The principle was somewhat further elaborated in the three-masted barquentine. Here the balloon jib, still carried before the bow, was raised on the foremast, the foot being lashed to radiating hullsprits, while mid and aft masts carried fore-and-aft canvas sail—a neat combination of wind and ether which greatly increased maneuverability.

But it was in ships like the galleon and the clipper that the science of sail really came into its own. Permanent masts on top, shipable sprits and booms below and around, these ships could so completely shroud themselves in sail that they resembled scudding clouds. Except in the chebec, which boasted upright masts and elegant lateens, topmasts were always raked. Mounted on movable block-and-beam arrangements, they could take up any angle of slant—for flying a sailship was a delicate matter of balance and the ship behaved aerodynamically like a free-flying kite. Yards could carry either silk or canvas, or both together in any combination. A ship could "keel" herself on the wind and tack against the ether, or vice versa. More simply, she could play wind against ether to move in practically any third direction, aided by a large rudder made of laminated wood or metal wrapped in ether silk.

There were other complications, of course. Since ship fields were invariably located on the outskirts of large towns, landing and takeoff presented the nuisance of ether whistle. Landing was less of a problem, since any crew worth its salt could put a ship safely on the ground using canvas alone, furling all ether sail just before entering the land-ether interference band. Takeoff, though, clearly could not be accomplished with canvas. One answer was to loft ships by means of huge gas or hot-air balloons, and only then to spread their silk. The simpler recourse adopted here in Olam was to restrict departure to a certain time of day (dawn in this case) when ships could gain altitude quickly without having to pass over the town. During that period, of course, everyone in the immediate vicinity wore earplugs.

Zhorga paused in front of his own ship, the *Wandering Queen*. Her timbers were in fairly good shape, but little else could be said for her. As on most other ships these days, her ether sails—what there was of them—were a mass of patches and sewn-up rents. For some time Zhorga had been flying overburdened and now, as he was forced to recognize, he had hit rock-bottom.

He hesitated, his mind half made up to go aboard, but instead he raised his gaze to the sky. In the clear night air the stars were strengthening; low over the horizon, visible even through the light of the lamps, shone a glowering red spot. Zhorga stared at the red planet, a reckless idea forming in his mind.

Then he began to curse again, the oaths becoming a monotonous grumble in his throat, and at length, an expression of disgust on his face, he turned and trudged away.

On the town side of the field, half a mile away, he approached a lone building outlined against the dusk. The building's narrow windows glowed from the light within, and were composed of strips of colored glass. A painted signboard picturing a clipper hung outside the door. The tavern was named, appropriately enough, The Ship.

Zhorga pushed open the door and let the comforting noise and confusion of the taproom sweep over him. The lamplight gleamed on burnished oak ceiling beams, pewter tankards and teak tables. Many of his crew were already there, including his first mate, Clabert. He ignored them and shouldered his way to the counter.

"Give me a bottle of ombril."

Clutching the bottle of pale orange spirit he moved to a table where other air captains sat in a huddle. Zhorga had some esteem among them; few owned their own ships as he did, but captained the vessels of merchants. He sat down grumpily, answering their greetings with grunts. The ombril, with its bitter, fiery taste, slid down his throat and warmed his stomach, sending heady fumes to his brain.

The talk was of the increasing tribulations facing the

air trade, and more specifically, of piracy. There had always been such depradations, of course, but latterly it had a different object. Pirates sought to rob ships, not of the cargoes they carried, but primarily of the ether sail on their masts.

"I heard that Ringebass was forced down in the Sanaman Desert, and every scrap of silk taken from him," said Hindemage, a scrawny and uncommonly ugly individual with a glaucomous left eye and a dirty red bandanna under his captain's hat. "He and his men would have died of thirst if a camel caravan hadn't come upon them."

This information prompted Zhorga to join in. "That's terrible. Something ought to be done," he said, choosing to forget that not too long ago, espying a small bark when on the other side of the world, he had done the same thing himself for what bit of ether silk was bent to her yard.

Everyone knew of his escapade over Olam that afternoon, and that he had been called to the Portmaster. But when asked about it Zhorga merely scowled and refused to speak, until he started on his second bottle of ombril, by which time drink had loosened his tongue.

"Business is all over," he said in a heavily laden voice. "I haven't got enough sail to carry a decent cargo any more. We damn near came down in the ocean a few days ago. Had to throw part of my freight overboard." To sink in the sea, now, that would be a disgrace. As it was the trip had left him without a penny of profit.

"What's the Portmaster have to say?" asked Hindemage, repeating someone else's question.

"Wasn't my fault," announced Zhorga grudgingly. "I'm short on good sail, that's all. I don't have a single piece that's without holes in it." In fact the Portmaster had imposed a swingeing return fine, which meant that next time Zhorga landed at Olam he would either have to pay it or have his ship impounded.

The others turned from him in that slightly awkward manner of those who see a defeated man in their midst. This tweaked Zhorga's pride, and it was for this reason, perhaps, that he blurted out his next words so impulsively.

"There's only one thing wrong, and that's that there's no silk to be had. The solution's obvious. All we have to do is get fresh silk."

"Oh yes, that's all." Everyone smiled and turned to new topics.

"I know where to get some," Zhorga interrupted forcefully, angered that he should be ignored.

Instantly he was the center of attention. Hindemage leaned close, sly and concerned. "Where?"

"Mars," Zhorga stated.

This time he elicited derisive laughter. Even Hindemage grinned crookedly, a chuckle escaping his lips. Zhorga reddened.

"What's the matter, you never heard of the place?" he roared.

"We've heard of it," Hindemage said mildly. "No one's been there since I was a boy. As a matter of fact there are no spacefaring ships in existence now, as far as I am aware."

Zhorga shrugged. "In principle there's no reason why any large, well-built ship shouldn't make the journey, provided she has ether sail enough. An air-sailing ship could be caulked for the voyage—"

"Principles are one thing, facts are another," Hindemage said quietly. "The notion is madness. The chances of getting to Mars and back in one of our ships are negligible."

"Even supposing there's silk to be had there," put in Ench, a squat bald man who captained a clipper. "If there is, why does no one from there ever come here?"

"Who the hell would want to come here?" rumbled Zhorga into his beard, and placing the palms of his hands on the table, he pushed himself to his feet and walked unsteadily toward the back of the tavern.

Outside, he relieved himself at the urinal and was about to return to the taproom when a slim figure accosted him. "Sir, may I speak to you?"

Zhorga looked at a fair-haired young man in a faded green tunic. The face was alert and mobile, eager one might say, and the hands rested on a wide leather belt.

"Who in hell might you be?"

"My name is Rachad Caban, Captain. Allow me to offer all assistance in your project. I overheard your conversation of a few minutes ago—"

"What on Earth are you talking about?" Zhorga screwed up his face, looking at Rachad suspiciously.

"Why, your voyage to Mars, Captain."

Zhorga gazed briefly at the red planet which still hung low in the sky. "What are you, a loon? What makes you think I can sail my ship millions of miles through space? I was joking, you fool."

"Since no one has tried, who's to say it can't be done?" Rachad rushed on, the words tumbling out of his mouth. "You will need a good astrologer to chart your course. Let me recommend my mentor, Gebeth the Alchemist. Gebeth can also advise you concerning chemical provisioning, so that we shall have sufficient air for the journey, as well as on other matters. Gebeth is learned in many ancient arts."

"We?" questioned Zhorga. "What is this *we?*"

"I will be honored to take part in the venture."

"A fool indeed, longing after a fool's fancies." Zhorga belched, steadied himself, then pushed past Rachad and into the tavern.

"Have you resigned yourself to a life on the ground, then?" Rachad called after him tauntingly, then skipped after him to make a final thrust.

"Remember, there is almost certainly ether silk on Mars, or indeed elsewhere in the solar family," he urged when they were just inside the door. "Also—Mars is nearing conjunction, which will bring it nearer to Earth than for several years to come."

"Anyone bringing back a cargo of silk from Mars at this time would make himself rich," Zhorga nodded in agreement. "It's unlikely anyone else would repeat the feat until the next conjunction."

These thoughts had already occurred, casually and glancingly as it were, in Zhorga's mind. Mars had been the main supplier of ether silk in olden times, for it lay far enough from the sun to make crystallization of the substance feasible. Zhorga reasoned that Mars had probably declined in the same way Earth had, with commerce falling off and interest in the outside universe fading. Nevertheless there would still be some traffic on Mars itself, as there was on Earth, unless civilization had collapsed altogether. So it was likely that silk was still being made there.

Sailing the *Wandering Queen* to Mars had been a wild, daredevil idea that Zhorga had conceived as being the only way out of his difficulties. It was a do-or-die idea— Zhorga would either succeed and make his fortune, or go out in a blaze of glory. Better than mouldering away on the ground, anyway, in his view.

But common scorn for the suggestion had caused it to be stillborn in his mind. Until, that was, he came back into the taproom, with Rachad still arguing at his elbow, to be greeted with general uproarious amusement.

"Captain Zhorga, the Martian ambassador!"

"Look out for space monsters, Captain!"

"He's the original monster himself!"

Zhorga glowered and went purple. His crew alone seemed unaffected by the hilarity and some of them, knowing their captain's ways, looked genuinely worried. Clabert, the wiry first mate, went so far as to approach him as he stepped to the bar.

"What's this about Mars, Captain? There's no truth in it, is there? If so you can count me out. That goes for the others too, I reckon."

Zhorga clamped a huge iron-like fist on the smaller man's shoulder and leaned close to him, intimidating him with his bulk.

"Don't think of running out on me, Clabert," he said in a low, confidential tone. "If I decide to take you to Mars that's where we're all going, see? We'll sail into the sun if I say so."

He shoved the man away from him and took himself through the main door. Hunch-shouldered, he went striding away beneath the star-canopied sky, importunately followed by a loping, hopeful Rachad Caban.

"All right," Zhorga said, "let's get to the business."

He sat uneasily in Gebeth's living room, a big rough man who felt incongruous in such cozy, enclosed quarters. His ham-fists rested on the table, at which also sat Rachad and the alchemist.

"First we must settle terms," said Gebeth mildly. "I will prepare your sailing instructions and give any other assistance I can. There will be no fee. Instead I make two conditions. Rachad here must accompany you, and you must make your Mars landing at the city of Kars, staying there until his business is done."

This Rachad and Gebeth had already decided, speaking privately in the laboratory while Zhorga waited in the other room. Gebeth had been astonished at the tale told by the two, and made no light matter of the dangers involved in the enterprise. But, seeing Rachad's keenness, and recognizing that the boy was a born adventurer, he had eventually consented to the deal which he now put before Zhorga.

Zhorga, however, demurred, hunching his shoulders and eyeing Rachad. "This pup has caused me enough annoyance already tonight, following me around and touting for business on your behalf. He is no sailor. There's no room on this trip for passengers."

"I'll be no passenger!" Rachad protested indignantly. "I'll work for my passage. I'll learn to work in the rigging, even."

"Well, it's no go. State your fee in money, alchemist."

"I'm afraid I look on this as a joint venture. I have stated my terms and they cannot be negotiated."

"Then I'll find another astrologer."

"If you wish, though I know of none in Olam as proficient as I claim to be." Gebeth smiled sourly. "There was a time when any captain worth his salt could do for himself what you need me to do for you."

Zhorga chewed at his beard, showing some annoyance. "It is not my fault. No airfarer knows much of astrology any more. There's no need to follow the celestial bodies, not really. One merely has to take note of the sun and the moon." He looked at Gebeth askance. "What possible business could you have in Kars."

"While we would prefer to keep that confidential, I suppose it is reasonable that you should want to know," Gebeth told him. "Briefly, we are students of alchemical works. There are texts in Kars we wish to obtain."

Understanding showed like a gleam of slyness in Zhorga's eyes. His gaze flitted round Gebeth's library.

"Gold! You think you can find the secret of making gold!" Forgetting his manners, he allowed himself to laugh lustily as if at a joke. "Dreams, ridiculous dreams."

"You do not believe in the Philosopher's Stone?" inquired Rachad.

"I believe the way to make wealth is not by messing about with crucibles and whatnot. The silk I shall bring back from Mars is gold for me, real silver and gold, more than you'll ever find in your dusty books." He scratched his side, looking at Rachad again. "All right, I'll take him. Half my lousy crew will probably desert anyway, so I might be shorthanded."

Glee came to Rachad's features. "We are as good as there!"

"Don't run ahead of yourselves," Gebeth said soberly. "Even Captain Zhorga may change his mind when he learns of the hazards ahead.

The alchemist puttered about the room taking down books and large dusty rolls of paper, all of which he dumped on the table.

"Before even planning the expedition you must satisfy yourself that you can actually manage your ship in space," he told Zhorga. "Remember that there will be no air or wind on which to keel your galleon or to use in opposition to contrary ether currents. There is only the ether. Therefore there is no question of steering in the same way you do on Earth, though to some extent there is a force that can be used in interplay with the ether, and that is the attractive force of the various celestial bodies. Hence the direction in which one launches oneself to begin with is of vital importance, since subsequent maneuvers take a considerable time to effect."

"I'm not that much of a dunderhead," Zhorga said. "I know the rules of travel in space: the longer you keep your sails out, the faster you go; don't try to tack against the ether wind—it can't be done, or hardly ever; find a current that's flowing roughly your way, toward the same half of the compass anyway, and tack across it to get where you want to go."

"That, in essence, is the procedure. Danger presents itself in the vicinity of the destination, for then one must lose the velocity one has accumulated during transit. This is done by making use of the eddies surrounding a planet, and is a tricky operation to say the least."

Clearing a space, he spread a large chart upon the table.

"I will make you a copy of this for general reference, though you must be guided mainly by the specific horoscopes I will prepare."

The chart was a map of the inner part of the solar family of planets extending as far as the Girdle of Demeter, as the region of rocks and planetoids beyond Mars was called. Marked on the map in a whirl of fine lines engulfing everything was the centrifugal vortex of ether that radiated out from the sun. It formed an intricate force field, streaming back into the sun at certain places, breaking up into eddies and whirlpools here and there, creating complicated flurries and rapids where interrupted by large bodies like moons and planets, but for the most part sweeping out and out like an expanding spinning top.

Zhorga pored over the chart, putting his face almost to within inches of it and examining it with intense concentration. Quaint illustrations were dotted here and there, accompanied by legends such as "Here run rapids," "This vortex will claim any ship," and "Here lie monsters."

"What's this?" he demanded, putting his finger on the last. "This, I assume, is not to be taken seriously."

"Hmm." Gebeth looked uncertain. "The chart is supposed to be factual. I would not ignore it."

"Pah!" Zhorga made an expansive gesture. "Many of these old mapmakers had fanciful imaginations. How many charts have I seen showing monsters in the sea, monsters in the air? Where are these monsters? They don't exist."

"Then you must use your own discretion." Gebeth laid the chart on one side and, taking an ephemeris, began to construct a geocentric horoscope.

"The day and hour of departure must be chosen with care. How soon will your vessel be ready?"

Zhorga stuck out his lower lip. "Three weeks, perhaps? Maybe longer."

"Let us see if we can find a suitable day. . . ." Consulting the tables, the alchemist marked his chart with planetary signs. He studied it briefly, then laid it aside and set to work yet again. This time he constructed, on transparent paper, a heliocentric horoscope, using a second set of tables. This he laid over the big main chart and began to trace various features from it, skillfully drawing curved lines to indicate the course of the ether winds, and so forth.

Rachad noticed that this horoscope differed from the chart in many respects. "You seem to be marking those vortices in the wrong places," he remarked. "Why is that?"

"The first map is a general one only," Gebeth explained. "As the planets move, their relationships to one another alter, and the flow of the ether winds is affected. This causes the eddies, vortices and rapids to move, too. They shift and waver, and some die down while new ones spring up. It's as if large stones were to be kept moving in a stream. Sometimes the configuration of the planets is such that the whole of solar space erupts into a violent storm and navigation is impossible."

"There are unpredictable times of bad ether weather on Earth also," Zhorga rumbled. "Could that be from the same cause?"

"No doubt of it."

The air captain grunted. "Then this astrology could be useful to sailors after all, if it can forecast storms. It's strange it hasn't been adopted. Though one knows, of course, that the direction of the ether changes with the positions of the sun and moon, and also with the moon's phases."

"It was used extensively once, and every captain possessed an ephemeris. But like much else it has fallen into disuse with the ending of transspatial communication."

The work finished, he nodded judiciously. "The time I have selected would seem propitious enough. Takeoff should be during mid-morning, say ten-thirty. Enter the slipstream above the atmosphere, set your sails to travel at an angle thus—" he indicated with a thrust of his pen —"and you will be on your way. But it will take skill. Mismanage the maneuver and you risk being carried by the slipstream round the curve of the world. If that happens you could fall into the Earth's lacuna—a dead spot in her shadow where there is no ether movement. Your sails will be becalmed. You could well end by crashing onto the moon."

Zhorga stared somberly at Gebeth's chart. "Then we'd better do the job right," he declared.

"Some practice forays into space would be well-advised before embarking on the main journey," Gebeth continued. "You must also learn the art of drawing up these charts yourself, so that you may interpret the changing planetary positions during the course of the voyage. Jupiter and Saturn, and the planets beyond, will produce little change since they move so sedately and in any case lie downwind. But it is the upwind planets, close to the sun, that you must watch, since they move with alacrity. Mercury, especially, exerts an influence out of all proportion to its size, lying only thirty-six million miles from the sun and completing an orbit every three months. All planetary ether fluctuations begin, in fact, with Mercury."

Zhorga nodded his understanding.

"Space captains would sometimes carry an orrery as an aid to quick judgment," Gebeth added. "Are you familiar with the instrument?"

"An orrery? No, what's that?"

The alchemist hesitated. Then he moved to a cupboard and unlocked it with one of many keys on a key ring. From the cupboard he lifted out an unwieldy gangling object, all orbs, nested armillary rings, cogwheels and gears.

Setting it down, Gebeth turned a handle. The gears creaked and tinkled; the variously sized orbs circled, each at a different rate. It was a perfect representation of the solar family, from the sun to Saturn. Even the relative distances were given some demonstration, though much scaled down as was inevitable. And the Earth even had the moon in attendance, whizzing round it on the end of a rod, thirteen times to every orbit of its own.

"See?" Gebeth said. "At one glance one can see how the planets stand in relation to one another."

"Indeed," Zhorga breathed. "Wonderful! Will you lend me this device, Master Alchemist?"

"I place considerable value on it," Gebeth said reluctantly. "But possibly I could donate it toward the success of the venture."

"They move—it's like magic!" Zhorga was enchanted —and hardly less so was Rachad.

Hypnotized, they both stared at the dancing orbs.

Chapter THREE

Ten days later Gebeth visited the shipfield to see for himself the vessel in which his protégé and his new-found pupil proposed to set forth for Mars.

Zhorga had sunk all his money into the scheme and work was well advanced. The hold was filled with goods which he hoped to barter with the Martians in exchange for silk. The caulking was all but done and when Gebeth arrived Zhorga was supervising the fitting of extra spars which he believed would improve the galleon's handling in space.

As Gebeth stood staring up at the ship two horse-drawn drays stacked with wooden barrels rumbled up. He stepped forward and spoke to one of the drivers.

"Are you from Hamshar's works?"

"That's right, sir." The drayman climbed down and began unfastening the lashings. "And there's two more loads to come."

The alchemist nodded. The barrels contained a chemical preparation that could be made to smolder slowly to release breathable air. It would sustain the crew of the *Wandering Queen* on their journey through space.

It was thanks to his own knowledge that Zhorga had been able to obtain the coagulated air so quickly, for only he knew where to find a manufacturer to make the stuff in quantity. Indeed Gebeth had made himself invaluable in many ways. He had supplied Zhorga with the pills, made up to his instructions by an apothecary in the Street of the Alchemists, that the crew members would take during the voyage to ward off the physical effects of space travel. They would be living in conditions of reduced weight once they left Earth, and part of the time, when the sails were furled or during maneuvering, they might experience null weight. Such conditions could rot the bones and weaken the heart.

Captain Zhorga's rough bellow sounded from above. Sailors came swarming down ropes dangling over the ship's side. The hold doors were opened and the barrels of chemical air began to be rolled inside, rattling up a short ramp.

Rachad's face appeared over the railing. "Gebeth! Come up!"

Gebeth climbed a gangway to a door halfway up the wall of the hull. He found himself between decks, with a passageway ahead of him and a stairway to his left. There was a strong bitter smell of the special pitch all chinks and seams had been filled with to make the galleon airtight. Rachad came down the stairs, a pleased grin on his face.

"Come up top, sir!"

He followed Rachad onto the main deck, which was alive with activity and a chaos of ropes and tackle not yet assembled. They wandered among cursing sailors until Gebeth could look over the starboard rail. He saw that yet another item of equipment had arrived and lay in a heap on the ground: a huge sheet of a flexible transparent material which was to be affixed to the hull to cover the sternhouse and part of the main deck. It would balloon up under pressure and meant that one could walk the deck under it without wearing a breathing suit.

"Come to the sternhouse," Rachad invited over the clamor. "It's quieter there."

They climbed to the quarterdeck and entered Captain Zhorga's cabin. It was as Gebeth would have expected: not too clean, jumbled, smelling of Zhorga's habitation. "Has the Captain found a role for you yet?" he inquired.

"Well, he uses me as a sort of cabin boy," Rachad said apologetically. "Running messages and doing odd jobs. But I don't mind. What an adventure!" His eyes gleamed and he looked through the windows in the slanted rear wall of the cabin. Gebeth noted that the panes had been covered with a second frame containing a single sheet of unbreakable glass, tinted against the glare of the sun. Even the sternhouse had been caulked, in case the outside bubble should fail.

A drawing of Zhorga's sail plan lay on the cabin table. Gebeth studied it briefly. An air sailing ship like the *Wandering Queen* was designed quite differently from the old transspatial ships, being closer in many respects to the old sea ships from which both were ultimately descended. Zhorga knew, therefore, that if he tried to sail in space as he did in the atmosphere the result would be a disaster; in space the ship would have no natural weight to keep it in balance. Instead he proposed to sail the galleon much like a cog. The ship would fly decks foremost, with the sails arranged overhead like a canopy. The hull's inertia would thus provide the needed drag on the sails, whose pull could then act through the ship's center of gravity, giving a stable system. This arrangement had one other important advantage, besides its simplicity: the ship's constant acceleration would give objects on board weight in the accustomed direction. One would be able to walk the decks.

Gebeth turned to Rachad. "How is Zhorga managing as regards his men?"

Rachad grimaced, then laughed. "He keeps them in line somehow."

In fact, on returning to the ship after his first meeting with Gebeth, Zhorga had been confronted by an anxious crew who, when he confirmed his intentions, had all quit on the spot. Zhorga had refused to hear anything about this collective vote of no confidence. He had half-bullied, half-jollied them into submission, keeping them by him mainly by fear and violence. He was forced to make regular visits to Olam's taverns and boarding houses to seek out deserters, driving them back to the ship with much roaring and bluster. Nevertheless he had let the more lily-livered go, losing thereby nearly half his crew —a loss he had made good by recruiting various desperadoes and adventuresome spirits he had found in the town, luring them with tales of riches. These at least were not against him, and even some of his original men —Clabert the first mate, for instance—were now behind him.

For the rest, their main hope was that the *Wandering Queen* would never take off, at any rate not for the void. None of them had dared attempt to sabotage the preparatory work, however; Zhorga's wrath in such a circumstance was something no one wanted to face.

"I must say I can't help feeling sorry for him," Rachad told Gebeth. "The *Wandering Queen* has become a standing joke. He is derided everywhere he goes. It will be awful if the thing flops. But it won't!"

"Departure time is close," Gebeth pointed out. "Zhorga ought to begin making his practice runs soon."

At that moment a sweating Zhorga entered the cabin

and greeted Gebeth. "Those curs work as though they were dying of consumption," he complained breathily. "Still, it won't be long now."

"There is one point I have not heard you mention heretofore," Gebeth said. "Rachad here tells me you don't actually have enough ether sail to make the voyage. You will, as a matter of fact, need more sail than is required for ordinary atmospheric flying."

Zhorga waved his hand. "It's being taken care of."

"Shouldn't your fresh sail be here by now? You'll need it for your practice runs. Where are you getting it from?"

Rachad knew already—and had informed Gebeth—that Zhorga had tried to persuade one or other of the owner-captains to throw their lot in with him, lumping their sail together with his. Without exception they had laughed in his face.

"You needn't worry about that," Zhorga said after a frowning pause. "One of the town merchants is giving it to me."

"You've certainly been trying hard," Gebeth said admiringly, gazing through the open door of the cabin to the decks of the ship. "Will you be ready on time?"

"Should be," Zhorga told him, "though I've only been able to do half what I'd like. There just isn't any more money and nobody will lend me a penny, dammit!"

"Won't your merchant partner finance you? He's already loaning you the sail, and that represents a considerable risk."

The big man moved his shoulders awkwardly, looking trapped and angry. "Don't pester me, alchemist. I can take care of that side of things."

He charged out again to continue berating his crew.

Every night, or nearly every night, Zhorga appeared at the alchemist's house to learn more of the art of preparing navigational horoscopes. After the airman had departed that particular night, there came a further knock on Gebeth's door. He opened it to see a group of men standing there, dressed in richly trimmed cloaks and soft hats of ermine and lambswool.

"We would have a word with you, Master Alchemist," said one, politely enough. Gebeth recognized Hevesum, a wealthy merchant of Olam and owner of a whole fleet of ships.

Puzzled but not alarmed, he admitted them. Five in all joined him in his small living room, and when introductions were completed he discovered that he was in fact host to all the ship-owning merchants of the town.

It was Hevesum who again spoke next. "We may as well be direct about our business here, Master Alchemist," he said. "Word has reached us that one Captain Zhorga, owner of the galleon *Wandering Queen*, plans to sail to Mars to bring back a cargo of ether silk. It is said that you are assisting him."

"In a small way," smiled Gebeth, pleased that his part in the project should have reached the ears of these gentlemen. "But what is your interest in the matter?"

"Only this," snapped Hevesum, while the other merchants all cast glances of venomous suspicion at one another. "We all know that the *Wandering Queen* bears little more than rags for ether sail—yet Captain Zhorga apparently claims to have procured silk enough for a journey to Mars! Tell us if you will be so good—where did he get this silk?" And at this several merchants' hands went unconsciously to rest on the hilts of dirks and rapiers, gestures which did not go unnoticed by Gebeth.

"About that I know little," he said, scratching the side of his jaw, "except that some merchant is loaning him some sail—one would presume in return for a share of the return cargo."

"There! I knew it!" exclaimed a tall thin man. "One of us is lying!"

"Be quiet, Druro," said a somewhat fat merchant named Gawing, more amiable looking than the rest. He turned to Gebeth. "What is the name of this merchant? He must have mentioned it."

"No, he did not," answered Gebeth with a shake of his head. "Indeed he seemed circumspect about the matter—with good reason I am beginning to think, seeing the attitude of you gentlemen."

"It must be from one of us!" Druro insisted. "Where else would he get it? We already know the other owner-captains scorn Zhorga's scheme."

"I am puzzled," said Gebeth. "Why do you object to this enterprise? What would be the harm in lending Zhorga sail—apart from the risk of losing it, of course."

"We recognized some time ago that the air trade is over," Hevesum explained brusquely. "And having laid other plans, we would prefer to keep it that way. Most of us are heavily committed to the building of sea-ships at Umbuicour." With a sudden movement he produced a small velvet bag tied with a cord. "It would be easy enough for you to ensure the failure of the expedition. A mistake on your charts, perhaps. Here is enough money to make it worth your while." The bag chinked as he tossed it to the table.

"That would not be ethical," Gebeth said. "And since a friend of mine is to be on board, I do not want the expedition to fail."

The merchants fell to arguing among themselves, for the most part accusing one another of reneging. Finally Gawing raised his hands.

"Silence, gentlemen, silence! Let us think calmly about it for once. Tell me, what chance has Zhorga of success?"

"None at all!" snapped Druro. "Not a hope!" And others added their agreement.

"That is my opinion also," Gawing replied. "So what are we worried about? Zhorga offers no threat—on the contrary his failure will discourage others. We are exerting ourselves over nothing."

"But *where* is he getting his *sail?*" Hevesum insisted.

"I will give you the complete answer: it is that Zhorga is a lunatic. He does not have any sail, beyond his pitiful rags, and he is not going to get any. Would any of us give it to him?" Gawing looked from one to the other. "Of course not! We are not fools. And the *Wandering Queen* will not even reach the stratosphere, let alone Mars."

Gebeth was ignored as the quarreling merchants discussed this aspect of the affair. Finally they left the house and he heard the sound of carriages drawing away.

For some time he sat pondering what he had just heard.

Although he mentioned the merchants' visit to Rachad neither of them succeeded in discussing the question with Zhorga, who became increasingly intractable on the subject. On the eve of the planned day of departure Zhorga announced that the ship, fully provisioned and fitted out, would sail on schedule the next day.

"But Captain," Rachad asked in a low tone later, "what of the sail?"

"It will be here," Zhorga answered briefly.

Many others of the crew were as mystified as he. That night Zhorga forbade anyone to leave the ship but instead sent out for some kegs of ale which was drunk without much merriment. Rachad settled down to sleep early, but throughout the night his rest was interrupted by thumps, shouts and bellows as Zhorga and the mate apprehended those who were trying to sneak over the side.

Dawn broke clear and bright. The ship ground stirred and seemed to shake itself, this being the hour of departure. Zhorga came from his cabin and gave orders to Clabert, whose voice then rang out over the *Wandering Queen*.

"We are taking off now? Without sail?" asked Rachad, joining Zhorga on the quarterdeck. His expression changed from puzzlement to despair as he began to doubt the man's sanity.

Whatever the Captain might have replied was lost for the familiar unearthly shrieking smote them all as the first ships to depart put out ether sail. Along with the others Rachad plugged his ears. Then he turned to watch with wonderment the sudden blossoming of pale blue sail, the miracle as big ships lifted off the ground and went streaming away with the sun behind them.

Now the *Wandering Queen* added herself to the dawn migration. A new shriek penetrated Rachad's eardrums as hands hauled on windlasses and the yards drew up Captain Zhorga's patchwork sails. A shudder ran through the frame of the ship. There was a groaning and creaking of timbers as futtocks, ribs and wales braced themselves to take the strain; and then the ether, the most powerful force known to man, more invisible than the wind and ungraspable by hand or eye, caught hold of the galleon and lifted her into the air. There was a jarring bump as she fell back a moment or two later, but the second time she surged free and up. Soon the panorama of the ship ground was below her. She entered the great avenue by which the vessels gained the open skies.

As soon as they were free of the interference fringe everyone removed their earplugs. Rachad was exhilarated. This was the first time he had flown and it was every bit as delirious an experience as he had imagined. The wind sang in the rigging and blew clean and fresh in his face. He noticed that running the length of the decks were lines to which some crewmen attached themselves by running ringhooks, presumably as a precaution against falling overboard.

When they were well clear of the ship ground they set some windsail for steering and moved off toward the south. The haphazard squadron of flying ships that had sprung up dissipated, the vessels dwindling in the sky as they all took themselves toward their various destinations.

Rachad still could not guess what was in Zhorga's mind, but eventually, since their course seemed purposeful, he hoped that he had arranged a rendezvous which would bring them their needed silk. A couple of times Zhorga altered course to bring them farther round to the south, so that they traveled roughly in an arc. The rendezvous would have to be soon if they were to make space today, for Gebeth had said they should enter the super-atmospheric slipstream before midday.

For about an hour they flew over rolling moors dotted with small woods and spinneys. At first there were villages and hamlets, but after a while they were passing over land that seemed wholly uninhabited. Zhorga paced the quarterdeck, anxiously scanning the sky and occasionally sweeping the horizon with a folding telescope. At last he gave a cry.

"There she is! Twenty degrees east, Master Clabert—and bring up the bombards!"

Tacks and braces were worked and the ship swung round. They were making, Rachad saw, for a ship that had appeared, somewhat lower in the sky than themselves. As they approached he recognized her as another galleon, the *Sperus,* he had seen on the ship field. Presumably she had taken off after the *Wandering Queen.*

Zhorga cackled. "There you are, my boy. The capital ship of Master Druro, merchant of Olam."

"So you *did* have a deal with one of them," murmured Rachad. Then he noticed the activity on the foredeck, where two heavy cylinders of black gunmetal were being heaved into place on raised platforms. He recalled what Zhorga had once mentioned—that the *Wandering Queen* had originally been a fighting vessel.

They drew nearer the *Sperus*, threatening to cut across her bows.

"Give her a shot amidships!" bellowed Zhorga.

Before Rachad's disbelieving eyes one of the bombards fired, bucking and giving off a cloud of smoke to the accompaniment of a loud explosion. He glimpsed the ball before it crashed into the other galleon and shattered some of her side strakes.

The crew, even Zhorga's old hands, responded with whoops and cheers.

"Heave to and descend!" Zhorga roared through a megaphone. *"Heave to and descend!"*

The answer was a running to and fro on the other's decks, a raising of more sail and a quickening of the *Sperus's* pace. Unlike the *Wandering Queen's* tatty silk her sails were whole and she had enough of them. She might well have got away but Zhorga, with a roar of rage, leaped from the afterdeck and bounded the length of the main deck to the bombards. Frantically he worked the aiming handles, then snatched the taper from a nearby sailor and put it to the touch-hole.

He was either very lucky or divinely inspired, because the ball struck the *Sperus's* middle mast. The mast splintered and broke away under the force of the sail it carried; the galleon swung wildly from side to side in the air, lost speed and began to fall alarmingly. The *Wandering Queen's* sailors guided her directly over the crippled ship, following her down.

Zhorga brandished a short broadsword, cursing violently and all but foaming at the mouth. *"Board her, you bastards!"* he screamed. "Get yourselves aboard!"

His own men hesitated, but some of the newcomers among his crew were no strangers to air piracy. Lines went over the side, and while the crew of the *Sperus* fought to stabilize their vessel they found invaders dropping onto their decks with sword, knife and pistol. The fight was brief and soon both ships were grounded on the heather-covered moor.

It was the work of but half an hour to strip the merchant ship of her silk and carry it on board the pirate. For good measure they set the *Sperus* on fire ("Well, she can't sail without silk," Captain Zhorga said), leaving her crew on the moor, and she burned merrily below them as they once again ascended into the air.

A few miles away they landed again. Zhorga glanced at the sun. Rachad could see the tension in his eyes.

"A couple of hours left to get ready," Zhorga muttered. "I don't want to miss that slipstream. By God, I wish we'd been able to make those practice runs."

His men were into the spirit of the thing now and responded well to their Captain's exhortations. They worked with a will to cut and fit the new sails, bending them to the newly added spars which would swing them into the "parasol" position once the ship reached space.

"But what when we return?" Rachad wanted to know. "We'll be arrested on the spot if we come back to Olam, or anywhere on the continent, I should imagine. Everybody will know what we did today."

"By that time we'll have a hold full of ether silk," Zhorga boasted, "and people will take a different view of us." He laughed briefly. "I asked Druro for sail and he refused, like all the others. But he's donated it anyway!"

He turned away and continued to supervise the work. The hour was eleven in the morning, half an hour past Gebeth's recommended time, when the *Wandering Queen* finally took to the air again, almost buried under blue sail, and soared proudly up toward the void.

Chapter FOUR

Clad like some billowing orchid in more than twice her usual spread of silk, the *Wandering Queen* seemed able to soar without limit. Up and up she went, climbing high above the commercial flying levels until the cloud layer merged with the ground below her.

The air thinned, producing a crop of headaches, nosebleeds and spells of dizziness. A silence and a stillness prevailed, broken only by the thrumming of the rigging and the jubilation of those on board.

Then disaster struck. A violent jet wind, flowing through the sky at more than a hundred miles an hour, hit the galleon without warning. She yawed, reeled, and then heeled over and was dragged on her side on a new and uncontrolled course.

It was a novel and terrifying experience for an air sailor to be at the mercy of an air wind. Ether silk, with its special porous construction, usually let air pass practically without hindrance. But even silk could not ignore a hurricane. Together with hull and canvas, it was ruthlessly seized and driven onward by the blast.

A world of confusion and dread exploded around Rachad Caban. The wind shrieked and squealed in his ears. It scoured him, speared him, slashed him with icy knives, pounded him with numbing hammers. It tore him from the capstan where he was stationed and rolled him down the deck until he met the balustrade, to which he clung with all his strength and thanked the gods that he had belted on a safety rope. That same wind carried others over the side and flew them out on their lines like kites.

On the quarterdeck, Zhorga's arms were wrapped around the wheel like steel bands, and he was screaming words which the wind instantly whipped away. Then, through the roaring of the jet wind, Rachad heard a sound which completed his terror: a cracking, snapping sound.

The unmistakable sound of timber giving way.

The spars were breaking up.

He sobbed. The galleon presented a dreadful, pathetic sight as she went wallowing through the air. Broken spars, tangled sails, all were trapped in the rigging. Men froze as they clung to the straps and handholds that dotted the decks, paralyzed and ready to die.

But not all were reduced to such utter helplessness. Incredulously Rachad saw three or four drag themselves along the common safety lines, carrying axes with which they chopped and hewed at standing and running rigging. At first their actions bewildered him; he envisaged the *Wandering Queen* dropping to earth like a stone. Then he realized that they were working to clear away the windsail, which had borne the brunt of the jet wind, and that the ether spars were relatively undamaged. Canvas, spars and rope, the shattered parts of the ship's superstructure, went whirling away into the distance.

The effect on the *Wandering Queen* was dramatic. Cumbrously she righted herself, swaying from side to side even though still sent scudding along by the hurricane. Captain Zhorga wrestled mightily with the wheel and the ship turned, wallowing and swinging. The ether sails billowed again with a series of crackling sounds, as they once more filled with luminiferous current.

Seconds later, as abruptly as it had come, the jet wind ceased.

The galleon climbed in an unearthly silence. They were above the jet stream, above the eight turbulent miles of the planet's weather. Here was a new realm: the stratosphere—tenuous, calm, extending, Zhorga believed, for more than a hundred miles until it finally petered out at the edge of space.

He had intended his men to don space garb adapted from sea-diving gear before reaching this height. Now they were befuddled from lack of pressure, gasping in the frigid air. Yet somehow they found the strength to haul aboard those who had gone over the side, and only then did they open the deck lockers and start struggling into the protective suits.

Fumblingly they ignited the powdered air in their backpacks. Then, utterly exhausted, they fell about the deck, hoping and praying that their captain had the good sense to abandon his foolhardy mission and turn back for home, while there was still a chance.

Captain Zhorga, however, did not have any such good sense. True, the hurricane had left him feeling shaken, but his ship had come through it and that was good enough in his book.

Already his mind was on the greater hazards to come. Far overhead sped the slipstream, a branch of the ether wind that instead of passing through the atmosphere split away and went racing over the top of it, like a breeze deflected by a ball. This slipstream was shallow but immensely strong and swift, and played a vital role in interplanetary sailflight. If approached correctly, it would send the *Wandering Queen* catapulting at top speed toward her target. Otherwise, there was a risk that it might bear her round into the Earth's lacuna, a static region where the ether did not move at all.

Zhorga lashed the wheel in position; from now on there would be no pitting the wind against the ether. Scorning to strap himself into his captain's seat, he stood by the poop rail, knowing it would hearten his men to see him standing there unafraid, prominent by reason of the large number 1 painted on his chest. Patiently breathing the acrid chemical air, he waited out the hours as the galleon continued to climb on the irresistible power of the ether. Spacesuits gradually swelled in near-vacuum. Stars appeared as the sky turned first purple then black, and the sun blazed with an unfamiliar fierceness.

With increasing anxiety he watched for the signs: a hastening of the ship's onward pace, an extra swelling of the sails, a new strain on the tackles.

They came; excited, he gave the prearranged arm signal. On the maindeck men clumsily worked the great ratchets, slipping and sliding on the planking. The three mainmasts that were mounted on those ratchets shuddered inch by inch toward their new settings, while at the same time sheet-ropes were taken in to bring the sails to the angle Zhorga wanted.

But before the maneuver could be completed there came a sudden shock so violent as to send Zhorga tumbling down the stairway to the maindeck. The ship seemed to be turning, tilting. He tried to get to his feet, but discovered to his horror that the deck had turned right over to form a sloping ceiling, and that below him there spread the shimmering blue sails, two hundred miles of space and air, and the blue-and-white expanse of the Earth.

He fell, howling. But already the deck had slipped beneath him again. He rolled, grabbed a handhold, and desperately tried to weigh up the situation.

The ship was spinning with a waltzing gyration whose center seemed to be somewhere between the maindeck and the topgallants. Men were either clinging to whatever was within reach or else were falling and tumbling through space like insects shaken from a tree. Evidently the galleon's entry into the slipstream had been too precipitate, and Zhorga had no doubt that she was now being carried inexorably toward the lacuna.

He saw that four or five sailors, swaying this way and that as the ship turned over and over, were still clinging to the nearest ratchet bar. He seized a safety line, gritted his teeth, and timing his efforts to the galleon's oscillations, hauled himself toward the bar.

He reached the men only to glimpse, through gridded faceplates, faces rigid with fear. He thumped and shoved them, but they reacted only by gripping the ratchet bar even more stubbornly.

He could not really blame them. It was not unknown at great heights for air sailors to freeze to the spars and to have to be pried loose. Roaring uselessly in the vacuum, he kicked and shoved more violently, almost knocking one man loose from his hold. At last they seemed to understand what they must do to save themselves. Following Zhorga's example, they made an effort to work the ratchet mechanism, their boots scraping intermittently on the revolving deck.

The ratchet moved a notch, then another. The mast shuddered and dropped, foot by foot, and shortly there was a change in the movements of the ship. The gyrations damped down. The stern rose, bringing the decks to a slope of nearly forty-five degrees, so that the bow pointed directly at the Earth and it seemed to the eye that the galleon was rushing headlong back toward the ground.

In fact, she was still in the grip of the slipstream. But now there was enough stability for the men to recover their wits and to work the remaining ratchets. The decks levelled; the onrushing slipstream began to do the work Zhorga had planned for it—lifting the galleon at a diagonal angle and at an ever-faster rate.

The acceleration was crushing. Even Zhorga's knees buckled, despite himself, and he sprawled full-length, scarcely able to breathe for long minutes that seemed like hours, as a colossal weight pressed him against the swaying deck.

Then the torture abruptly vanished and was replaced by a novel feeling of lightness. Zhorga lunged to his feet, looking about him and experiencing this new sensation with enjoyment.

His pleasure did not last long. Staggering toward him came a crewman who mouthed at him appealingly from within his helmet. Zhorga saw that he clutched the fabric of his suit with both hands, and that air was escaping from a large tear. For a moment Zhorga stood nonplussed, wondering how to save the man. But already it was too late. The sailor collapsed, gaping like a fish, and turned blue.

Zhorga hesitated, aware of many eyes watching the scene. Then he glumly unhooked the dead man's safety line, lugged the corpse to the side, and threw it unceremoniously overboard.

After this, Rachad was alarmed to see a spirit of mutiny appear in the crew, many of whom ignored orders, refused to work and huddled together in a sullen group. Zhorga waded in to restore discipline, aided by Clabert and a few other stalwarts. In the silence of the void brief scuffles took place, made more weird by the thuds and clumps that were transmitted along the timber of the deck and through the soles of the boots of those present. But the disaffected men lacked the determination to put up any real resistance, and before long they were back at their posts, helping to put into effect the final stage of Zhorga's launch plan—the parasol canopy with which he intended to sail across the vast gulf between Earth and Mars.

The masts were levered erect and the upper yards swung fore and aft. The outboard sprits and booms were raised above the level of the decks. Clambering up the ratlines, men hammered in pins and rings so as to reeve new running rigging and rearrange the sails. When the sails were finally run out, they formed a multi-tiered canopy over the *Wandering Queen*.

The ether wind filled them immediately, and the galleon, in a smooth majestic movement, responded by swinging round to present her bottom to the sun. For a short time she oscillated to and fro, like a pendulum, but then became rock steady.

Zhorga breathed out a sigh of relief and immense satisfaction. All his careful calculating of weight and balance had paid off. The ship was trim. The inertia of her hull perfectly balanced the forward impetus of the sails.

There was a long pause in which no one moved. Every man gazed about him, the harsh sound of his own breathing loud in his ears, and saw a sight that perhaps had been familiar to his grandfather. Earth shone to port, a stunningly beautiful shield. Farther off floated the moon, small and brilliant.

The sun could not be seen. It was below the hull, blowing ether straight into the sails. Yet the scene on deck was far from dark. Apart from the glow of Earth and moon, there was a shimmering blue radiance cast down by the sails—a ghostly glow of reflected sunlight.

A more fanciful ship would never have made it, Zhorga told himself proudly. A clipper, a chebec—even a more elaborate galleon—would by now be lying in tatters on the ground, or at best be helpless in the lacuna.

To one side of the taut sails he found a prominent red spot, and stared at it avidly and hungrily, for a long time.

Angry, challenging Mars stared back.

The real mutiny did not come until many hours later, by which time a great deal of work had been done. The transparent cover known as the air balloon had been fixed and sealed to the hull, covering the sternhouse and part of the maindeck, and was now inflated. The ship's interior had also been filled with air. The caulking had been checked seam by seam, and any leaks made staunch.

An urn of powdered air smoldered in Zhorga's cabin where, in the presence of Rachad, he conferred with Clabert over the disposition of watches and other matters. The three men swayed slightly in the weak gravity the ship's steady acceleration provided, though their feet remained firmly planted on the deck due to the lead weights with which their boots were shod.

Rachad waited for a break in the conversation. "What about me, Captain?" he then asked eagerly. "You said I could learn to work in the rigging."

"Very well," Zhorga agreed. "But keep your face out of direct sunlight as much as possible. It's always been a bane to space travelers—Earth's atmosphere filters out the harsher rays, apparently, which cause skin diseases." He nodded to Clabert. "Find a place for him—"

He broke off at the sound of boots treading the deck outside. Someone had come through the balloon sphincter, even though the whole crew was at this moment supposed to be recuperating down below.

Zhorga did not seem at all surprised. With scarcely a pause he took down the cutlass that was clipped to the cabin wall, then flung open the door. He stepped out, while Clabert and Rachad crowded the doorway behind him.

Four men stood under the air balloon, their faces bearing a ghastly pallor in the eerie light of the sails. Obvious leader of the party was Sparge, a bear of a man recruited just before the voyage from one of Olam's taverns—an unsavory character, Zhorga recalled, who rarely got work because of his reputation as a troublemaker. The others came from Zhorga's former crew. All were armed—Sparge with a saber and a flintlock pistol, the others with knives and axes—and all had removed their helmets.

"The game's over, Captain," Sparge said bluntly. "We've talked it out among ourselves, and we are agreed that as we value our lives we're turning back. The ship's in our hands, so lay down your cutlass and we'll settle it in peaceable fashion."

"Do *you* aim to pilot us to earth?" Zhorga asked Sparge, looking at him askance. "For you may be sure I won't."

"We'll go down on the night side, where there's less turbulence. Then since there's a charge of piracy hanging over us in Olam, we'll divide everything between ourselves and split up. That's our plan, Captain, and it makes no difference whether we take you alive or dead."

"If you imagine I'll give up this enterprise now, you don't know me," Zhorga said. He wasted no more time in words, but launched himself at Sparge, ignoring the gun that was pointed at his chest. So sudden was the attack that Sparge failed to fire, and Zhorga knocked the muzzle of the pistol aside.

Blades clashed and rang as the two hacked at one another. It was exaggerated, awkward swordplay. Chary of moving their feet for fear of losing control over their bodies, they swung grotesquely this way and that, while Sparge's followers edged nervously forward, looking for an opening.

To avoid being surrounded, Zhorga backed himself against the rail, near the wall of the air balloon. It was then that Sparge found a moment in which to aim his flintlock, and he fired.

The shot, deafening in the enclosed space, was both clumsy and stupid. The ball missed Zhorga and punctured the air balloon behind him. The balloon began to deflate with a shrill whistling noise, but Zhorga, as if unaware of it, grinned and pressed a fresh assault.

Everything had happened so fast that neither Clabert nor Rachad had so far been able to react. But now, without thinking, Rachad plunged past the three with axes, dodged Sparge and Zhorga, and threw himself toward the puncture.

It was about the size of a fingernail, and as he got closer the evacuating air became like a miniature whirlwind. He slapped his hand over the hole. Air pressure immediately clamped his palm to the slick material, and he could feel the hole sucking at his skin like a ravenous little mouth.

"*A patch, bosun, a patch!*" he yelled desperately. He closed his eyes, frightened by the grunting of men and the clanging of steel behind him. He guessed that the balloon had already lost a fair amount of air, for he felt dizzy and short of breath.

Then the clashing stopped. A hand fell on his shoulder.

He opened his eyes. It was Clabert, with a patch. The bosun helped him to force his hand sidewise of the puncture, substituting the square of adhesive. It flew to the hole, sticking itself down and sealing the puncture.

Sparge lay on the deck. Blood oozed from a wound in his neck and flowed down into his suit. The other three mutineers cowered against the starboard rail, weapons hanging in limp gloves.

Zhorga spoke. "All right, Boogle. Who organized this charade?"

Boogle rolled his eyes. He was a stooped, cadaverous figure and he looked even more deathly in the light of the sails. "Sparge and Boxmeld mostly, Captain," he muttered, then broke into a spluttering rush of words. "We don't want to die in space, Captain. The *Queen* isn't built for this kind of thing. Mars is too far away.... Let's go home."

Clabert grunted with disgust. "Just look at it."

"They've got a touch of panic, all right," Zhorga agreed. "I've quenched mutinies before. We'd better go down below and stamp on this one."

"What about these three?"

"Take their helmets off them and leave them here."

The would-be mutineers put up no resistance as they were disarmed. Zhorga found powder and shot in a pouch on Sparge's belt and loaded the flintlock, handing it to Clabert together with Sparge's saber.

He handed Rachad an axe. "Hold this for show, lad, but if it comes to a fight—best stay out of the way."

Rachad nodded. Little else was said—Zhorga seemed completely in command, completely confident. They suited up, then carried the additional helmets and weapons through the sphincter, stowing them in a locker on the open deck.

With the loping steps they were already used to, Zhorga led the way to the air-shed, a double-doored cubicle erected on the maindeck which acted as an airlock and gave access to below decks. One by one they passed through it, pulling themselves hand over hand down the companionway beneath until they were standing in the short corridor that led to the common messdeck. Here they removed their helmets and placed them on the companionway steps. A murmur of voices came from the end of the passageway, where a glimmer of lamplight outlined the frame of a door.

Zhorga beckoned. Lead boots thudded quietly on timber as they crept to the end of the corridor. Then Zhorga pushed open the door, and without a pause stepped through.

Faces turned, and froze to see Zhorga's bearded visage. Zhorga glowered around him, taking in the long compartment with bunks down both sides and a board table down the middle. A barrel of powdered air threw off a faint smoke which dissipated quickly into breathable phlogiston. He had known there were not many weapons aboard; as he glanced here and there he saw axes, knives, a couple of swords—and one more flintlock, lying on the table in front of Boxmeld, who was regarding him with a calculating eye.

Zhorga pointed his cutlass at him. "Sparge got what he deserved, Boxmeld—and the same is in store for you, unless you give yourself up and take whatever punishment I mete out."

Standing to the rear, Rachad wondered if Zhorga's apparent confidence was not misplaced. What if the whole crew were ready to rally behind Boxmeld? How could Zhorga possibly cope?

Boxmeld clearly had the same thought. He came to his feet with an unpleasant smile and turned, addressing the others. "Well, do you want to follow our good captain into eternity, boys? Do you want to die out here, where no one will even find our bodies? Of course you don't—*so get them!*"

As he snapped out the last words he snatched up his pistol. But Clabert was too quick for him; his shot took Boxmeld in the throat, and the renegade fell slowly back with the blast still resounding on the air.

His death was hardly noticed by those who attempted to rush the newcomers. Zhorga and Clabert found themselves shoulder to shoulder, facing a dozen angry and determined men. Rachad, heeding Zhorga's earlier advice, dodged back into the passageway, and peered between the straining bodies to try to see what was happening.

Zhorga realized that few of his crewmen had stomach enough to fight. Even so, the odds were heavily against himself and Clabert, encumbered as they were in their spacesuits. He slashed and swiped, ripping cloth and spilling a spray of blood, at the same time taking a nick in the cheek.

Momentarily the mutineers drew back from the ferocious blades. "Give up!" a voice cried hoarsely. "You haven't got a chance!"

At that moment a loud pounding noise came from the far end of the messdeck. A door that led to a storeroom burst open. Through it piled four men whose faces Zhorga had noticed were missing from the gathering—those same diehards who had already saved the ship when she had been caught in the hurricane.

Yelling wildly, the four raced the length of the messdeck, shoving aside any who stood in their way and grabbing up chairs to attack the renegades from the rear. For a while the scene resembled a tavern brawl. In the confusion Zhorga managed to disarm one of the swordsmen facing him, snatching up the weapon and tossing it to his new allies.

Axes and knives were no match for three skillfully wielded swords, and suddenly the fight did not seem so uneven. Even so, more blood was spilled before the mutineers lost heart, threw down their weapons and backed grudgingly against the bunks. Three were dead; four others lay injured.

Zhorga called for Salwees, a sailor who doubled as barber and amateur surgeon. While the wounds were being dressed he turned to Bruges, one of those who had come bursting in from the storeroom.

"Thanks for your intervention," he said. "I was wondering where you were."

"We couldn't get loose straight away," Bruges replied. He grinned crookedly. "They took us by surprise, you know. But you needn't worry about us—we're with you, all the way."

Zhorga nodded. He turned to face the rest of the crew, who were staring ashen-faced. "So, you want to go home," he rumbled. "Well, there's only one thing I can say to you—put the thought out of your minds. It's Mars we're bound for, and Mars is where we're going. When we come back, you'll all be rich."

"We'll never get there!" a sailor backed against the bunks protested in a tremulous voice. "The ship's simply not up to it. Already we must be way off course!"

"It's true we're a few degrees off," Zhorga admitted in an even, reasonable tone, "but it's nothing we can't compensate for. We're navigable; we can correct errors." His voice became suddenly impatient. "Do you think I can't read an astrolabe?"

"You can't correct for space monsters," another voice muttered.

"Don't talk nonsense. There are no such things," Zhorga retorted firmly. "Now listen to me, all of you. Instead of quaking in your boots the way you are, you should be feeling proud of yourselves. You've proved that a wooden hulk like the *Queen* can be taken up into space, given enough sail—and enough guts—and that's an achievement. Everyone will look up to you when you get back to Earth—and you'll get back, never fear. You'll be wealthy into the bargain, if we return with a hold full of silk. Thanks to you, the interplanetary trade might even revive.

"Now there's nothing much between us and Mars, so from now on I anticipate an easy journey," he continued. "As for turning back, well, I wouldn't try it even if I wanted to. We're in space now, and you can't backtrack on your course just like that. If you could, you'd find the Earth had moved on and you'd likely never catch her. These things have to be planned a long time in advance. To put it bluntly, to go back we have to reach Mars first."

Zhorga's words, consisting mainly of half-truths, were greeted by silence. Nevertheless he knew the rebellion was over. He hoped his men understood now that if they wanted to stay alive there was only one person they could rely on—himself.

Back in his cabin with Rachad, Zhorga sat down and began to brood anew over a problem that had occupied him ever since the sail canopy had been extended.

It would not have reassured the crew to know that the dangers of takeoff they had so narrowly survived were not, in Zhorga's view, anything like so hazardous as the business of landing on Mars. The tricky part of traveling to a downwind planet lay in being able to shed the velocity that had been gained on the way over, if one were not to go streaking through its atmosphere like a meteor. The recognized way of doing this was to fly past the target planet at short range, allowing its natural attraction to pull the ship into circum-planetary orbit. The ether itself could then be used to reduce speed, during as many circuits as were necessary.

But Zhorga did not trust his sense of computation too far. If he missed planetary capture he would find himself hurtling out into the Girdle of Demeter. So he was left with the alternative method: tilting at Mars head-on, going for dead center, and braking on the retroactive shock wave the planet created in the ether flow. If, that was, the *Wandering Queen's* timbers were equal to the strain.

The prospect so worried Zhorga that he had scarcely begun to think about the homeward journey, for which different tactics altogether were required. To travel to an upwind planet one sailed against the solar system's general rotation, so as to lose angular momentum. The massive attraction of the sun would then draw the ship inward, enabling her to match orbits with the target planet and land.

But once again the theory was simpler than the practice. How much angular momentum should be shed? Guesswork would not be enough.

Zhorga sighed, rose, and taking a handful of powdered air from a walnut box, poured it into the smoldering urn. Wearily he rubbed his face with his hand, then suddenly noticed that Rachad was watching him attentively, aware of his troubled mood.

"You'd better bed down here in the sternhouse for a while, Rachad," Zhorga rumbled. "Some of the crewmen might have it in for you."

The *Wandering Queen* swept on through the blazing darkness, gaining velocity all the time. Zhorga's thick black hair, Rachad saw for the first time, was streaked with gray.

Chapter FIVE

For all Zhorga's assurances, the voyage of the *Wandering Queen* continued to be fraught with difficulty. The continuous beating of the sun on the ship's bottom caused her interior to become stiflingly hot, but what was worse, softened the caulking, making it bubble and leak. The crewmen were obliged to spend much of their time making good these breaches, and some became so terrified of asphyxiation that they tried to sleep in their spacesuits, only to be forcibly dragged from them for the sake of conserving the powdered air.

Zhorga became concerned at the damage the heat was doing to the costly essences and expensive wines included in his cargo—damage which, he now saw with hindsight, could have been prevented if a reflective screen had been fitted under the hull. But annoying though this was, there were more serious worries. For one thing, chasing Mars across the sky was proving not nearly so simple as he had imagined. His first attempt, guided by orrery and astrolabe, to make a course change by bracing a few sails had ended in the ship swinging wildly off-center, forcing him to issue a hasty countermand. The rules of aerial flight, he was discovering ruefully, were not all good for space.

But gradually he was getting the hang of it. The sun receded and the ship cooled, and life aboard her settled into a routine. Fear faded in most into a mulish resentment, even to growing pride. And there were always a few to whom every moment was a glorious adventure....

Blue silk billowed and strained all around Rachad. Occasionally the sails rippled as they met some tiny irregularity in the ether flow and the ship trembled ever so slightly. Mostly, however, everything was rock-steady. It required an effort of the imagination to realize that the ship was moving at all.

Having finished his daily task of checking tacks and pulleys, he was making his way along a yardarm. Below him, the maindeck was deserted. Overhead he could see Mars, glowing like a red warning lamp, and to one side, as if below the level of the deck, was an equally brilliant blue-white star he knew was Earth.

Suddenly something seemed to flash past him, so close as to make his heart jump. A meteor, he decided apprehensively—the one accident a spacefarer could do nothing to avoid. Making sure his safety line was clear, he stepped off the foot-rope, let go the yard, and floated gently down until hitting the deck. Then he unhooked his line, coiled it neatly and clipped it in place near the deck lockers.

It happened again. A flash, a fleeting impression of something hurtling aslant the deck, this time narrowly missing the midmast.

A swarm, he thought with fright. A third object approached, more slowly, visible as a pale white ball which thudded into the deck, splintered the planking, and rolled before coming to rest against the airshed.

Rachad saw Clabert and two others working forward. They seemed to have noticed nothing, the sound of the impact being conducted poorly, perhaps, through their lead-soled boots and mingling with the thuds and thumps one heard when busy in a spacesuit. It occurred to him to warn them, but instead he turned to peer in the direction from which the meteors were coming, and thought to detect a whole swarm of tiny glints, distinguishable from the starry background by their motion.

He hurried to the white ball and picked it up. It was about the size of a large melon, very regular in shape, and not at all what he would have expected a meteor to be. Judging by the ease with which he was able to move it, he judged it to have the density of wood rather than stone, and its pale rind-like surface made him think of a hard-shelled fruit. One side seemed partly decomposed and was friable under the pressure of his hands.

Very odd, Rachad thought. He decided to give the object closer inspection. He tucked it under his arm, passed through the airshed, and made his way to the mess deck.

He now messed with the rest of the crew, having been unceremoniously booted out of the sternhouse by Zhorga once the men seemed more settled. Few of them were friendly toward him, however, and he met only hostile glances as he walked in, set down the ball on his bunk, and unscrewed his helmet.

The stench of the crew quarters invaded his nostrils, but within seconds he ceased to notice the familiar thick odor. He unfastened the suit's toggles and pulled apart the self-sealing inner lining, ducking his head through the brass ring and pulling the suit down over his shoulders. He withdrew his arms from the sleeves and picked up the ball with his bare hands. It was as cold as ice—colder. It seemed to suck the heat from him. He dropped it back on the bunk, his fingers numb.

Then he became aware of Boogle standing over him. The sailor spoke in a hoarse whisper. *"What you got there, boy?"*

"It dropped on the deck," Rachad said, blowing on his aching fingers.

"So that was it . . . we heard the thump. . . ." For once Boogle's bulging eyes were fixed in concentration as he leaned closer to the pallidly shining ball. Then, with a hysterical shriek, he staggered back.

"Oh God! Look at this, mates!" he called out breathlessly. "He's copped a space dragon's egg!"

Rachad blinked, and gave a nervous laugh. "Nonsense!" he declared. "Space dragons don't exist. This is a piece of rock, that's all, that probably drifted in from the Girdle of Demeter."

He fell silent, uncomfortably aware of the crowd that rapidly surrounded him in answer to Boogle's cries. He caught a whiff of superstitious panic.

Boogle pointed with a trembling finger. "Don't you recognize it, any of you?" he hooted. "A space dragon's egg, that's what it is!"

"It's a dragon's egg, all right," another voice said hotly. "I saw one in Indie, once—de-animated."

"Well this one won't be!" Boogle snapped back excitedly. "Our little Captain's pet has brought a dragon into the ship, that's what he's done! And we're all done for!"

"Get rid of it!"

Boogle's last words had ended on a wail, and echoing wails answered them. The panic mounted. Men went for spacesuits. Some so much forgot themselves as to dash for the companionway unprotected.

"All right!" Rachad yelled in exasperation. "I'll get rid of it!"

He picked up the ball, intending for some reason to transfer it to the table before suiting up and taking it back topside. The ball was no longer cold; in fact it seemed improperly warm, and in the next moment or two a network of fine cracks appeared on its surface, which then broke open. A gray tentacle, ending in a pincer which clicked audibly, emerged and waved in the air.

With an involuntary cry of horror Rachad dropped the space egg. Around him were screams and a general rush.

"Don't be fools!" he shouted, nonplussed. "A thing that size can't hurt you."

But he was proved wrong for the second time. The monster remained small only for as long as it took it to emerge from the egg. It seemingly had no central body. It was a matted mass of tentacles, of lumps and nodes. Each tentacle was either pronged, pincered or bladed, and many of them were also barbed and suckered.

Defying any laws of matter Rachad could envisage, it swelled and grew, the tentacles thickening, growing stronger, lashing about them and seizing the legs of the table, which it shook in an impressive show of strength.

And it continued to grow, with lightning speed. Later Rachad remembered little of the next few minutes. In fact, he was among the first to be suited and to go clattering along the short corridor to the companionway. Others attempted to pull their suits on as they ran, while some had left their helmets behind and, too afraid to go back for them, cowered in the corridor together with those lacking suits at all, unable to go either way.

Rachad, however, joined the press at the airshed (which was so hastily operated that both doors were momentarily levered open at the same time, only to be slammed shut again, fail-safe fashion, by the internal air pressure). The crew streamed out onto the deck, some climbing the ratlines, others huddling together behind whatever cover they could find.

Taking himself to the port rail, Rachad looked out again. The white flecks were more easily seen now. They were closer. And even as he looked, one burst into life!

At first it was only a burgeoning patch, writhing and

slowly expanding. But then it seemed to explode into a fiery smoke which billowed and spread and roiled, towering over the *Wandering Queen*, until finally it took on definite shape and became solid.

And now it stood revealed as a giant version of the tentacled creature on the mess-deck—a monster huge enough to crush the ship to matchwood!

It seemed aware of the passing galleon, for it came onward, propelling itself by some means unknown, blotting out space and becoming even more vast as it approached, its tentacles jerking this way and that in a frantic dance as it reached for its prey.

Rachad was stupefied. The monster, he guessed, was three or four times the size of the ship, and any one of its pincers could have snipped a mast easily. In color it was predominantly gray, but the skin had an oily sheen which seemed to glow with hundreds of transient hues.

While Rachad was frozen at the rail, his shipmates clung to one another or else fell to their knees, sobbing uncontrollably inside their suits. In no time at all the space monster was upon them, expanding about them, the stars glimmering through its reticulated body. Its tentacles reached out to embrace the ship—

Then there was a flash, a flare, an explosion of light. The galleon rocked, tipped, began to spin.

And it was over. The ship re-stabilized, her attitude corrected at once by the ether's constant action. Of the space monster, Rachad's dazzled eyes could see nothing.

He passed a hand over his faceplate, forgetting for a moment that he could not rub his eyes. How could such a huge beast disappear so completely? How, indeed, could it grow so incredibly swiftly in the first place?

He blinked hard, and when his vision cleared and he looked about him, he discovered, at least, what had caused the explosion.

The space monster had been demolished by a single shot from one of the bombards. Bosun Clabert stood on the foredeck, his hand resting on the weapon, which somehow he had lifted onto its firing platform. His other hand held a lighted taper, of the kind that would burn even in the void.

Even he must have been surprised by the result of his action. Rachad turned away, staring into space. The distant milky glints, he noticed, were still there, sweeping slowly by.

After a while of apprehensive waiting those on deck began to wonder why the ship had not yet been burst asunder by the monster left swelling down below. There was conferring with Captain Zhorga under the air balloon. He decided instantly to investigate.

Since most were loath to join the expedition betweendecks, Rachad found it easy to attach himself to the party. Zhorga and Clabert went first, ready with pistols. The others carried sabers, alert to chop at tentacles.

There was no need. The monster had grown to the size of a pony, and then died. Its tentacles were scattered forlornly about the mess-deck, and were already beginning to corrode and shrivel, looking like dead wood.

As they removed their helmets they were met by a new smell that had added itself to the usual stench: a smell of rottenness, sweet and corrupt. Rachad prodded the creature with his blade. The flesh of it flaked away, like ancient paper.

"These beasts must be without substance," Zhorga mumbled. "Blown up, merely, like paper balloons. But for what reason?"

Clumsily Rachad knelt and tore away a piece of tentacle. Even while he held it, he saw that it was crumbling, fading. Soon the whole creature would be nothing but dust.

"Homunculi," he mused. "I should have thought of it before."

He straightened. "Yes, that has to be it. The creatures are solid enough, Captain—for the brief time they live, that is. But they are not natural. They are, in fact, alchemical weapons left over from ancient wars."

Bruge grimaced in perplexity. *"Alchemical?"*

Rachad nodded. "In ancient times it was known how to generate synthetic beings, such as small, manlike beings known as homunculi. Also bizarre beasts which were used in battle."

"It makes sense," Zhorga rumbled. "Space warfare was rife at one time, that's well known. Strewing these eggs in the path of an enemy ship would be a good tactic. Presumably they lie dormant until a ship comes near and triggers them off, then they burst into life and attack in the manner we've witnessed."

Rachad nodded gravely, pleased with his knowledge. Some of the semi-legendary lore he had heard from Gebeth was useful after all.

Bruge seemed doubtful. "Small threat if they are so easily disposed of," he said.

"After all this time they must be almost exhausted of life force," Rachad answered. "Long ago they would have been more formidable—though even then, creatures that grew at such an unnatural rate can't have lived for more than a brief time. The type of matter they are made of is a product of alchemy, compounding fresh mass out of itself but quickly collapsing again."

A grunt came from Patchman. "It's lucky this one hadn't the strength to reach its full size," he observed, indicating the beast on the deck, "or we wouldn't be talking together now."

At this remark Zhorga nodded, and looked sternly at Rachad. "It's a rule of space travel, young man, never to take anything onto the ship until you know with absolute certainty what it is."

Rachad, his conceit damaged, hung his head, as far as he was able in his suit. He coughed.

"I don't want to spread alarm," he said, "but I spotted hundreds of space eggs floating not far from us. Even if they came close enough, though, I doubt if scarcely any of them would have the power to germinate."

Despite his reassurances there were mutterings. The fear so recently banished reappeared. Zhorga turned to his followers.

"I'll take a look at this myself. The six of us may have to arrange a special watch by the bombards for a while. But not a word of what you've just heard to anyone else, understand? The slobs we have crewing for us fall to pieces at the first hint of trouble."

They nodded. And without another word the six began to chop up the disintegrating monster, ready to be carried above and cast over the side.

When his watch ended Clabert reported to Zhorga's cabin. He found the Captain poring over the chart table, having just prepared a new heliocentric horoscope. Near to hand was Gebeth's orrery, meticulously brought up to date.

As Clabert entered he lay down the pair of dividers with which he had been checking distances. "And what mood are the men in now?" he asked wryly.

"They do what they're told," Clabert told him in a low voice. "But then they don't have much choice. There's nothing they can do—it's too late for them to think of turning back now." He paused. "Patchman and Small have taken the second watch forward. The others are below."

"Still pretty scared, eh?"

"Yes, in spite of having it proved that space monsters aren't anything supernatural."

Zhorga chuckled without humor. "And all cursing their captain, as usual!" Crew dissatisfaction rarely bothered him. He knew from experience that he could simply browbeat most men into obedience, and that was his method.

"They'd be more frightened still if they knew what I know," he said somberly. "Come and take a look at this."

His stubby finger pointed to a mark he had made on the chart. "Here's where we are, halfway between the orbits of Earth and Mars. Here's Mars . . . and you'll see how close our path will shortly take us to the trailer here."

Clabert drew in his breath. Every planet generated a type of vortex known as a trailer, which it dragged along with it some millions of miles downsun.

Directly behind a planet, the ether flow tended to be relatively smooth. Nevertheless there were latent tensions which eventually broke out in a series of flurries and rapids, culminating in the large and dangerous etheric whirlpool.

"I thought we were going to miss that by a good margin," he grumbled.

"So we were—but my calculations are off, of course, due to early discrepancies. We could still change course to give it a wide berth—but then we'd risk never catching up with Mars." Zhorga rattled his fingers nervously on the table. "No, we shall have to run the flurry, I'm afraid. Bit of a nuisance. Still, there's no *evident* danger. Just means we'll pass too damn close to the vortex for comfort, that's all."

Both men were silent for a while. Both knew all too well what being caught in an ether vortex meant. There was no way out of it, except by discarding all silk, which meant being left adrift without sail power. Toward the center the forces were so intense that ether silk was broken up, first to shreds, and then to dust. The eye of the vortex then carried that dust along with it forever. If the *Wandering Queen* should ever be fated to arrive there, she would probably find a good many old wrecks waiting for her company.

"This is for your information only," Zhorga rumbled. "So you'll know what to expect. We'll have trouble on our hands if the others get to hear of it. They'll want to change course."

"What about Bruge and his clique? Shouldn't they know?"

Zhorga shook his head. "The fewer the better. Keep your mouth shut."

Gloomily he rose and clomped in his lead footweights to the rear of the cabin, where he peered out of the slanted casements. It was strange, he thought. Space seemed so changeless and impassive. It gave no hint of the invisible, raging power that was propelling his little ship onward, either to riches or destruction.

"Well look—it's the fine young lad who wanted to feed us to the dragon!"

Ignoring Boogle's taunt, Rachad divested himself of his suit, put out the powder in his backpack, and climbed onto his bunk. Others who were seated round the long table looked up with sullen interest as Boogle followed him, grimacing into his face.

"Hope you enjoyed your star-gazing," he hissed. "Maybe I'll come up after you next time and make it permanent. All it needs is a knife to cut your line, and one good shove!"

"Shut up, and go away," Rachad said wearily. Ever since the fight a few days ago with the space monster—still referred to by many as a dragon—some of the crew, led by Boogle, had begun to use him as a whipping boy to give vent to their fear and frustration, diverting to him the resentment they felt against Zhorga. Rachad did not think any real harm would befall him, but he was thinking of asking Zhorga to let him sleep in the sternhouse again.

"Leave him alone, Boogle, or you'll answer to me," Small called from the other end of the mess.

Boogle scowled down the table, then spoke to Rachad out of the corner of his mouth. "They say it was through talking to you the Captain got so set on this enterprise, alchemist. You put a spell on him, like as not. Well, I've lost good friends for it, and I'll get you sooner or later. Here—Mars—I'll find a way."

"Boogle!" Small bellowed.

Reluctantly Boogle moved away, and Rachad lay back on his bunk, appalled by the man's hatred.

He closed his eyes and shortly dozed off. He was not sure how much later it was that he woke up feeling that the bunk was shivering under him.

He sat up. The bunk *was* shivering. On the table, plates and utensils clattered and vibrated.

Then the whole ship began to sway. Side to side, up and down, as if she were caught in a wavering current, while at the same time she leaped forward, accelerating sharply.

He swung off his bunk, but his knees almost buckled under him with the unaccustomed weight, so harsh was the acceleration. There came a violent lurch. Utensils and other loose objects fell and rattled.

The lamps flickered. Rachad's stomach contracted. He could hear the ends of the ship's beams jiggling against one another, groaning and squealing, and he could imagine what that would do to the caulking—though the special pitch had a rubbery consistency that allowed for a certain amount of free play. He gripped a stanchion, and in common with everyone else present, looked about him in a questioning, wondering way.

Suddenly a trap door banged open at the farther end of the mess deck. Through it struggled Captain Zhorga, coming up from the hold where he had been inspecting the cargo. His face was livid, and even while he was only halfway through the trap door his gravelly voice smote through the room.

"Get on deck and take in the sail, every one of you! We've hit the rapids!"

At first there was no reaction, as if his words had no meaning. The men watched dumbly while he staggered to his feet and strode toward them, reaching for his spacesuit.

"Don't you understand?" he roared in fury. "It's too soon! We're headed for the trailer!"

This they *did* comprehend. There were gasps and throaty wails; then a strange silence, broken only by sobs and grunts of effort, as the men began to struggle into their suits. Zhorga, lashing up his toggles, approached Rachad.

"You too, boy. This is a *real* emergency."

In a daze, Rachad began to pull on his canvas garment. "What happened?" he asked in a hushed tone. "We were supposed to miss it by a million miles!"

Zhorga pulled a face. "Gebeth's chart gives the wrong damned position, I suppose!" he grated, telling the truth as far as he understood it, but neglecting to mention how fine he had tried to cut his course. "Get moving or we're all finished."

He rammed on his helmet, screwed it tight, and thrust a taper in Rachad's hand. Rachad performed the service of lighting his backpack and the Captain lumbered off, the first to head for the airshed.

The crew poured onto the deck and scurried for the capstans. Zhorga was desperately hoping that, by clewing up all sail as quickly as possible, the rapids would lessen their hold on the vessel and her deadweight momentum would be enough to carry her past the vortex—through the rim of the vortex, even—without being dragged into it.

The gigantic degree of luck this would require, however, was not with him. The billowing, elaborate canopy had, indeed, begun to break up, and the star clouds were shining through the gaps, but most sails were still full-spread when the entire ship keeled over about twenty degrees.

The transition came so quickly that scarcely anyone or anything on board was disturbed. But everyone knew what it meant. It was like taking a curve at high speed, but with the deck tilting, compensating for the change in direction, so that the only physical effect was a sudden swing to one side coupled with a momentary increase in weight.

The *Wandering Queen* had been seized by the vortex. Mechanically the crew continued to work the windlasses, fighting the dawning realization that they were doomed. And bleakly Zhorga stared ahead of him, fancying he saw the stars move as the ship swept along on her new, inwardly spiraling path (though the turns of the spiral were so huge that the impression must have been in his imagination) and wondering what he could possibly do now.

Eventually as many as there was room for gathered under the air balloon, where it was possible to talk. The rest looked on from outside, hands pressed enviously against the transparent sheeting. For once Zhorga's face was white as he stood facing his crew, helmet under one arm, his back to the cabin door. Many were openly weeping. Others raged impotently, shaking their fists at him but not daring to come closer.

Endpress's face was distorted. "A fine testimony to your leadership, Captain!"

"Follow me, he said," another blurted between ragged sobs, "I'll see you through, I'll take you all the way to Mars, he said, and instead we're all going to die in the trailer...."

"We should have killed you in Olam!"

Finally Zhorga became impatient with the imprecations. "SHUT UP!" he roared. Then, in a lower tone: "I'll get you out of this."

Endpress's response was a hysterical laugh. *"How?* No ship ever got out of the trailer!"

"I need a dozen good men," Zhorga said. He glanced around him, peering into space. It seemed as if he were searching for something. He cleared his throat. "The rest of you can get below, where it's safer, and wait. Five men I have already—Bruge, Patchman, Zataka, Small, and the bosun. Seven more. It will be dangerous work and I can't even promise that you'll live through it—but you'll have a chance of saving the ship."

"Bluff!" someone jeered. "It's just bluff!"

Zhorga waited no longer. He waded into the crowd, struck the last speaker in the mouth with his canvas-covered fist, and then began grabbing and shoving, selecting the most stalwart and pushing them to one side where they were watched over by the flintlock-wielding Clabert.

There was surprisingly little resistance. They all knew from the look in Clabert's eyes that he was ready to shoot down any one of them like a dog. "This should do it," Zhorga gasped, panting. "The rest—get below decks and hang on for all you're worth."

"Captain! Take me to!" Rachad pushed his way forward, but Zhorga merely waved him back. "Sorry lad, no amateurs. Get below."

Rachad turned away crestfallen. Zhorga entered his cabin and returned with his folding telescope. While the dismissed men made their way, silent and suspicious, to the mess deck, he put the spyglass to his eye and swept space to port, searching out something he had glimpsed a few minutes earlier.

There it was: a cloud of milky-white points, moving slowly against the starry background. He muttered to himself, his brow ridged in concentration, then turned to his skeleton crew.

They stared back at him, their faces displaying a frightened gauntness. He spoke to them in a gruff, mumbling voice, stumbling over his words.

"This is the end, you're thinking, and maybe you're right. But don't give up yet. There's still a chance for us, and we're going to take it."

He swallowed. "So now we'll do a spot of real space sailing. You'll work on the side windlasses, fore and aft, in groups of three. All you have to do is watch for my signals, *and obey them*, no matter what happens. Those of you I trust are armed, and if you see anyone desert his post or ignore a command, cut him down without delay."

"You can depend on it," Bruge rumbled.

"One more thing—use double safety lines. If things go right we'll be tossed about a bit. And *whatever happens*, stick to where you are."

One of the pressed men spoke up nervously. "Just what is going to happen, Captain?"

"You'll see."

Zhorga climbed to the quarterdeck from where he would direct the operation, and watched as the twelve, willing or not, went to their posts and readied themselves. His desperate gambit was about to begin.

In the swirling world of the vortex, maneuvering a sailship was not the type of proposition it would have been anywhere else. For practical purposes, in fact, it was virtually impossible. At present the ship swept on smoothly; the vortex was a well-ordered system and its in-turning stream scrupulously obeyed the pattern of forces that had given rise to it. But should she seek to escape the voracious whirlpool she would find the effort futile, and similarly, should she for some reason turn to head deeper into it she would soon encounter the sliding ridges, ripples and minor eddies that the progressive turns of the spiral produced as they surged against one another at different rates of travel. These turbulences would turn the ship back onto her former course: thus she was doomed to run the gamut, to spiral round and round, ever faster, on an ever-narrowing circuit, to destruction.

Within these strictly defined limits, however, there was room for a degree of mobility. At present the sails were lashed to their yards, even the minute area they presented being enough to keep the ship implacably in the power of the vortex. Zhorga gave the signal to unfurl a small mast on the starboard side, and as this was done the ship swung round and moved at a portward angle to the current.

Four stunsails were sufficient to steer the galleon. The *Wandering Queen* swayed, tossed in the tumultuous stream, as Zhorga guided her toward the swarm. The glints brightened; for all his tension, he breathed a sigh of relief. The eggs were within range!

Half an hour later he suddenly found himself surrounded by the egg swarm. The eggs drifted and hurtled by, some bouncing off the hull and deck. He replaced his helmet in case one should rupture the air balloon, and continued to peer anxiously to see if any of them would react to the ship's presence.

Not all were absolutely sterile. Some burst into abortive life, sprouting insignificant creatures that lashed about themselves feebly before expiring. Then, when Zhorga had almost given up hope, there came what he had been waiting for.

Instinctively he threw his arm before his face. A writhing patch of nebulosity had blossomed into existence. In little more than a minute it had expanded and solidified into a full-grown monster—and, like its earlier brother, this monster moved toward the ship, sensing her, reaching toward the only mode of life it knew: to attack and destroy.

And Zhorga unhesitatingly gave the order for his men to steer the galleon straight for the heart of the lashing beast!

Even the best of them recoiled with horror when it was

realized what was required of them. But only one broke and ran, loping with ten-foot strides back along the shed toward the airshed. Zhorga saw Clabert raise his pistol. A puff of smoke from the flintlock followed. The runner's body jerked suddenly, and rammed against the airshed, then to go rolling across the deck and lie motionless.

Now the others hurried to obey Zhorga's order, though whether they understood the purpose behind it was questionable. The ship turned toward the monster, which as it neared seemed to fill the sky. Zhorga clung to the lashed-down wheel to steady himself as the ship gathered speed. For hideous moments the frantic tentacles seemed to enclose her—but they were made to reach out for a fleeing prey, not to snatch at something coming in close. Miraculously, it seemed, she had slipped swiftly between them—and then she crashed into the web-like body!

The concussion was less shattering than Zhorga had feared. The monster yielded and vibrated. The *Wandering Queen* was like a great cumbersome insect caught in that web, and the beast seemed not to know that it could, if it chose, use its massive tentacles to pluck her out.

Yet the monster continued to charge on its former course, and though the galleon was not broken by the impact her change in momentum was bone-cracking. For all his strength, Zhorga was torn from the wheel and found himself flung hard against the thick covering of the air balloon, which mercifully held. For a while he was confused, and afterward deduced that he must temporarily have lost consciousness. He only knew that eventually he recovered his wits to find himself resting lightly on the deck, but with practically no discernible weight.

The monster was gone. It had disintegrated, its brief, truncated life had collapsed. But, as Zhorga took note of the almost imperceptible level of acceleration, and observed that the galleon had already swung lazily round so that her decks again lay beneath Mars, he knew that the space beast had served his purpose.

The basis of his suicidal strategy had been his reasoning that the creature was not composed of ether silk and so was unaffected by the vortex. It was simple chance, he had decided, that had sent the eggs drifting through this region. He had speculated that the monster's dread strength might just be enough to tear the *Wandering Queen* free of the ensnaring current before she was drawn too deeply into its coils.

He had not seriously expected the plan to work. He had expected the galleon to be torn to pieces, bringing himself and his crew a quick death, instead of a lingering one in the eye of the whirlpool, full of misery and—what was worse from his point of view—recrimination.

He relaxed, feeling peaceful, basking in his triumph. The rest of the voyage, he told himself, would be relatively plain sailing. Until Mars was reached, anyway.

He wondered if the brave men on the main deck had all survived, or if more had been added to the death toll so far.

A wry thought occurred to him.

They would be dying, he admitted sourly, in the cause of trade.

Chapter SIX

Zhorga's prediction proved correct and the *Wandering Queen* journeyed on through calm ether for the remaining distance to Mars. The temperature dropped sharply and the ship grew bitterly cold. He gave permission for braziers to be lit which burned *chak,* a combustible charcoal-like preparation which gave off heat but no stupefying fumes or irritant smoke.

There was ample time to make good the damage done by the space dragon. The midmast had cracked and so was cut down, the sails being redistributed among the remaining spars as best as could be managed. Zhorga reckoned he still had sail power enough. Mars was smaller than Earth and so had less gravity to contend with—it was only the shock wave that worried him.

The target planet became first a glowing ruby, then a red disk which Zhorga studied through his spyglass, and at last a full-blown world floating ahead of them, in its own way as fascinating a sight as Earth. At closer range its fiery redness mellowed, and was relieved by other features—the glittering white and blue of the half-frozen polar seas, the clouds of various types: white for water vapor, orange (like dyed cotton wool) for atmospheric dust, and gray for the sooty by-products of the air fires which showed up against the general background as blotches of a deeper, maroon red. Zhorga explained that these burning areas had been ignited in ancient times to release warmth and breathable air onto the planet, for once it had been uninhabitable.

The hazy dark triangle of Syrtis Major was easy to find, but he searched it in vain for any sign of Kars, its major city. At length, however, the planet became like a vast wall and it was time to act. He ordered all crewmen lashed in their places, and all sail taken in, so that the galleon coasted in free fall.

Then he waited for the telltale signs. Eventually they came, chiefly a rocking to and fro of the vessel as the first ripples of the shock wave lapped against the furled silk.

Deeper into the wave he would harness these retroactive ripples, using them to slow the ship down and make it safe for her to enter the atmosphere.

He unfurled one small sail: the aft topgallant. For a second or two it flapped, then filled with the retroactive eddy as though trapping a fall of water and bellied toward the deck, which in response tilted sternward.

The red wall which was Mars swung, tilted vertiginously, and vanished beneath the hull as the topgallant turned the ship through a hundred and eighty degrees like a weathercock turning in the wind. She was now falling Marsward bottom first, and for the first time in months the sun shone directly on the deck—a sun shrunk to half size, giving off a wan, clear light.

Zhorga ordered more sails cautiously unfurled. The shock wave snatched at them, buffeting and shaking the galleon with terrifying force. Agonized, he wondered if the tackles could take the treatment. Already the deceleration was bearing him down toward the deck. But soon the whole sail canopy had been unfurled and the galleon was on full brake.

Gasping, crushed by the thunderous deceleration, those on board lay stretched out on deck. The timbers groaned and protested, and the ordeal went on and on and on, seemingly without end.

It was, in fact, impossible to gauge its length, for no one stayed conscious. Zhorga was not sure how many times he blacked out, how many times he dimly recovered his senses to find the ship shaking and shuddering all around him. He only knew that, in the end, he became aware of a series of decided bumps, as if the vessel were bouncing down a flight of steps. This, he decided later, betokened the ship's passage through the shock wave's inner isoclines, for suddenly everything became marvelously calm. The deceleration slackened and became merely mild. The sails no longer vibrated or rucked wildly.

The ship was through the shock wave's leading fracture zone. Here the wave manifested as an easy swell, making it an easy matter to control the ship's rate of descent.

Zhorga, trying to bring life back into his aching limbs, grinned with triumph. Far from being the most dangerous maneuver he had attempted, the deceleration had proved in many respects to be the easiest.

He had made it!

The ship swooped over Mars, moving southward away from the dead center of the shock wave. Shortly she encountered the beginnings of the normal circum-planetary flow, the sort of ether movement Zhorga understood best. He ordered the crew to dismantle the sail canopy and prepare for aerial flight.

Masts, booms and yards shifted jerkily into position. Zhorga was so intent on the operation that he was not the first to spot the object that came hurtling round the curve of the planet, and which expanded rapidly from a tiny wedge into a long elegant shape. When it was pointed out to him, all he could do was stare.

It was a ship, orbiting in free fall below the violence of the shock wave, all sail taken in. But what a ship! She was, he judged, nearly a quarter mile in length, and at first she seemed so strange, her appearance so unexpected, that he was confused.

Abruptly she put out a sail, an oddly-shaped sheet of silk, and with incredible skill altered course to go flashing by the *Wandering Queen* at close quarters. Now her immensity was overpowering and her length seemingly endless. Her burnished wood shone in the sun, and her decks seemed jewelled, bedecked with satins and velvets. Colors glowed along her hull, which was decorated with unfamiliar designs. At her stern a stiff pennant bearing a black emblem added to her outlandish appearance.

Her design owed nothing to seagoing or airgoing influences. Her tiered decks would have made aerodynamic nonsense. This was a ship built for space alone. What was more, her masts and booms were so unbelievably long—longer even than the ship herself—that the vast expanses of silk they could presumably carry would have attained speeds too great even for interplanetary travel.

Such enormous speeds were useful in only one area: travel from star to star. This was an interstellar ship.

Zhorga was stunned. He had heard of these interstellar leviathans, of course, but never in his life had he expected to see one. What could be her business on Mars?

In a fragment of time she had dwindled into the distance—but as she did so she seemed to eject a smaller part of herself, which sprouted brilliant blue ether silk and advanced toward the *Wandering Queen* again, swiftly catching up with the galleon and pacing her a short distance away.

The daughter craft reminded Zhorga of a dragonfly. Its sails resembled a dragonfly's double wings, being extended on flexible rods which could be warped, curved and twisted by means of control lines. The hull was long and black, except for two transparent domes within which figures could be seen peering across at the Earth ship. Like a dragonfly, too, it could hover and dart, displaying perfect control. Zhorga realized that he faced a sailing technique beyond his wildest dreams.

Zhorga tore his gaze away from the sight. The task of adjusting spars and rigging still had to be completed. Stalking across the deck, he attracted the attention of Clabert, and managed to get the work back under way.

The new activity seemed to displease those aboard the dragonfly. The craft spat out a glimmering flare which stitched a magnesium-bright necklace across the bows of the *Wandering Queen*, which by now had almost adopted the attitude of aerial flight. In the forward dome, the watching figures gesticulated across at the galleon, pointing upward and astern.

Zhorga easily guessed their meaning. They wanted him to accompany the dragonfly to a rendezvous with the mother ship. But how could he? He did not have that kind of maneuverability. Could they not see he was practically helpless to go against the ether current, Mars's version of the slipstream?

He signalled Clabert to continue and soon all was in readiness to enter the atmosphere. A second glowing missile crossed the stem of the ship. Zhorga realized glumly that he had no choice but to hope that the captain of the dragonfly would be content to follow the *Wandering Queen* down, and would forebear from doing her any damage.

But he had reckoned without the impetuosity of certain of his crew, who had received lessons galore from their master on rashness. Unseen by Zhorga, Bruge, Small and Patchman levered one of the bombards out of its storage pit, loaded, primed and fired it, all in the space of a minute.

The ball missed the dragonfly proper, but tore a rent in one of the silken wings. Aghast, Zhorga yelled futilely in his helmet, but the dragonfly's response came almost immediately. Its third glowing shot hit the *Wandering*

Queen amidships and exploded with a dazzling blare of light.

Zhorga distinctly heard a soft WHUMPH through the brass of his headpiece. Momentarily he was blinded. Then his vision cleared to see that a number of side strakes were smashed, and a section of deck lay propped against the rail, having come adrift from its beams.

On the foredeck, the fighting spirit was unabated. By now both bombards had been manhandled onto their firing platforms. They were fired as fast as they could be reloaded, all balls going wide. In return, the dragonfly sent yet another fire-dart which fell among the rigging and devastated the spars, scattering fragments of wood, rope and silk in all directions.

And then a rapid whisper of air against the sides of the hull signalled the end of the battle. The ship was entering the atmosphere.

Mars's air was in a sense artificial, being produced by the air fires (though these had burned for centuries and could not be put out). The continuous addition of phlogistonic gases from the burning areas was offset by a boiling off, or evaporation, of air from the top of the atmosphere, which consequently met space abruptly, not gradually as did Earth's. Almost, the atmosphere had a surface of its own, and the *Wandering Queen* was now plunging into that surface.

It had been Zhorga's intention to skim the atmosphere, dropping into it as he got the feel of the local ether currents. Now it was too late. With so many sails gone, or in tatters, control was lost, and there was little that he could do to take effective command anyway.

The susurration intensified. Density, Zhorga knew, would increase rapidly. The desperadoes at the bombards gave up the fight and scrambled to return to their posts as the galleon swayed under the impact of rushing air, scudding along as if driven by a storm.

The sound of the atmosphere became a buffeting roar. Down and down fluttered the *Wandering Queen*, spiraling and corkscrewing with the aerodynamics of a sycamore seed. It was only her inherent airworthiness that gave her any chance at all—that and the efforts of groups and individuals who stubbornly hurled themselves onto capstans and windlasses, using their instincts amid the chaos to try to bring the ship some measure of stability. When she was only two or three miles from the ground some windsail was released; temporarily it brought the ship out of her spin, sending her lurching crabwise in a stiff breeze. For a minute Zhorga thought a controlled landing might be possible after all, but the damage among the spars was too great. The ship skidded around the Martian sky. She dipped, and entered into a steep, curved descent.

The crash, when it came, was a prolonged, titanic thunder. Timbers, masts, spars and sails shattered, splintered, tore. Zhorga, like everyone else who was not actually killed, was knocked cold.

In the restricted view through his faceplate, Rachad saw that he lay on gritty soil. His head ached abominably —not just from the knock he had received from the inside of his brass helmet, but also because his backpack was nearly extinguished and the air inside his suit was foul.

He struggled to sit up, anxiously feeling himself for broken bones, and discovering none, applied himself to unscrewing his helmet. At last the headpiece came off; thankfully he drew in a lungful of cold, thin air with a slightly burnt odor, not at all strange to him after the acrid chemical air he had been breathing.

Unsteadily he came to his feet.

So here he was standing on Mars, he thought shakily. The pull of the planet seemed oddly burdening after so much time in space. Evidently he had been thrown from the *Wandering Queen* on impact, for he was still attached to his lifeline, which led to the wreckage of the ship. For a while he stared at this wreckage. The crash had almost completely crushed the galleon, scattering timbers over the surrounding ground. A few remaining spars leaned crazily, trailing sail.

Bodies lay unmoving. Casks and demijohns from the cracked-open hold spilled their contents onto the sand. It seemed to Rachad's numbed mind, as he gazed at the scene, that he was the sole survivor.

He turned to survey the landscape. The ship appeared to have come down in a semi-desert region. He saw a rock-strewn plain, the sandy ground ranging in color from reddish-brown to orange and dotted here and there with stunted shrubs. Beyond the horizon there jutted up a range of hills and scaurs.

The sky was mauve, shading from grayish-pink to purple. Near the mid-heaven was the wan, half-size sun, casting a gentle, undecided light, and if one looked, one could make out glimmering stars.

Altogether it was a world sufficiently novel in appearance to hold considerable charm, albeit an alien charm, but Rachad was unable to take pleasure in the sight. He unhooked his safety line and wondered unhappily where he might be. Certainly nowhere near the city of Kars, and probably not even in the region known as Syrtis Major.

Behind him he heard the sound of falling timber. Captain Zhorga, unhelmeted like himself, was emerging from the wreck. Rachad hurried to meet him, but Zhorga ignored him and immediately bent to unscrew the helmet of the first body he came to.

With a start Rachad realized that he had been negligent. He was *not* the sole survivor, and his inaction might be condemning others to suffocation. He hurried to copy Zhorga, who grunted with pleasure to see him.

"I might have known *you* would come through all right," he congratulated sourly.

"A pity about your ship, Captain."

Zhorga sighed, and spared a glance for his ruined merchantman. She, at least, would never take to the air again. But he judged there was enough timber and silk to build some sort of flying raft to explore the surrounding countryside, and perhaps to ferry his men and goods to the nearest town. Thoughts of that, however, would have to wait. His first duty was to his dead and injured.

There was more movement from within the wreck. Clabert and Patchman appeared. Zhorga went over and talked with them.

Rachad pulled off a helmet. The man inside was Boogle and he was dead, his neck broken.

More men were stirring, climbing to their feet groaning and looking about them with awe. Rachad straightened, and then he heard a familiar noise—a whistling noise, the interference effect of a ship sailing too close to the ground.

Something long and dark went hurtling by overhead. It was the dragonfly, sails outstretched, its pointed tail trailing like a sting. It executed a neat turn, swooped, and put down with poise and precision on the gravelly soil.

Between them Zhorga and Rachad had by now checked all the bodies that still lay motionless on this side of the ship, and had found three who breathed and three who did not. Rachad retreated toward Zhorga, as did most others who were able to walk. The air captain glowered at the alien craft as a ramp dropped from the side of the dragonfly. A party of about eight to ten men, marching with springy step, emerged and advanced in a squad.

All but the leader, who carried a holstered pistol, bore long-barreled guns with bell-shaped muzzles. And they wore spacesuits,—elegant garments, slim as cat-suits, made of some silky, deep purple material, the backpacks moulded into them and making only slight humps, an armorial device—a rampant star beast—stitched on each man's breast. The helms were likewise close-fitting, the faceplates a single curved piece of tinted glass.

The squad halted. The leader stepped forward, and with a flick of his wrist slid back his apparently flexible faceplate.

The face that stared at Zhorga with steady blue eyes was of a man about thirty. A confident, military sort of face, sporting a neat brush moustache. "Why did you ignore my instructions?" the officer inquired incisively, in a guttural but fluid accent unfamiliar to Zhorga. "Why did you open fire on me?"

Zhorga spluttered his indignation before answering. "*Ignore?*" he said in a strangled voice. "How in hell could I—"

He took a hold on himself. "What do *you* mean by shooting down a peaceful merchantman?" he said angrily. He spread his arm to indicate the scene of destruction. "Just take a look at what you've done! Do you know who we are? We are Earthmen! We've just completed the crossing from Earth—the first to do so for two generations. And the first thing that happens when we finally make it is that we get smashed up by you!"

"From Earth?" the officer echoed. He looked suspiciously at Zhorga, and seemed puzzled. "The sunward planet? I would hardly have thought your vessel fit for such a journey. I was sure you were Martians, trying some stupid attack on the *Bucentaur*."

He sauntered past Zhorga, suddenly noticing the bottles, chests and bales that were scattered over the ground. He kicked at a cask. He raised his eyebrows.

"Trade goods," he remarked on a note of surprise.

Zhorga was silent. The officer returned to him. "Well, I suppose anything is possible. At any rate, we'll soon get the truth out of you. I'm taking you all up to the *Bucentaur*. Baron Matello's ship," he added, seeing Zhorga's frown.

Bruge, his temple discolored and swollen by a massive bruise, moved closer to Zhorga. "Tell these murderers to get lost, Captain. All we want is to be left to go about our business."

The officer bristled. Zhorga, nervously aware of the bell-muzzled weapons he faced, coughed ostentatiously. "I have many dead and badly hurt," he complained.

"All the more reason to cooperate with me," the officer said briskly. "On the *Bucentaur* your injured will be attended by the baron's excellent physicians." Suddenly he became impatient. "Come now, Captain—you are hundreds of miles from any settlement. Just what do you think you are going to do? Mars is not a hospitable place, I assure you."

Zhorga, in fact, was attracted by the prospect of seeing the fabulous starship at close quarters. "What about my trade goods?" he demanded.

The officer laughed. "We are not in the shipping business, Captain. The baron will decide what will become of you. Now—"

Zhorga hurriedly deliberated, then nodded, trying to give the proceedings an air of negotiation. "We'll come with you," he said.

The star officer regarded himself as a gentleman. Without argument he allowed time to bury the dead, which was done in shallow graves, heaped over with the crumbly Martian soil.

Litters for the badly injured were improvised from bits of planking. Of more than forty who had set out with Zhorga from Olam, twenty-six men limped or were carried into the hold of the dragonfly. On entering the craft, Zhorga realized that it was actually an armed lighter for ferrying men or goods between the starship and the ground, for the hold was more roomy than he would have guessed from outside. He peered up a ladder that led to the foremost of the two transparent domes, and was surprised to see that the coxswain was seated, and worked an elaborate arrangement of wheels, levers and pedals.

Could one man alone really fly a craft of this size, he wondered? Where would he find the strength to warp all the sails and hold them against the ether?

A star soldier nudged him along. Captors and captured alike hunkered down with backs braced against the walls, gripping handholds set into the floor while the injured were strapped down to similar holds. Almost before they had settled themselves the ramp was closed and the floor lifted under them, subjecting them to the ear-piercing shriek of the ether (though it was somewhat less shrill, Zhorga noticed, than it would have been on Earth) before they shot aloft and streaked spaceward.

Why, this vessel was practically crewless, Zhorga told himself. How was it done? Presumably with the help of very ingenious mechanical devices, he deduced. Reduction gears and multiple pulleys, ratchets, escapements and slip-levers. The running rigging was probably controlled by mechanisms as complicated as the inside of a clock.

After a while the rush of air against the hull ceased. They were in space. Perhaps half an hour later there was a series of thuds and shocks that told Zhorga the lighter was docking.

They were aboard the *Bucentaur*.

Chapter SEVEN

Baron Goth Matello, Margrave of the Marsh Worlds, Protector of the Castarpos Moons, and a loyal subject of his liege-lord, His Most Majestic King Lutheron by whose leave he held all his titles, raised a gold goblet to his lips. Ingeniously designed for free-fall, the goblet was capped by a gold cupola punctured with scores of tiny holes like a pepper-pot. The cover prevented the sharp-tasting wine from floating away as a liquid sphere; the wine's own surface tension, on the other hand, prevented it from seeping through the perforations.

The sucking action of drinking, however, easily overcame this weak restraint. Baron Matello sucked, drained the goblet, and tossed it to the serving maid who had handed it to him.

He turned to Captain Veautrin. "Have they been down in interrogation?"

"Yes sir," Veautrin replied. "They all tell the same tale, right down to the details. The inquisitor is satisfied that their story is true. They really did sail from the third planet."

"All right, let's see this captain of theirs. Things are so boring around here that anything is a diversion."

Veautrin walked to the door in cling-slippers. He opened it, and beckoned. A burly, bearded man entered, moving awkwardly in the cling-slippers he also now wore (like everyone else aboard the *Bucentaur* for as long as she remained in orbit). On his head was a battered cap displaying a tarnished badge of rank; he stood chewing his beard, gazing uncertainly at the baron, who reclined against a high-backed chair, legs carelessly outspread.

Zhorga saw a man some ten years younger than himself, with a broad face framed by a close-clipped fringe beard. The baron bore that direct look of someone used to exercising authority. But there was also a certain ruffianly quality about him—it was a fighter's face.

His eyes were brooding and restless, brown in color but

with a luminous orange tint Zhorga had never seen on Earth. He avoided meeting those eyes directly. This was a man one did not trifle with—indeed the whole power and massiveness of the interstellar ship, its unabashed grandeur, was such that Zhorga felt overawed. He knew that he must tread carefully with the baron. It was true that he and his men had been received civilly enough so far—ten men, in fact, were currently in the ship's sick bay. But on the other side of the coin Zhorga recalled his recent interrogation. The interview had been entirely verbal, but the instruments of persuasion—ready in case his words lacked the ring of truth—had been clearly on view.

"Well, Earthman," the baron said in a loud voice, "what do you call yourself?"

Zhorga cleared his throat. "Captain Zebandar Zhorga, sir—at your service."

"You are an air captain, I believe."

"In the main, that is true," Zhorga nodded. "I can now, however, claim some experience in space."

"Yes—I am curious about this exploit of yours." The baron smiled patronizingly. "Something of a pioneering flight, I gather."

Zhorga saw no reason to hide his pride in the fact. "The first space voyage from Earth in nearly two generations!" he boasted.

"I can believe it," said Matello dryly. He signaled to the nearby serving girl, holding up two fingers. She did something with a peculiarly fashioned carafe that rested on a magnetic tray, and approached with two full goblets. Matello took them both and tossed one through the air to Zhorga.

Zhorga caught it and stared at it in puzzlement.

"Drink—it's a goblet of wine," Matello said patiently. He demonstrated the use of the cupola, as though explaining something to a savage. Zhorga followed suit, then as he got the hang of it swallowed the wine greedily, emptying the goblet with gusto. The baron signaled the girl to refill it for him, then relaxed, sipping at his own.

"How did you drink in space on your own ship?" he asked.

"Oh, we just stuck a tube in a water cask. We had a bit of weight most of the time, anyway."

"Spatial travel generally needs careful preparation. Evidently you had to improvise a great deal. Tell me about this voyage. Begin at takeoff."

Zhorga did not need telling twice. Mentally he had rehearsed this scene many times, though the imaginary setting for it had been the taproom of The Ship in Olam. Down in the bowels of the *Bucentaur* the inquisitor had already once cut off his flowing narrative with an irritated "that's enough."

Bearing in mind that the baron was also unlikely to look kindly on any long-windedness, Zhorga tried to keep his story concise. He recounted the perilous ascent into space, described the difficulties of keeping the galleon trim and maintaining a course; told of the brush with the vortex and the encounters with alchemical monsters. Captain Veautrin stood by impassively, showing no reaction even when Zhorga, with some bitterness, described how the lighter commanded by himself had effectively destroyed the *Wandering Queen*.

The baron listened in fascination. When Zhorga had finished, he chuckled.

"Don't blame Captain Veautrin too much," he said. "He was only doing his duty. You, no doubt, mourn the loss of your galleon—so think how I feel about a threat to my *Bucentaur*! An odd-looking ship like yours, appearing out of nowhere, was bound to arouse suspicion. But there's something you haven't told me. What were your reasons for embarking on this venture? They must have been pressing."

"They were simple enough," Zhorga said gruffly. "We came to Mars to trade. The merchants on Earth are running out of ether silk with which to ply the airways, and it is our hope to obtain some here."

At this the baron threw up his hands and uttered a half-horrified, half-delighted exclamation. "But my dear fellow! Your efforts have all been for nothing! It is absolutely certain there is no silk to be had here!"

Zhorga stared at him blankly. "My lord—"

"There can be no doubt of it. This wretched planet has declined almost to a state of savagery. The people are barely capable of ploughing the dirt—there are so few of them, anyway." He shook his head, smiling with amusement. "No, I'm certain you won't find a shred of silk. We've been here for nearly a month now, and yours is the first flying ship we've seen."

Zhorga was dumbfounded. Somehow this possibility had simply not occurred to him. It was as if his mind had unconsciously put a block on the subject.

He clenched his fists and gritted his teeth. What a farcical joke he had played on himself! What a fool he would look in the eyes of the men he had dragged with him across space! Momentarily Zhorga's spirit was crushed. He stood with his back ramrod straight, gazing emptily ahead.

"I may pay a visit to Earth myself, when I am finished here," the baron was saying lightly. "It is reputed by some to be the birthplace of space travel, not to say of mankind itself. If, that is, it is the same planet I am thinking of."

"I seriously doubt it," Zhorga rumbled absently. "Ether silk cannot be manufactured there; the sun is too close. So it cannot be the origin of space travel. Or of mankind, either, for the same reason. Both must have arrived there from outside."

Matello shrugged. "Not worth a visit after all, then. Well, Captain, what are you going to do now? No ship, no silk to buy."

"*Hmmmmm. . . .*" The sound, a combination of chagrin and reappraisal, came from deep within Zhorga's chest.

What, indeed, was he going to do? He was crushed, defeated, his plans destroyed.

He glanced wildly about him, sensing the vast bulk of the *Bucentaur* all around. He thought of the *Wandering Queen;* thought of the ships he had grown up with and struggled with all his life.

Suddenly it seemed to him that he had not really appreciated what it could mean to him to be standing on a starship. True, he had lost the *Wandering Queen*—but was it not ridiculous to be still obsessed with the need to take ether silk to Earth, a dilapidated backwater? Ridiculous—when this great ship could take him to a new life among the stars!

He took a deep breath. "My future lies in your hands, my lord. You have destroyed my ship. You have left me stranded. It lies in your power simply to abandon me here, or—"

He stopped. Matello frowned, looking dangerous. "Or?"

"Earth was never the place for a man of adventure.

Swear me into your service. Permit me to wear your lordship's coat of arms."

Captain Veautrin's rigid expression told Zhorga that he had committed a considerable *faux pas*. The baron tossed away his goblet, which went spinning across the room.

"And your men? You would desert them?"

"Any who want to grub on Mars, let them," Zhorga said, blinking. "As for the others, swear them in, too."

"To serve with the Margrave of the Marsh Worlds," the baron said harshly, "is accounted an honor. It is not something to be handed out to any passing rabble of merchants and air sailors."

Zhorga persisted. "I've been a fighting man in my time," he claimed. "I was a midshipman on the *Victorious*— one of Earth's last fighting ships."

"Oh, you're a fighting man!" Matello echoed mockingly. "What weapons do you know?"

"I prefer the cutlass or the broadsword."

Matello had not lost his good humor; he sensed an opportunity for sport, of which there had been precious little since his departure for Mars. He rose and crossed the room to open a wall cupboard. Within, weapons were clipped to a rack—swords, pistols, long-barreled shooters.

He selected a pair of matched blades and returned to hand one apiece to Zhorga and Veautrin, before stepping back to lounge once more in his chair, though there was little need for it in the null gravity, the special cloth of his garments adhering crepe-like to the thick-piled upholstery.

"Match yourself against the good Captain Veautrin here," he drawled. "He'll be only too pleased to accommodate you."

Zhorga tested his sword for balance, difficult though it was to assess in free-fall, and probably immaterial anyway. The weapon was broad-bladed and somewhat longer than he was used to. The metal, however, was excellent— much springier and tougher, he judged, than anything to be found on Earth.

He turned to Veautrin, who stared expressionlessly back at him, his sword pointing military-style at the floor.

"To what limit?" Zhorga asked the baron.

" 'Til one of you yields."

Veautrin took a step back, saluted Zhorga, and took up a formal stance, one arm extended behind him, his sword thrust forward and down, and apparently expecting Zhorga to do the same. His was obviously an impeccable kind of swordsmanship.

Zhorga was trained in a rougher school, however. With a growl he charged at Veautrin, wielding his blade in a whirl of savage strokes. Veautrin easily parried the flurry, stepping neatly in his cling-slippers—while Zhorga found himself tromping clumsily like an elephant.

Then Veautrin's blade found an opening. Its tip hacked at Zhorga's cheek, narrowly missing his ear. Zhorga knocked the sword aside with a bellow and a clang of steel. His blood spilled into the air, forming floating globules which he batted with his free hand, splitting them into a fine mist of droplets.

He regarded the waiting Veautrin with a more cautious eye. The fellow was used to free-fall swordplay; Zhorga was not, and besides he was out of practice. Just the same, he told himself, he had better put up a good show or he would be booted off this ship and onto the red desert below.

Cunning would be required.

He charged again at Veautrin, apparently in the same manner as before, but at the last moment changed direction. As he had anticipated, Veautrin was impeded by his cling-slippers and was unable to take advantage of Zhorga's momentary defenselessness. As he lunged past the starman, Zhorga swung round and kicked him behind the knee—a trick he had learned on the *Victorious*. Veautrin buckled and in the next instant Zhorga's whole bulk collided with him. In a moment the star captain was knocked to the floor, his sword arm pinned down by Zhorga's knee, and Zhorga, teeth bared, held aloft his own blade in both hands, directing the point at Veautrin's throat.

"Yield," he grunted.

Veautrin twitched his sword arm. Too late, Zhorga realized that he lacked the planetary weight to hold his opponent to the floor. Already he had made the mistake of lifting one foot from the carpet, and the other remained attached only by the sole. Now the remaining inches of grip-felt came free, and Veautrin sent him floating into the air, spinning slowly, unable to reach his adversary and feeling ridiculous.

With a chiming sound his sword was struck from his

grasp and went flying toward the ceiling. As it bounced back, Veautrin deftly caught it. Then he tugged Zhorga to the floor by the skirt of his jacket and handed him the weapon hilt foremost with a curt bow.

"Your play has merit, though it lacks finesse," he said.

Baron Matello was laughing loudly and clapping his hands. "Well done! The best bit of clowning I've seen for a long time!" He turned to the victor. "Well, Veautrin, what do you think of him?"

The captain looked Zhorga up and down. He might have been appraising a horse. "He'll be all right, once he's been put through the drills. A good reliable type, basically—if he'll accept discipline."

Privately Zhorga marveled as he dabbed at the blood that still oozed through his beard. The two were discussing a fealty oath that could bind him to the baron for life—yet nothing had even been mentioned to him of the baron's own allegiances, his ideals and aims, even though Zhorga was obviously quite ignorant of them. It was apparently of no consequence, for instance, that he did not even know the name of Matello's monarch.

All this accorded with what he had heard of the mentality of these great star nobles, who lived in an atmosphere of unquestioning obedience and treated their bondsmen as personal property without any opinions of their own. Zhorga tried a new tack. "Perhaps your lordship would be generous enough to give us passage to the star worlds and allow us to fend for ourselves thereafter. In return, let us work for you during your stay on Mars."

"But what use would you be to me?" Matello said petulantly. "It is not as if you had any special knowledge of Mars, or could help me in my mission."

"That depends, of course, on what brings you to this planet," Zhorga said in a low voice.

Matello was silent for a moment. Then he grunted.

"Well, what does it matter if you know? Mars, at one time, was a venue for those seeking a thing of value called the Philosopher's Stone. It has come to my knowledge that a book is hidden here somewhere, said to contain the ultimate alchemical secret. Alchemy, as such, doesn't interest me—but I have reasons for wanting this book."

He gestured to Veautrin to return the swords to the cupboard rack. His florid tones became complaining.

"Where, however, is it? The towns are in ruins, scarcely anyone in them can even read. It could be under any square foot of sand."

Zhorga blinked, and looked astounded. "That is all you know, my lord? That the book is on Mars?"

"That is all."

Zhorga grinned. His eyes gleamed. "Then I can be of use to you after all!"

"You're sure your mentor had nothing else to add? No hint of an address? No idea of what quarter of the city to look in?"

"No, my lord," Rachad lied, trying to sound as guileless as possible. "He only knew that I should go to Kars."

They stood on a rise overlooking the ruins of the ancient city. Around them were parked the *Bucentaur*'s three lighters, which had ferried some hundreds of men to the site. Included in the work force were Zhorga and his crew, transformed now into a small squad and wearing the baron's uniform, but without his coat of arms. They stood at ease alongside the others, awaiting instructions.

Matello was reflective. "Not a great deal to go on for one young man on his own in a strange land," he mused. He had been firm but courteous toward the youth, not wishing to terrify him unduly. He was aware, anyway, that Rachad had already seen the torture equipment in the interrogation room. And indeed, the boy had volunteered his information with alacrity, though disappointingly it did not amount to anything more than the snippet already provided by Captain Zhorga.

"To know that the book exists at all is already a great deal," Rachad said defensively, "let alone in what city it is hidden."

"And with that," Matello sighed, "you came all the way from Earth."

"With respect, my lord, you came much farther with even less. Even a small chance of obtaining so precious a secret is worth taking."

Matello shot him a sarcastic glance. Rachad continued: "My master advised me to pose as a seeker or even an adept, and to inveigle myself among the alchemists and secret societies he thought would exist here."

"Hah! I wish *he* could be here to answer for his advice." Matello rattled the map he was holding. It showed Kars as it had been in former days, before war and decay had overtaken it. At one time the city must have been a thriving, colorful place, but now it presented mostly piles of tumbled masonry, shells of buildings, broken towers and jutting pillars. True, it was even now not entirely abandoned. Among the decrepit piles of sand-colored stone were signs of movement, and on the edges of the sprawling ruins ploughed fields extended.

And the main street plan could still be made out, at least as regards the wider avenues. Rachad craned his neck trying to see Matello's map. He had already learned to recognize the squiggly symbol that marked the temples, of which Kars, it seemed, had been crammed full. Rapidly, almost despairingly, his eye raced over the parchment—and then stopped. There it was, clearly written in the graceful Martian script! The Temple of Hermes Trismegistus!

Rachad's heart beat faster. He looked out over the dead city, trying to locate what he had seen on the map. Could that be it over there—that half-tumbled building with sloping walls, that might once have resembled an athanor?

Yes, he decided. That was it.

With a grunt Baron Matello took up a pen, dipped it in a little bottle of ink, and divided the map into sections. "We'll start here," he said, subdividing one section still further into a number of blocks. Beckoning his officers to gather round, he allotted one squad to each block. "Tear everything apart," he ordered. "Pay special attention to temples—these ancient Martians seem to have gone mad on religion."

The officers shouted commands. Nearly five hundred men trotted downhill, and the inhabitants in their path, living in shacks and makeshift dwellings, fled at their approach.

The work was quickly organized. Block by block, street by street, uniformed men swarmed over the ruins, showing a preference for those that seemed to have been public buildings. Soon the air was filled with dust and resounded to the crack of hammers and the crash of falling masonry.

Rachad, wearing not the baron's uniform but his own tunic and breeks, attached himself to Zhorga's squad at first. But after an hour's work he contrived to slip away, glancing behind him constantly to make sure his departure was not noticed, and set off across Kars, orienting himself by recollecting Matello's map.

It was like a journey through a dream landscape. The city's buff and orange stone was weathered, so that the ruins had a mild and rounded rather than a shattered appearance. He clambered over fallen columns and ascended heaps of rubble, but for the most part walked along what had been magnificent thoroughfares, many of them almost clear of detritus.

He became aware, too, that eyes were watching him from the surrounding ruins, though he caught only glimpses of the watchers as they darted from sight. He felt little fear of being molested; it was obvious that the people hereabouts feared the visitors from the stars.

At one place he came to a street used as a market or bartering place and lined with booths and stalls offering food, cooking utensils, coarse and ill-cut garments, ornaments, and so on. But both vendors and customers had departed.

At last he came to the building he had picked out as the Temple of Hermes Trismegistus. Set apart from the surrounding structures, it was still impressive even though derelict. The space around it was now partly filled with tumbled stone and masses of a creeper-like weed sporting innumerable scarlet flowers. Rachad paused before an almost intact portico. Over the entrance a large relief carving blazed forth, depicting the Worm Ouroborous, its body arced in the familiar perfect circle, its tail in its mouth. Reliefs also adorned the square flanking columns— on the left a caduceus, the health-giving Hermetic staff entwined by two snakes, on the right a two-headed Hermetic androgyne.

He crossed the threshold and stepped through a vestibule. Beyond that was a square, darkened room. Finally he found himself standing under the sky again, in a spacious interior whose roof had collapsed to deluge the floor beneath with spilled bricks, pieces of rafter, and tiles of assorted pastel hues. Like all others in the temple, the walls sloped inward. There were several doors to the chamber, and through a gap in the opposite wall Rachad saw more chambers.

His attention was caught by a sarcophagus-like marble dais on which, all covered with brick dust, there stood crucibles, alembics, and a small furnace. The equipment was scanty for any real alchemical efforts, Rachad thought. He guessed its use to have been ceremonial and the dais to be an altar, for as a backdrop to it was a mural showing the alchemical marriage of the sun and the moon, in progress within a glowing flask.

He rapped his knuckles on the marble top. Could this be the book's hiding place? The idea seemed logical. He tried to remove the top, but it resisted his efforts.

He set off to explore the remaining rooms, hoping to find something with which to break the dais open. He found nothing, and returned to the altar. It was then that he heard the tramp of booted feet. Into the temple burst Zhorga, closely followed by several of his squad.

They all halted on seeing Rachad. Zhorga's eyes were bright and wild as they darted about the chamber, and he seemed immensely pleased with himself.

"So this is the place, eh?" he crowed. "I knew you wouldn't be able to stay away from it for long!"

Crestfallen and surly, Rachad lowered his head. "You followed me," he accused tonelessly.

"Damned right we did, and lucky for you, too. It stood to reason you knew more than you were letting on. The baron would have given you back to the inquisitor if I hadn't persuaded him to let you lead us to it, and you know what that means." He gave a deep sigh of satisfaction. "Well, have you found it yet?"

"No."

"Any ideas?"

Rachad shrugged. "I was going to look in that altar."

"Smash it," Zhorga said brusquely to those behind him. Patchman went forward with a sledgehammer and swung at the plinth, cracking the marble after several heavy blows.

Zhorga placed a paw on Rachad's shoulder and watched the work greedily. "This is good news for all of us," he murmured. "The baron will swear us into his service if that book turns up. He's promised me that much."

Rachad felt suddenly dismayed, even bitter. Zhorga, long his hero, seemed to be changing his nature. "What happened to your independent spirit, Captain?" he said scathingly. "I never thought to see you selling yourself to a master—I wouldn't have guessed you'd betray me, either!"

Zhorga's reply was heated. "I'm giving Matello the book for all our sakes!" he hissed. "He'll take us to Maralia, the star country he comes from—or would you rather spend the rest of your life on Mars?"

"You'll still be a serf. How does it feel?"

"A soldier-at-arms! It's an honorable profession—I've been one before. As for not being your own master, that's how things are in the star worlds—so get used to it." Zhorga dropped his arm from Rachad's shoulder wearily. "I don't know what you imagined you were playing at. You couldn't possibly get the book back to Earth."

"Oh, I don't know," Rachad said, brightening. "We could smuggle it aboard the *Bucentaur*. The baron might decide to visit Earth, and then we could sneak away with it. Gebeth could make gold. We'd be rich."

"Forget it," Zhorga snorted. "Anyway I've already sent a message back to the baron. This temple will be aswarm before long."

Rachad's face fell. "What's going to happen to me?" he said nervously. "The baron knows I tried to trick him."

"Don't worry," Zhorga said sourly. "He thinks you acted out of loyalty to Gebeth. That's the complexion I've put on it—you understand? He appreciates loyalty. Also, he thinks you're a genuine student of alchemy."

Rachad did not fail to notice the sarcasm in Zhorga's voice. "You think differently, of course," he sulked.

"Oh, it's gold you're after. I understand that well enough. But you'll have to give up your dreams. Forswear everything and give your allegiance to the baron, unless you want to be left behind on Mars."

Somewhat grumpily Zhorga left him and went to supervise the work. The alchemical apparatus crashed to the floor and the dais finally broke. Rachad rushed forward. The dais was indeed hollow; but empty.

"We'll dig underneath," Zhorga decided.

Rachad retreated. Shortly afterward Matello arrived, his whole retinue in train. The baron was in high spirits. He bustled about the temple, peering here and there, donating advice as to how the building was to be razed. Then he retired to watch from a safe distance, relaxing in a chair his servants provided.

Cursing Zhorga in his mind, Rachad skulked well out of the way. He had to admit that Zhorga had acted for the best as he saw it—but what would Rachad's own position be if the book were never found? After all, there was no proof that it even existed. The inquisitor, however, might be unimpressed by his protestations to that effect.

He need not have worried. Although Matello would have persisted until every stone in the temple had been ground to a powder, in this event such thoroughness proved unnecessary. A fluted column, pulled down by means of a rope, smashed open as it struck the tessellated floor. Within a hollow space lined with alabaster a soldier found a heavy object wrapped in cloth of gold.

He took it at once to Matello, who unwound the glittering wrapping. He uncovered a massive tome with covers of solid lead nearly half an inch thick, engraved very skillfully with an iron stylus and then beautifully colored by rubbing powders or paints into the incisions.

Matello summoned Rachad and passed the book to him. "Is this what you sought?"

Gingerly Rachad accepted the book. It was so heavy that he nearly dropped it. On the front cover was an engraving of the philosophic tree, the signs of the elements hanging from its five branches. Below it was a somewhat less picturesque symbol that was cool and almost luminous in its simplicity: a blue square inscribed within a silver triangle, inscribed in turn within a golden circle.

Awkwardly he turned the book over. The back cover bore a single colored engraving which almost sent him reeling. A face glared out of the lead plate. An ancient, wild face that seemed to be alive. The skin was a dusty gold, veined with gray and silver. The hair exploded wildly in all directions to frame the face like a sunburst, and was gray mingled with rivulets of dull silver, a mixture of tones it shared with the beard. The eyes were a more brilliant, penetrating silver, lacking pupils but seeming ferociously, pitilessly aware.

Rachad made a quick guess that this was the symbol known as the lead man, who became first the quicksilver man, then the silver man, and finally was transformed into the gold man.

He turned the book over again and opened it to the frontispiece, where he read:

THE ROOT OF TRANSFORMATIONS

Including Also

The Art Of The Fulmination Of Metals

"The title is the correct one," he informed the baron. He turned more pages, but immediately observed that a sizable proportion of the leaves had been removed and that the spine gaped bare where they had been.

"My lord," he said quickly, "half the book is missing!"

Matello grinned in triumph. "Then we have found what we were seeking! The other half already lies in the Aegis."

Taking the volume from Rachad's hands, he rose to his feet. "Let's get aloft. It will be a pleasure never to have to set foot on this miserable planet again."

Perplexed, Rachad followed the baron as, cloak flying behind him in the light breeze, he went striding away through the ochrous city. Soon all the others followed too, pouring from the destroyed temple, raising a cloud of orange dust as the procession made for the lighters that stood ready to convey them to the giant sailship orbiting overhead.

Tearing the meat from a chicken leg with his teeth and throwing the bone across the banqueting hall, Baron Matello leaned toward Rachad. "Well, young man," he teased, "do you think you could make gold now?"

Rachad, who had been poring over the alchemical book, pursed his lips. "After sufficient study," he said brazenly, hoping that Matello was too ignorant to gainsay him. "Provided I were supplied with the missing pages."

In fact, he found the book almost impenetrable. For one thing, it was written in so many different languages —even different alphabets! And although supposed to be an explicit commentary, it was couched in the same cryptic style that characterized alchemists throughout the ages, replete with poetic expressions and arcane symbology.

Some passages were more or less intelligible. Such as: *"When the artifex depicts colored flowers, surrounded by griffins and dragons, he indicates the sublimation of sul-*

phur accomplished by means of an athanor of infusoration, or in other words by fulmination; for if this operation is carried out with sufficient intensity and duration the flowers will be seen. Likewise, when the reverse of the fifth page shows the blood of young children gathered together and giving forth serpents, the artifex indicates the intensive fulmination of quicksilver. . . ."

To impress the baron with his alchemical training, Rachad had been explaining the terms in this passage. "Chiefly, of course, the book speaks of the *primus agens*, the materials with which one must start," he said airily, parroting Gebeth. "Ordinarily alchemical treatises never clearly reveal that. It is the essential secret."

"Little would it avail you to know this secret, locked away on Earth," the baron retorted. "Your Earth metals are of no use for transformation, even I know that. It's celestial metals that are needed—metals with special properties found only among the stars."

He drained a goblet and stuffed more bread and chicken into his mouth. Taken aback, Rachad pondered this revelation. It was an aspect he had never thought of before—though of course the baron's words could not be relied on. It was likely that he was simply repeating something he had heard.

Rachad's sudden discomfiture must have shown, for the baron laughed. Rachad allowed his gaze to wander down the long table, where there sat a comely young girl who for some time had been drawing his glances. Her name, he had heard, was Elissea; she was Matello's niece.

She smiled. He smiled. Shyly, he closed the book and resumed eating.

The baron had given him a favored place at the table, being curious—though it seemed to Rachad in a half-hearted way—to know what he could tell him of the book. The *Bucentaur* remained in orbit; but Rachad could not help but marvel at how well the comforts of the dining table were adapted to the state of free-fall. Clingslippers, together with garments that clung almost as effectively to the special plush of the chairs, made the lack of gravity close to irrelevant. The diners drank from closed goblets punctured with tiny holes as in a pepperbox. The food, all solid—bread, meat, cheeses, confections and fruit, pastries and pies—was wrapped in paper napkins and, so that it did not float away, was spitted with skewers which were stuck into cork boards. Apparently the cooks were not discommoded by this restriction, for the repast was delicious.

Belching with satisfaction, the baron rose to his feet. "In two hours we depart for Maralia," he announced. "But first, I honor my pledge. Bring them on!"

At these words Matello's private secretary seized the alchemical book from under Rachad's nose and made off with it. All those at table—mostly the baron's senior officers—hurriedly rose also, whether or not they had finished their meal. Serving girls and footmen unfastened the clasps that locked chairs and tables to the floor, steering the now floating furniture to the sides of the hall.

Baron Matello seated himself on a throne-like chair farther back in the banqueting hall. The main doors opened. Through them came Captain Zhorga and his crewmen, looking about themselves nervously.

Mingling with the others, Rachad sidled toward the door. He knew what was coming; perhaps if he could slip away, he thought, his defection from the proceedings would pass unnoticed.

It was not to be. Near the door he came face to face with Elissea, and stopped, entranced by her pert face and smiling eyes. "You came on that ship from Earth, didn't you?" she said. "Uncle says it was very brave of you."

He laughed jauntily, and could not resist lingering. Soon he found himself boasting of his experiences, while in the background he heard, like a continuous murmuring, the voices first of Zhorga and then of the others as one by one they took the fealty oath. Eventually he reminded himself that he should leave; but suddenly Matello's voice rang out.

"And where is the lad who was apprenticed to the alchemist? We mustn't leave him out; I need him on my staff."

Rachad felt himself pushed forward, reluctantly.

Then he realized he would never have got away with it, and resignedly approached the baron to kneel before him, offering his hands in the attitude of prayer as had been shown to him earlier. Nearby stood Matello's secretary, ready to prompt him.

The baron clasped Rachad's hands in his. Slowly, though the words stuck in his throat, Rachad repeated the oath the secretary read out to him, swearing obedience, loyalty and truthfulness. With what seemed a measured perfunctoriness, the baron responded, accepting him into his household and promising protection and fair treatment.

When his hands were released Rachad stood up and walked away. It was done. He was under oath to Baron Goth Matello, Margrave of the Marsh Worlds, Protector of the Castarpos Moons, and liege to his Majesty King Lutheron the Third of Maralia.

Chapter EIGHT

Elegantly the *Bucentaur* raised sail and receded from Mars, curving round the Girdle of Demeter and then hurtling outward on the plane of the ecliptic.

In little over a week the orbit of Pluto had fallen far behind, even though the starship had extended but a few of her sails. Then, in interstellar space, the journey proper began.

For now she had moved into conditions of incomparably greater power than was available within the solar family; conditions from which the sun, like a mother, protected her planets with her own etheric atmosphere. Out here were ether winds on a stupendous scale, amassed from the outputs of billions of suns, creating processes affecting the entire galaxy.

This colossal system of invisible motion was what made interstellar sailflight possible. As the *Bucentaur* eased herself into the stream that was to carry her toward Maralia, her passengers sedated themselves and took to deep-cushioned bunks. The crew, too, took drugs that helped them to withstand the period of acceleration, though the potions were of a kind that did not bring on stupor, and in a well-drilled sequence more and more sail was run out.

The ship's velocity mounted, became stupendous.

Then, after a few days, a remarkable change took place. A barrier seemed to have been broken, heralding new, pleasanter conditions. The sails remained at full stretch; but the bone-breaking pressure abruptly dropped to a comfortable one-half Earth normal which bore no relation to the ship's actual rate of acceleration. The Earthmen on board were puzzled by this, especially when they were told that maneuvers which logically should have torn the ship to pieces (such as sudden changes in direction) could now be tackled without danger.

Rachad Caban, bunked deep down in the starship with the rest of Zhorga's men, recovered his strength somewhat more quickly than the others. For the first time since coming aboard the stupendous *Bucentaur* he found himself unsupervised. He decided it would be a good opportunity to go exploring.

He wandered at length up companionways and through corridors which were still deserted for the most part. Eventually he found a hooded door, and on passing through it emerged, without warning, onto the main deck.

The view was breathtaking. The deck, the size of a large playing field, consisted of an immense expanse of polished planking waxed to the color of light honey. At least a hundred capstans studded it; and swelling over the major part of it like a giant glass cocoon was an enormous transparent air balloon.

There were towering superstructures whose nature was not immediately clear to Rachad. Farther down the deck, docked in special bays, were the three lighters, plus the fast reconnaissance craft, which the *Bucentaur* used for planetary contact—though she could, if the need arose, put down on most planets herself.

In order that Rachad and everyone else on board could stand upright on the floor, the ship currently traveled deck foremost. Rachad knew, however, that she could just as easily move stemward, sternward, sideways or even bottom first. On enormous booms extended from either side of the hull were arranged the sails that made such maneuverability possible; he now turned his attention to these.

They were even more spectacular than the deck itself, curving away and away into the void, their farther limits vanishing in the distance. And there were colors. Not just the shimmering blue Rachad was familiar with, but thousands of dazzling rainbow colors that crawled across the sails in ever-shifting moiré displays.

Rachad stared hypnotized, gaping in a dazed rapture.

Suddenly a slap on his face rocked him back on his heels. A voice snapped at him harshly. "Keep your eyes off the sails—the silk will trance your mind!"

Rachad swung blankly to his attacker, shocked out of his reverie. He found himself facing a neatly bearded sailor in a body-hugging striped tunic.

The sailor's stern expression softened slightly. "Never look at ether silk when we're in star travel," he instructed in a more kindly tone. "The luminescent patterns are because we're moving faster than light, and they're not like anything you've ever seen before. They'll leave you dazed for the rest of your life."

Rachad touched his stinging cheek. "I—I didn't know," he faltered.

"One of the Earth lubbers, eh?" the sailor said, gazing at him condescendingly. "Don't know much about star flight, do you?" He gestured upward. "Take a look overhead."

Rachad obeyed. At first he thought there was something wrong with his eyes. It wasn't like looking into space at all. The blackness was *incomplete*. Violet curtains seemed to be swirling behind the void, reminding him of dark oil poured on water. Set against those curtains, the stars were a startling sapphire blue. And they *danced:* they wove, darted, spun, leaving contrails of lavender light.

"Space will get more purple as we accelerate," the sailor informed him. "Already we're doing better than a hundred lightspeeds."

"Why do the stars move?" Rachad asked shyly.

"It's an illusion. When the sails get up to lightspeed they disturb the ether. That distorts space. And if space around us is different, everything is different. That's why we only have one-half gravity—roughly Mars-weight—when by common sense we should be smeared against the deck."

"*Space* can be distorted?" Rachad echoed incredulously.

"We'd never break the light barrier otherwise. If it weren't for ether silk, light would be the fastest thing there is." The sailor smiled, grunting reflectively. "It's a weird experience when space starts to waver and we overtake light. Time seems to slow down, to stand still. I must have gone through it a hundred times. You wouldn't know anything about it, of course, sound asleep in your bunk."

The starman spoke with the pride of one who considered himself a member of an elite. Rachad struggled to understand his words. He was conversant, of course, with the general principle that the larger the sail the greater the velocity. Theoretically if one had a sail spanning the entire macrocosm, its speed would be infinite.

But the idea that light had a speed of its own was something that had never occurred to him. He did not understand why this speed should be so significant, nor why it should comprise a "barrier." He did recall, though, that Gebeth had once described light as a compound of ether and fire; and that according to some sages the motion of the ether winds was more apparent than real—the ether did not actually "move" at all, but conveyed a vibration or tensioning force in some way.

The sailor left to go about his business, giving him a parting warning to keep his eyes off the silk. Rachad strolled about the deck for a time, but grew nervous; always the shimmering sails seemed to lure his eyes. Shortly he went back below, through the hooded door.

He felt no desire to return to his quarters, however. He walked aimlessly through the quiet corridors, passing men and women all clad in some version of the baron's livery (as he himself now was). Everywhere he seemed to be tantalized by closed doors. Until, that was, he spotted Elissea, the baron's niece, stepping along a passageway wearing a flowing robe cinched fetchingly at the waist.

He quickened his steps, but before he could catch up with her she had disappeared behind a door of paneled wood. Rachad halted before it, lifted his fist to knock, but instead, swallowing at his own temerity, he turned the knob and opened the door gently.

Quietly he stepped into what was evidently a private bedchamber. Elissea was alone, seated at a dressing table. She turned, startled to see Rachad, her expression one of shock but also of veiled excitement.

"Is *this* how you conduct yourself on Earth?" she accused coquettishly.

Rachad was flustered. "Forgive me, I. . . ." Afraid lest someone should happen along in the corridor outside, he closed the door behind him.

She rose and sauntered toward him. Her eyes were dancing. "Why, you look terrified. Is this the brave hero who faced space dragons?"

He looked away, stung by the taunt. "Excuse me. I will leave."

"No, wait. Come here." Taking him by the elbow, she led him to a wide, plush bed and sat him down beside her. "Why so gloomy? I should have thought everything was going well for you."

He snorted. *"Well?* Hardly! I didn't embark on this adventure meaning to leave home forever. I've lost everything—my freedom, my. . . ." *My chance to make gold,* he finished silently.

"Shsh." She put a finger on his lips. "Don't *ever* let my uncle hear you talk like that. It's treason."

"So what?" he muttered with a shrug.

They were silent. Then he turned to her. "Well, never mind about that. Tell me what it's like where we're going—in Maralia."

"Where we're going is to my uncle's own domain, the Castarpos Moons. It's only a small corner of Maralia, and rather dull and gloomy, really." She let loose a sigh. "That's why I came along on this trip. I thought it might be fun. It hasn't been so far, though."

"Well, we must, er, see what we can do," he stuttered, and his arm went round her waist. Excitement mounted in him. At the same time new ideas began to invade his brain. All was *not* lost, he told himself. New frontiers lay ahead—and there was *still* a chance, he thought stubbornly, that he could somehow get hold of the alchemical book, still a chance that he could learn the secret of making gold.

Apart from that, he speculated, allowing his thoughts to spiral crazily, what if he were to become related to Baron Matello? Married to his niece?

Unaware that there was no chance of a commoner marrying into the nobility, Rachad sank down onto the soft bed with Elissea, and soon, for a while, forgot all his ambitions and disappointments.

For two months the *Bucentaur* sailed along a glittering star arm, traversing several degrees on the great galactic circle by which interstellar flight was reckoned. In the latter half of the voyage her crew, showing great skill, guided her onto invisible running contours which the layers of ether wind created as they slid against one another—for the interstellar ether was far from homogenous but formed tunnels, streams and inclines as it swirled and boiled around the stars. The *Bucentaur*'s sails were able to gain leverage on these contours and use them by which to decelerate, so that as she approached the borders of Maralia her velocity steadily dropped.

Finally she fell below lightspeed and began picking her way through a vast natural obstacle that lay between Maralia and the region of space in which Sol lay: a great screen of cosmic rubble, a Girdle of Demeter on a stellar scale. It was the chief reason, in fact, why ships rarely penetrated in that direction.

Zhorga spent his time being put through a military training routine by Captain Veautrin, together with a squad selected from his former crew. At first it irked him to be under the tutelage of a younger man, but he applied himself to the drills with zeal and grew to like Veautrin, who in many ways was a man after his own heart, though less hasty in his judgments and more disciplined in his actions.

Toward the end of the training period Zhorga expressed an interest in how the *Bucentaur* was run. He had heard that her captain commanded her from a control room deep within her hull (though there was a second, rarely used bridge towering over her main deck) and he was puzzled to know how this was done. As a favor Veautrin arranged a visit to this control room.

There, by chance, Zhorga learned of the nature of the enemy he might well spend the rest of his days fighting.

The control room was a large, wood-paneled chamber. The captain, a spare, bearded figure, sat in a straight-backed chair on whose arms were fitted a number of wheeled handles. Occupying the opposite wall, receiving his full attention, was an extraordinary device which answered Zhorga's question.

It consisted of a circular screen nearly ten feet across, made of milky-white frosted glass. At first Zhorga thought that it was a porthole into space, or that it was painted, for it showed the rock-strewn void through which they were passing. Then the captain twirled one of his handles. The picture expanded; they seemed to hurtle dizzily through space, toward a distant group of irregularly shaped asteroids.

Captain Veautrin leaned close, muttering an explanation to Zhorga. "A system of lenses, prisms and mirrors projects a view of external space onto the glass screen. The system can also function as a telescope of enormous power, as you have seen."

"An invaluable aid," Zhorga remarked, getting his breath. Once again he was astonished at the technical excellence of the starship. Compare this with his own fumbling journey to Mars!

"It would be difficult to cross these reefs without it,"

Veautrin agreed, "but in essence the device is simple. It works on the principle of the *camera obscura.*"

The image of the rock cluster had stabilized in the center of the screen, quartered by its cross-hairs. Again the captain fiddled with the handles and the rocks shifted, moving toward the circumference where the screen was scored with calibration lines. He turned his head and spoke to the officer standing behind him.

The first officer took a couple of steps and barked an order into a speaking tube. Shortly afterward the floor shifted slightly under their feet. As the ship changed course, the asteroid group disappeared from the screen.

The captain relaxed. The screen continued its scanning, sweeping space to and fro in search of danger.

Veautrin explained that by means of speaking tubes, of which the control room had many, one could communicate with most parts of the ship. Then he pointed to what looked like a locked desk, which with the lid off, he said, disclosed a battle plan of the *Bucentaur,* useful for directing her armament—though she was not primarily a warship.

Zhorga nodded, taking everything in. He wondered if the day could come when he might command such an interstellar ship himself. Probably not, he conceded. He was too old to learn so many new tricks.

They turned to leave, but a murmur behind them caused them to halt. All eyes had turned to the glass screen, which now showed a veritable jungle of asteroids through which the captain was trying to find a safe gap, having reduced the ship's speed still further. But that was not all. There were also—ships, their images small but unmistakable, sliding through the rock fields.

A single word, harsh with hatred, came from the first officer.

"*Kerek!*"

Veautrin nudged Zhorga. His expression had changed to one of restrained ferocity. "Stay," he grated. "As well you see what Maralia may soon be up against."

The screen zoomed and refocused, bringing into closer view a drove of strange vessels. To Zhorga they appeared like nothing so much as ancient sea-galleys, crudely adapted for space. Their hulls were clinker-built, of overlapping planking, and to the gunwales were welded the sides of leathery coverings, or bags, which bulged by air pressure over what were presumably decks, and in which were cut square windows. The ships were driven by crescent-shaped lateen sails, vast in proportion to the loads they carried, supported by enormously long outriggers, so that seen head-on the craft looked like some grotesque species of blue-winged butterfly.

Veautrin agreed bitterly when Zhorga remarked on their makeshift appearance. "They are exactly what they seem," he said. "Galleys taken from the oceans of the Kerek world. It's astonishing how well they are able to travel in interstellar space. But then the Kerek have a talent for improvisation—as well as an insatiable appetite for conquest! Yet they were completely unknown until fifty years ago, when the secret of ether silk was unwisely introduced there."

"The Kerek are not human, then?"

"Indeed they are not!" Veautrin spoke with what, for him, was an uncharacteristic degree of passion. "They are monsters with a terrible ability—the ability to enslave the minds of men, to capture the human will, though just how this is done is still a mystery. Their hordes are constantly swelled by incorporating seemingly willing slave-soldiers in this way, from their conquered worlds." His voice fell. "And that's not all. They also have a practice of converting these worlds into likenesses of the Kerek world, creating new atmospheres, even climates, by planting fast-growing forests and lichen beds from their home planet. Kerek-forming, the process is called, and a pretty unpleasant business it's supposed to be."

A hollow laugh came from behind them. "Yes, Zhorga, even your native Earth may be Kerek-formed before long. Like the smell of sulphur compounds, do you?"

It was Baron Matello, who had already received a message by speaker tube. He strode over to stand by the captain, peering at the glass screen.

"They're coming this way, I see."

"I think they mean to attack, my lord."

"When they get close enough, hit them with everything we've got. Just like the jackals to be lurking in these reefs."

"I have already given the orders to prepare, my lord."

Kerek craft were clearly not handled as carefully as those of Maralia. One, striking an asteroid, shattered to dust which exploded in all directions. But the rest came on, magnified by the viewfinder so that every detail of their construction became visible.

The battle board was unlocked. The *Bucentaur* prepared to engage the enemy. As the Kerek ships came near all her subsidiary craft quit her decks, approaching the attackers from their flanks, spreading out to give the giant starship's guns and catapults a clear line of fire.

The captain ordered a full salvo. Seconds later the ship shook and thundered to the bark of the bombards and the loud, snapping *twang* of fire-darts being shot off. The effect of the bombards, which discharged a type of spreading shot, was not seen, but that of the fire-darts was dazzling even on the shifting field of view of the glass screen. For a moment space coruscated and seemed to catch fire.

Only one of the glimmering fire-darts found its mark. A Kerek galley began to burn, glowing as some sort of seething fluid spread all over it.

There was a second salvo, to which the lighters added their fire. Zhorga was surprised that the Kerek failed to answer with any armament of their own. He saw no sign that they even possessed any. Their one tactic, it seemed, was to board.

The leading vessel came through the barrage. It swooped down toward the starship's superstructure, but then was hit by a bombard and apparently lost control, crashing into the maindeck and ripping down the air balloon like so much paper.

From the broken hull crawled and staggered two score or so space-suited figures. Most were man-shaped, but a few were four-legged creatures, with narrow, rearing bodies and long necks. The forelegs were longer than the hind legs, and together with a pair of grasping limbs the creatures looked a little like miniature giraffes with arms. These, Zhorga imagined, were the Kerek.

But they all, men and aliens alike, fought with equal ferocity as the *Bucentaur*'s commandoes rushed to engage them. They wielded outlandish blades that were oddly curved, almost circular. They aimed ring-shaped devices which hurled spinning discuses capable of slicing a man in half. They gave no quarter nor expected any, and soon a bloody brawl was in progress.

The captain shifted the scene away from the deck, back

to the Kerek flotilla. Two more galleys were blazing in the darkness. The rest were withdrawing, beaten off.

"They're licked!" Zhorga exclaimed loudly.

Baron Matello cast him a sour glance. "A small squadron like that is no great threat to a ship of our size, but the Kerek can rarely resist a chance to attack," he told him. "When they really move, their fleets number thousands."

He turned back to the screen, fretting. "A damned nuisance just the same! This close to Maralia!"

"Strange we should come upon them accidentally, space being so vast," Zhorga ventured with a frown.

Matello ignored this, but Veautrin spoke quietly to Zhorga. "It's no accident. The Kerek have some instinct that helps them find ships over immense distances." His lips quirked. "Yet one more facet of the 'Kerek Power.' "

Before Zhorga could ask the meaning of this phrase, the screen focused back on the maindeck, where the last of the intruders were being efficiently butchered. Clouds of vapor puffed from slashed space suits, shining briefly in the light of the deck lamps before dissipating into the void.

At the troop sergeant's orders a prisoner was taken; overwhelmed, disarmed, and then dragged down below. Minutes later, under heavy guard and with a sword point at his neck, he was brought into the control room.

Zhorga was somewhat startled to see that the renegade human cut an impressive figure. He stood tall and proud, his head held high. His space suit was a magnificent piece of work, made of honey-colored metal inlaid with what looked like silver and gold. The helmet, however, had been removed, and his face reminded Zhorga very much of Captain Veautrin—young, moustachioed, with blazing but steady eyes, and blond hair. But a foul smell, like the odor of rotting eggs, seeped from him, and the handsomeness of his features was made bizarre by a proboscis-like gadget clipped to his nose, enabling him to stomach the odious mixture of gases that made up the Kerek atmosphere.

"You want to see one? Here it is!" Baron Matello intoned somberly. "A human turned Kerek!"

His expression a mixture of contempt and pity, the starship captain rose and gazed at the prisoner. "Were you born under the Kerek?" he asked mildly.

The prisoner seemed unconscious of the proboscis,

which dangled and danced as he spoke but did not prevent him from speaking clearly. "No," he said, "I am from Frujos, of the Anderra system, which came under the Kerek Power in my youth."

"Why were you sailing these reefs?" Matello demanded suddenly.

"You know the reason. Kerek ships rove everywhere."

The man's manner was disconcertingly rational and self-possessed. "You would do well not to resist, but to join with us," he declared. "Cease your opposition. Live in vigor and harmony with us, not against us. Ours is the better life! We know true joy under the Kerek Power!"

"As slaves of the Kerek?" Matello snorted.

The prisoner's voice took on a ringing tone. "Not so! We are no slaves, for the Kerek also are under the Kerek Power. With us, all are equal and together as brothers."

"Kill him," Matello said gloomily. "Throw his body overboard with the rest."

The warrior put up barely any resistance as he was hustled from the room. Zhorga heard chopping sounds from the other side of the door; then something heavy was dragged away.

Baron Matello grunted. "Hah! The Kerek Power!"

Without another word he swept from the room.

"What is this 'Kerek Power?'" Zhorga asked Veautrin, as the two of them also turned to go.

Veautrin took his time about replying. "It has never properly been accounted for," he said. "It is only known that it is a mental force that can command human and Kerek alike. Some say it does not exist as such and is only a form of collective hypnosis—others that it is a living entity that can reach out across space." He shuddered. "Already whole kingdoms have fallen to the Kerek. If they are not stopped the outlook for the galaxy itself will be bleak. But the Kerek will be stopped! They have to be stopped!"

Zhorga felt chill. Why had this menace never been mentioned to him before?

It could only be because it was such an ever-present shadow that it was taken for granted.

They stepped out into the corridor. The *Bucentaur* swept on, sinuating through the asteroid shoals toward the clear void beyond.

Chapter NINE

For all his grandiose titles, Baron Goth Matello's actual standing in life went little way toward satisfying his true ambitions for himself. In fact his highest rank—Margrave of the Marsh Worlds—was really worth least of all, for the Marsh Worlds were a dismal group of border planets not even worth taxing, but which it was his onerous duty to defend. Also largely empty was his title of Baron (by which he was formally addressed in keeping with Maralian tradition, it being his only hereditary title), most of the barony he had inherited having been gambled away in his impetuous youth, when he had been overmuch addicted to the card table and the dueling field.

To Rachad or Zhorga, or indeed to any Earthman, he was incredibly wealthy, but in his own estimation Matello regarded himself as poor. What he aspired to was a dukedom: a goodly crop of rich worlds where a man of expansive appetites need not feel cramped.

As it was, his base these days was the unprepossessing Castarpos Moons demesne, of which he was official Protector, and his one concession to undeniable luxury was the *Bucentaur*, his magnificent personal starship to buy which he had taxed his holdings till they bled. As the giant starship swung down toward the pitted surface of Arp, largest of the moons, those on deck were able to look down on the huddled town of Corrum which was Matello's residence. Not long after she had landed, in a premanent dock on the edge of the town, a procession of horses and carriages suddenly issued forth from her, to go clattering through the narrow, winding streets, making for the craggy manor-castle that loomed on high ground.

Castarpos, the moon system's primary, a vast striated world on which no man had ever set foot, bulked huge in the sky. By contrast the sun was small and amber, and seemed to add a burnished hue to everything it touched in the perpetually gloomy landscape. The sight of his domain afforded Matello no pleasure, however, and he kept the curtains drawn as his carriage passed through the town, mulling meanwhile over the plan that was forming in his mind.

During the journey from Mars he had been discreetly informed that an improper liaison had developed between the young Earthling, Rachad Caban, and his niece Elissea. He would have been quite within his rights to kill the youth immediately; but he had chosen to do nothing, and on the contrary had gone out of his way to show the impudent youngster every consideration, giving no sign that he knew what was going on. Caban, he had decided, was just the man to carry out the scheme he had in mind. He was audacious, self-interested—a chancer if ever there was one—and he even had some alchemical knowledge, which was excellent for Matello's purpose.

Ensconcing himself in his stone fortress, Matello spent some time disposing of household affairs. That evening, he sent for Caban.

Nervously Rachad entered a vaulted hall of modest proportions. A fire blazed in a huge grate, adding a wavering glow to the light of the cressets. The baron sat at a large table that might have been of teak, but was more probably of a local material. Near him was a flagon and two goblets. He was thoughtfully tapping the lead cover of the alchemical treatise he had taken so much trouble to obtain.

At the other end of the hall Rachad saw something odd. A cloud of yellow dust hovered in the air over a large iron tank. Traces of the same dust were scattered about the floor.

Rachad coughed, and bowed.

"Ah, it's young Caban!" Matello greeted jovially. "Come over here. Try some of this."

Rachad approached. Matello filled a goblet with murky brown liquid and handed it to him. Rachad looked at the beverage doubtfully before sipping it. The stuff had a thick, aromatic flavor. He swallowed, then spluttered as it scorched his throat.

"The local vintage," Matello told him. "It's brewed from berries grown on the upland plateaux. Rough stuff, but not bad once you get used to it. Drink!"

The order was peremptory. Rachad forced himself to gulp down the wine, feeling his stomach burn and his senses reel.

"Now sit down," grunted Matello with a grin. "We have something to discuss. How best make use of *this*."

Once more he tapped the book. In his woozy state, Rachad wondered how long he could keep from revealing that the book was of little help without its supporting text, the *Asch Mezareph*, which thanks to his silence had been left behind on Earth. "I am to help you make gold, my lord?" he said, slurring his words a trifle. "You have an alchemical laboratory?"

Matello threw back his head and laughed loudly. "What, me make gold? What in space for? Not far from here I can show you a moonlet composed entirely of gold."

His eyes twinkled to see Rachad's startlement. "I can see that you're a real backwater boy. Maybe gold's something special back on Earth where you come from, but here in Maralia it's worth no more than iron. Real wealth takes the form of *power*. Power over men, over territories."

Rachad lowered his head, biting his lip. He should have thought of this before, he realized. Out here among the stars there would be a plenitude of every kind of material.

He looked up. "Then why *do* you need the book, my lord?" he asked, puzzled.

Matello slammed his goblet on the table. "Not to make gold, you may be sure! This book is bait. I need it to help me to get a man inside the Duke of Koss's Aegis. Do you understand me?"

"No, my lord."

Matello sighed. "I feared not."

"What is this 'Aegis,' my lord?"

"An aegis," Matello answered, with self-conscious patience, "is an impregnable fortress. It is built of adamant, a substance which is absolutely indestructible, and once inside it there is no known weapon that can harm you, and no way that the fortress can be breached. Now, as to the Duke of Koss, who lives in its protection—" Suddenly Matello rose to his feet. "Let someone else give you an indication of his character."

Beckoning to Rachad, he strolled to the far end of the hall, stopping at the iron tank. As he followed, the fog of yellow powder stung Rachad's nostrils and made him cough. He looked into the low tank, and recoiled with a gasp.

"Don't be afraid," the baron murmured. "He's as civilized as you or I."

Rachad guessed that the tank was deeper than it appeared from the outside and was set into the floor. It was filled to within a foot of the brim with fine yellow powder, resembling flowers of sulphur. The powder was waving and rippling. "Swimming" just beneath its surface was an undulating shape.

"Flammarion!" Matello said in a loud voice. "I have with me the young man I mentioned."

The swimming shape surfaced. The creature was gray in color and resembled a stingray, with a waving, flapping cape. From beneath it came slim tentacles which tapped the sides of the tank, but Rachad could not properly see what else the cape hid. He forced himself to be calm as the beast flopped part of itself over the side of the trough, splashing out gouts of bright yellow powder.

"I sense you, humans. Greetings, Rachad Caban."

"Er—greetings," Rachad stuttered. The creature's voice was soft and human-sounding, yet somehow *larger* than a man's without being louder.

"This is Flammarion," Matello said to Rachad, "a master builder from the other side of the galaxy. He it was who built the duke's Aegis, long ago, and he and I are now united in a common purpose—somehow to break into that aegis. It is an ambition not altogether unique to us, for the duke has many enemies."

He turned to the tank. "Tell Caban your story, Flammarion. It is best he should know the background to his mission."

There was a pause, while the alien creature flapped and stirred in the powder-bath. "It is a sad tale, a pathetic tale, one that can only bring bathos and pity," the voice said mournfully. "I am an acknowledged expert in the building of aegises. I alone know the secret of adamant, a material impervious to any weapon, unaffected even by alkahest, the universal solvent. No gun, arbalest or sonic trembler can break it, no acid can corrode it. It deadens even the shriek of Vurelian war trumpets, whose vibrations pass through stone and steel to kill those within."

Flammarion paused again and went surging through the powder. "Thinking to employ my talents in foreign parts of the galaxy, I traveled to that region where humans dwell. Here I was commissioned by the Duke of

Koss to build an aegis for him. I labored mightily, constructing, I believe, the best example of my skills so far. Finally the work was finished, the duke took up residence, and after a decent interval to allow inspection, I presented myself before the gate to collect my fee: two tons of heavenly water, a rare commodity much prized by my kind."

The voice of the alien became burdened with dole. "His answer was direct and most unkind. 'If the Aegis is truly invulnerable as claimed by you and specified by contract, you have no means by which to enter and extract payment. You cannot hurt me; here I shall remain forever. Begone!' Oh, cruel injustice! Since then I have remained nearby, trying by this stratagem and that to force payment from my client."

Matello chuckled. He plainly enjoyed the tale. "Someone should have warned Flammarion about the man he was dealing with. What a churlish, unjust, detestable fellow he was! And that, mind you, was fifty years ago. So you can see how long poor Flammarion has been waiting."

"Fifty *years*?" Rachad echoed.

"Yes. Flammarion built the Aegis for the old duke. A very strange man, driven by an incomprehensible hatred for everything and everyone. There was no one he did not treat with the utmost contempt, even the king, and he earned literally thousands of enemies. Even now, countless families bear him a grudge. His final act of contempt was to shut himself away in the Aegis and to ignore all of existence. He's dead now, of course, and his son rules the Aegis as Duke of Koss. But he seems to have inherited everything from his father—his habits, his temperament, his interests, and also his enemies, including Flammarion, whose grudge is perfectly straightforward."

"Does the younger duke never venture outside either?"

"He's never been outside the Aegis in his life, to my knowledge. He was born there. It's his world."

Rachad pondered. "But how long can Flammarion wait?"

"He has a long life. And he comes from a race that never accepts a bad debt—it's a peculiar psychological obsession all his kind have. For a bargain to be reneged on is a completely unacceptable tragedy."

"And you are helping him to collect his fee?" Rachad said. "That's very noble of you."

Now Matello laughed loudly, and plumped himself down in a nearby chair, signing Rachad to another. Looking perplexedly at Flammarion, Rachad obeyed.

"With your innocence you could be the king's own clown, Rachad! No, our partnership is based on mutual advantage, for there is much at stake for me, too. You see, the duke's behavior has become a matter of serious concern for King Lutheron. The Kerek threat looms large, and Maralia faces the biggest threat yet to her existence. The king cannot afford to see so large a dukedom as Koss left in neglect, unable to come to the nation's aid with all the strength it might. And meantime the duke ignores all messages and will admit no one—not even the king himself."

"Then why doesn't the king deprive the duke of his domains, and given them to someone else?" Rachad asked.

"Ah, there you've put your finger on it. That is what the king would dearly like to do, but he dare not. The other nobles jealously guard their rights, and would never permit such a precedent, even against one they hate. The king would face rebellion. But there is something else the king can do. He can declare the duke *fair game*. That is, any man of noble blood who can dispossess him, by killing him or taking him prisoner, comes into his title and all his worlds. This the king has done—and that's what I am about. I aim to make myself Duke of Koss!"

The baron's eyes blazed. "The king would be glad to see a man of my experience take over the dukedom. I understand military matters. I'll soon knock it into shape."

"Are there other contenders, my lord?"

"Not one!" Matello tittered. "The task is regarded as impossible. The king's declaration was made more in desperation than in hope. But I have a plan."

Matello leaned forward, his arm on his knee, wagging his finger at Rachad. "Nothing in the whole cosmos will lure the duke out of his Aegis. We have to get inside somehow. But how? There's only one possibility. We have to get it opened from the inside, by someone in our pay."

He sighed. "The gods know we've tried. Now and then the duke's servants emerge on various errands, but only those who were themselves born in the Aegis, and they are all damnably loyal to him. No, we have to find someone—a stranger—whom the duke will actually invite into the Aegis, of his own free will."

"You mentioned a mission for me, my lord," Rachad said with a feeling of apprehension. "Do I come into this somehow?"

"You do." Matello leaned close to Rachad, fanning his cheek with his wine-laden breath. "Among the duke's passions is an interest in alchemy. It's he who possesses the other half of the book we took from that temple in Kars."

He leaned back, grinning. "Do you begin to get my meaning? The last man to be taken into the Aegis was an alchemist, about ten years ago. Amschel is his name. The duke recruited him to try to perfect the Philosopher's Stone in accordance with the book he had, though I don't know where he got it. But obviously he's failed, because for two or three years past the duke's agents have been looking for the missing part."

Matello broke off his tale to walk to the table, where he refilled his goblet and came back swigging it, the flagon in his other hand. "It was then we had a bit of luck," he said. "Flammarion here had already heard of the whereabouts of this book, over a hundred years ago. He's a much traveled being, you see. Probably nobody else in Maralia knew of it."

"So that's why you wanted the book."

The baron nodded. "The duke has already let one alchemist into his fortress. He'll do the same for another—if it's somebody who's bringing him what he's looking for."

"I? . . ."

Matello nodded again.

"My lord, I'm not sure I can pass myself off as an adept."

Matello guffawed, his eyes twinkling. "Now the truth is out! But you know some of the pattern, which should suffice for a while. *The Root of Transformations* is your real passport into the Aegis, the rest is just decoration. I'm absolutely sure the duke will fall for it—but I can't use one of my own men or his agents might get wind of the deception. It's got to be somebody like you, from a distant, unknown place, and with that peculiar foreign accent of yours. Flammarion will tell you what you're to do once you're inside."

Suddenly Matello emptied his goblet, filled it again and handed it to Rachad, himself sipping from the flagon. "Well, what do you say? I won't compel you to it, because this is a job that has to be done willingly. But I'll be damned annoyed if you refuse."

Rachad thought over the proposal. It frightened him. But at the same time the idea of such an adventure, of playing such a role in Maralian power politics, was almost irresistible.

"Do you trust me, my lord?" he had the temerity to ask. "What if, once in the Aegis, I sided with the duke?"

"Unlikely," Matello rumbled. "I can't see you wanting to spend the rest of your life in an adamant fortress. If you crossed me, your life would be worth nothing outside it. Besides, you have so much to gain, young Caban. You'll be able practically to name your own reward. *Both* halves of the book will be yours. I'll send you home to Earth with a hundred tons of gold, if that's what you want. Or you can stay here in Maralia, where King Lutheron will no doubt heap honors upon you." The baron's voice became silkily persuasive. Rachad thrilled.

He made his mind up. "So what am I to do?" he demanded.

"To begin with, simply take up residence down in the town. The duke has an agent there, I'm aware of that. You must on no account let it be known that you have any connection with me. Pose as an alchemist, and put it discreetly about that you are in search of a missing alchemical text, which you may name. The duke's man will lose no time in finding you, and you may both then discover that each has what the other is looking for. From then on it should be plain sailing."

"He will try to buy it from me, of course," Rachad commented.

"And you will absolutely refuse. You will insist on being allowed to study the other part of the book, and on discoursing with Amschel, who has attempted to follow its principles. Since the duke will not let either out of his control, he will have no choice but to invite you inside."

"First he will want to be convinced that the book is genuine."

"Then part with one page of it," Matello replied with a shrug. "Amschel will authenticate it."

Rachad nodded. "And if I open the gates of the Aegis —what then? Do you have it under siege?"

"Everything is made ready. It is under constant observation, and nearby I have a small force hidden underground. They will rush in as soon as the Aegis is opened. There are only paltry defenses within, I believe."

He paused, while Rachad carried on thinking. "You'll find the duke a strange fellow," Matello said softly. "They say the Aegis is a madman's world. What goes on in there is unbelievable."

"What I can't understand," Rachad said with a trace of asperity, "is why anyone in Maralia should be interested in alchemy at all, with gold so common. Why is the duke so keen on it?"

"You echo my own views," laughed the baron gruffly. "Yet philosophers still strive for the secret of transmutation, for whatever obscure satisfaction it gives them. As far as I can see it's a perfectly useless exercise—although alchemy has been known to produce some interesting weapons of war. I once heard tell of alchemical bullets that speed up indefinitely after they leave the muzzle. If they miss their target, they accelerate up to lightspeed."

"I have seen better than that," Rachad said hurriedly. "When we journeyed from Earth we were attacked by alchemical monsters that grew from seeds."

"Yes, so I've been told. Well, young man, can I count on you?"

"Yes, my lord," Rachad said definitely. "You can count on me."

"Good!" the baron said, with great satisfaction. He drank deeply from his flagon, then raised it aloft.

"To the opening of the Aegis!"

And he laughed so wildly and so long that Rachad felt chilled in his bones.

Leaving the hall, Rachad made his way through the dank-smelling castle until coming to the ladies' apartments. Once he hid in a window recess as a servant girl chanced to pass by. Gazing through the panes, he saw that the amber sun had set. Castarpos alone illuminated Arp, with a shifting, uncertain glow, while below the castle Corrum twinkled dimly.

When the way was clear he eased himself into Elissea's boudoir, secreting himself behind the arras until she came in, when he leaped out at her, laughing softly.

Afterward they lay together on her large, soft bed. "I have to leave Arp soon," he told her brashly.

She scowled prettily. "Oh? And where are you going?"

"On a secret mission for your uncle." He smiled mysteriously. "It's very important."

She raised herself on one elbow to lean over him. "When will you be coming back?"

"That depends. Later I might go back to Earth. I'll take you with me. We'll live together in Olam. . . ." He stopped, realizing that the boast was vain.

A bullet that carries on accelerating, he thought. He tried to imagine how it was given the necessary properties. Quicksilver for mobility, ether to provide constant impetus. An amalgam of quicksilver and ether was not the easiest thing to bring about.

He would ask the artifex Amschel about it, once he was inside the Aegis.

Chapter TEN

"Caught you!"

Leaping from his bed, Rachad seized hold of the intruder who was in the act of stealthily lifting the lid of a clothes chest, and dragged him to the window. In the pale light of Castarpos the burglar blinked, his face paper-like, his throat feeling the prick of Rachad's copper-pommelled poniard. It was Suivres, the Duke of Koss's agent in Corrum. Just as Rachad had expected.

Outside the dank attic room, the town lay sleeping, looking like a slumped forest, its streets winding upward to the castle on the summit of the hill. Contemptuously Rachad pushed Suivres from him.

"Thief! Thought you would make off with my property, eh? Easier than dealing honestly, isn't it?"

Suivres cleared his throat, and looked about him until he spotted an oil lamp gleaming in Castarpos's light. With commendable aplomb he reached in his pocket for a flint and struck a spark onto the wick.

He turned to Rachad as the lamplight filled the room, not in the least abashed. He was dressed in puffed breeches and a tight-fitting doublet. He had a dried, somewhat weary face, the eyes pale and restless.

"I merely wished to confirm that you do indeed possess the remainder of the text," he said in a matter-of-fact voice. "No theft was intended. After all, so far you have only produced one page."

"Which you have taken to Amschel to have authenticated."

"True. And it is authentic." Suivres looked around the shabby rented room. "Where? . . ."

Rachad grinned. "Not here. I'm not as stupid as I look. I have it in a safe place, never fear." He looked at Suivres speculatively. "I see you did not have the courtesy to return my page."

Suivres shrugged. "There is one aspect of this business that puzzles us," he said. "What are you doing on Arp? There is no other alchemist within systems of here, that

I know of. Hardly the place to come if you are really searching for the matching half of the book."

"It's simple enough," Rachad replied instantly, his mind tumbling over itself for an explanation. "While I was in the Ragnak system I heard that someone here was making the same inquiries as myself. So here I came to follow it up."

"Ha ha! That someone was myself, putting out feelers on the Duke's behalf." He straightened, and seemed to make up his mind. "Very well, then. I am authorized to take you to the Duke, with the book. We leave in a few hours. Where *is* the book?"

"How do we get there? How far is it?"

"Only a few light-years. We travel by horseback to where I have a ship hidden, some miles over the horizon."

Rachad felt nervous now that the moment of departure was approaching. "How can I trust you?" he said irritably. "Once we are away from here it will be easy for you to have me murdered and seize the book for yourself."

Suivres raised his eyebrows in an offended manner. "Really! You insult my liege-lord to think he could behave in such a fashion!"

"Really!" Rachad snorted. He had heard plenty about the eccentric duke during the time he had been living in Corrum. His name was mentioned in mumbles and whispers. There were endless tales of the perversions and grotesques practiced within the sealed-up Aegis, where none of the normal standards of mankind was observed.

"The stories rife about the Duke do *not* give one confidence in his conduct," he pointed out stiffly.

"All of them exaggerated. . . . Many of them, at any rate." Suivres waved a hand dismissively. "The Duke is noble, a gentleman. Now what's the matter with you? You were keen enough before."

Rachad bit his lip. Perhaps his best guarantee of safe conduct was that he had managed to pass himself off as an adept. Very likely Amschel was as eager to meet him as he was to meet Amschel.

"All right. I'll collect the book, and meet you in two hours."

"Excellent. Join me outside the town, on the polar road. I'll have steeds waiting."

After Suivres had gone Rachad dressed himself and sat down for a few minutes to think. Far-off Earth seemed appealingly cozy and safe now that he had begun to immerse himself in the rough-and-tumble of Maralian society. Maralia was so *big*. And yet it was but one of many star countries. This part of the galaxy, it seemed, was a confusion of kingdoms, empires, principalities and even one or two independent republics.

And over it all spread the shadow of the Kerek. Rachad knew now what fear went with the speaking of that name, and that the position of Maralia, indeed of any human nation, was insecure. There were times when his brash self-confidence faltered, and he felt out of his depth. Especially when he thought of the hated and unbalanced Duke of Koss, a decadent hermit who, so it was said, despised the whole cosmos.

But Rachad's heart sank when he thought of the coming exploit. Entering the Aegis seemed to him now like descending into a deep hole from which there was no escape.

The horses provided by Suivres were of a long-legged variety bred specially for Arp, and they fairly leaped and clattered along the road that followed the contours of the slate-colored landscape.

Rachad had approached the meeting place with caution, but there was no evidence that Suivres planned anything treacherous and gradually his fears had abated. In his saddlebag was the lead-covered tome he had recovered from its keeper, his landlord (who had not taken kindly to being awakened in the middle of the night), and by now Baron Matello would have been informed of his departure. No doubt he was already sending word to his secret camp near the Aegis.

For two hours the loping Arp horses cantered along the highway, until eventually Suivres reined in and turned off to lead the way across slablike terrain which gave off ringing *clicks* when struck by the horses' hooves.

Behind them the road passed out of sight. Their steeds slithered down shingle into a deep gully masked by snake-like trees which bore broad olive-green leaves. There, hidden by the overhanging branches, was a ship.

Though of spacefaring design, she seemed even smaller than the *Wandering Queen*, especially as she currently showed neither masts nor booms. Urging his mount forward between the trunks of the slippery trees, Suivres uttered a low *halloo*. Men appeared, wary and with drawn weapons at first, but quickly recognizing him.

Soon, with much sweating and groaning, the ship was being hauled on runners to the shallow end of the gully, where she stood under an open sky. Rachad went aboard while the horses were stripped of packs, saddles and bridles, and set loose. Sprits went out; sail was raised and found a current despite the nighttime hour.

Stealthily the ship wafted into the air, and before long had gained space. Casting out her whiplash rods, on which she then bent extraordinary lengths of silk, she went hurtling away from the amber sun.

For speed the smaller starship could not match the *Bucentaur*, and the journey lasted a week. They cruised through a small cluster of stars which glowed in a dozen colors, looking like a splendid, dazzling brooch. Finally they approached an aggressive, furnace-like sun, its surface whirling visibly white and red.

Three planets endured the vagaries of this contentious star. The ship slanted down toward the largest of them: a craggy world of gravel and granite.

The Aegis was set amid mountains, and seemed itself an artificial mountain, jutting up from the tumbled and chaotic slopes, lustrous gray in color, like graphite. Slanting pilasters buttressed its sloping walls, creating an effect, Rachad thought, not unlike that aimed at by the builders of the Temple of Hermes Trismegistus. But clearly no outward show was intended in this case. No crenellations crowned its heights. No window grills or firing slits relieved its sullen immensity. The Aegis brooded, looking inward, separated from the rest of existence.

The starship alighted on a downward slope and reeled in her sail rods. Rachad, clutching his precious tome to his chest, followed Suivres onto the gravely surface, shivering in the cold wind. It was hard to imagine that the obdurate, seamless mountain ahead of him was in fact under siege. Yet somewhere nearby, if what Baron Matello had said was true, an armed force hid, provisioned, presumably, from the mining towns that dotted the planet.

They trudged up the slope. "If the Aegis is impassable, how do we get inside?" Rachad asked, catching his breath.

"That is arranged with considerable circumspection," Suivres answered wryly.

The vast fortress loomed over them. They made for an oblong outcropping that protruded from the foot of the Aegis. Although it was hard to see how anyone could have been watching, a part of the oblong slid aside, revealing a square chamber within.

Suivres pointed to the poniard in Rachad's belt. "Get rid of that. No weapons are allowed within the Aegis."

Reluctantly Rachad threw the poignard to the ground, and they stepped into the casemate. Behind them the panel closed up again. Light shone from a square gap in the ceiling, but it was impossible to see what, if anything, lay beyond it.

"This is the main gate?" Rachad whispered anxiously.

"Only a side door. The main entrance hasn't been opened in fifty years." Suivres raised his voice, calling out to an unseen guard. "I, Suivres, bring the guest who is expected!"

Rachad touched the wall of the chamber. The adamant of which it was made was smooth and silky—but hard as diamond.

Suddenly the wall facing the main bulk of the Aegis slid upward. Beyond lay the interior of the Duke of Koss's lifetime retreat.

As he stepped through the portal, a bewildering melange of impressions swamped Rachad's senses. There was the sound of flute music, drifting on the air as if through countless chambers. And then there was the air itself—so flooded with innumerable intriguing scents that it was like dark wine. The air was heavy, heady, with this meld of scents, which seemed to have been present for so long that it had fermented, producing an indescribably decadent aroma.

Guarding the portal stood a line of pikemen in pied livery of lilac and yellow, the chest blazon consisting of some sort of geometrical figure. They stepped aside, allowing the newcomers to pass between a gathering of people dressed in sumptuous but subdued colors, staring at Rachad curiously but silently.

Behind them lay a sybaritic scene that was hard to reconcile with the harshness of the moutain landscape outside. Indeed it was quite unlike what Rachad would have expected on entering any normal castle. Where were the inner defenses, the keeps, the sloping ramparts? The Aegis needed none, he realized. Its defense relied *in toto* on its adamant walls.

Instead, the portal opened onto an arcade richly hung with plush drapes of plum red and deep purple. On either side extended cross passages and staircases. At the far end were two broad sets of steps, one ascending, one descending, suggesting that the Aegis was as extensive below ground as it was above (a fact already known to Rachad through his talks with Flammarion). Up from the depths of the lower stair-passage there drifted a sparkling mist, or smoke, which thinned out into streamers and curlicues.

Yet despite the arcade's size, it lacked spaciousness. The Aegis's obsessively self-enclosed nature pervaded it, making it almost claustrophobic.

Rachad's eyes rested on a huge statue that commanded the near end of the arcade. It was of a figure in a flowing robe, tall but with broad shoulders. The hair was cropped short and hung in a fringe over a bulging brow.

The face was extraordinary. It bore a pained, sneering, almost insane look—a look of ultimate rejection. The eyes stared straight ahead, as if fixed on something incomprehensible and horrifying.

This, Rachad thought, must be the Duke of Koss.

Suivres halted. Someone else had entered the arcade and was walking unhurriedly toward them. It was a man dressed in a loose, flowing purple robe, a man who might have been the model of the statue, except that he was slimmer and somewhat younger in appearance. The statue, Rachad realized, was of the old duke. This was the present master of the Aegis, the son and successor.

The resemblance between the two was striking, and yet markedly different. The second duke appeared austere rather than brutal, distracted rather than insane, an aesthete rather than a man of power. His eyes seemed permanently glazed, except when they focused, for long disturbing moments, on some object—as they did on Rachad, making him feel naked and transparent.

Hastily Rachad copied Suivres's low bow. "Your Grace," Suivres said humbly, "may I present Rachad Caban, an artifex, owner of the fragment we seek."

"If all is as it seems, you have indeed done well, Suivres," the duke murmured, his faint voice sounding to

Rachad like the distant piping of the wind. "I shall reward you."

"To serve Your Grace is reward enough!" Suivres replied ardently. It was evident that the duke inspired enormous respect in those around him, so much so that as he drew closer, with effete movements and giving off a waft of pungent scent, Rachad found himself trembling.

"Give His Grace the tome!" Suivres hissed out of the side of his mouth. With a start Rachad handed over the lead-bound book, noting as he did so that though barely above forty years of age if his appearance was any judge, the duke's swept-back hair was streaked with gray.

Gracefully accommodating himself to its weight and bulk, the duke opened the volume and for a minute or two seemed deep in thought, his face bent to the beautifully colored pages. Eventually he nodded slowly, and again looked directly at Rachad.

"It has an authentic air. Have you studied the *Asch Mezareph?*"

"Er . . . I've examined it," Rachad replied hesitantly.

"You seem very young to have had any extensive alchemical experience . . ." the duke observed pensively. "What operations have you performed?"

Rachad felt obliged to evade the question. "I owe everything to my master and mentor," he said. "He sent me in search of the knowledge we lack, entrusting the book to me for the purpose."

The duke pondered this. "Well, we shall find much to discuss in this text, you and I, not to speak of Master Amschel. Come, let me conduct you through my realm."

Due to some acoustic effect the flute music faded as they approached the steps at the end of the arcade. The duke turned at the head of the stairs, smiling faintly at Rachad. Then he descended the steps, becoming shadowy in the thickening mist.

A tinkling sound reached Rachad's ears as he encountered the first coils of the sparkling smoke. Stepping down the staircase was like floating through a cloud. The tones, initially random and inchoate, increased in volume and texture, coalescing as he moved into a collage of shifting, novel melodies of incredible complexity and color.

The duke's voice drifted to him. "Does the melody mist please you? The smoke is composed of crystal particles, each emitting a tiny tone. In addition the crystals have a vibrational empathy with one another; they respond to each other, creating elaborate webs of sound that movement translates into tunes and harmonies. No composer could equal the inventiveness of the mist . . . music, I find, is a unique adjunct to the stirrings of the soul. . . . My Aegis is everywhere pervaded by music. . . . One could become lost in music. . . ."

The murmuring voice went on, droning against the ever-meshing, ever-separating and commingling maze of melody, which was beginning to lull Rachad into a state of helpless fascination, especially as the melodies were so alien to his ear. But then they reached the bottom of the steps and, a little farther on, emerged into clearer air.

The duke stopped and stared straight ahead, his face slack, his eyes vacant. Then he turned and looked blankly at Rachad.

"Eh? What? Oh yes, it's you again."

They strolled across a mosaic floor strewn with what looked like rose petals. The music had faded to a tinkle, like the sound of a running stream in the background.

"You have seen the statue of my father," the duke said. "He was a much maligned man. They called him a criminal, a traitor, a thief . . . whereas he was merely a philosopher, whose disgust with life led him to construct his own artificial life. In those days many famous philosophers and artists were invited into the Aegis . . . they settled here, and have brought up a generation who have known only the Aegis. . . ."

"But do outside affairs never interest you, Your Grace?" Rachad asked.

"Never. The outside world does not exist, as far as I am concerned. Here we have created our own cosmos. . . ." The duke made a wry mouth. "Would that I could seal off the Aegis from the rest of space and time altogether, to live self-existent, and alone. . . . Amschel has spoken of the possibility, once the Great Work is completed."

"But you depend on the outside for *some* things, surely? What about food?"

"The Aegis needs no supplies, either of food or of fuel. We grow food in our own culture gardens. And as for light—" He directed Rachad's attention to the lamps that illuminated the concourse through which they were passing, milky hemispheres set in the ceiling and giving forth a clear white glow.

"The bowls are filled with a luminous substance which retains its glow for five years," the duke told him. "It can then be revived by means of an alchemical process."

"Extraordinary!" Rachad said. "I've never heard of that before!" For some reason it impressed him even more than the melody mist. Yet still he felt compelled to press the point of the duke's isolation. "But tell me honestly, Your Grace—could you really stay aloof if Maralia were faced with a Kerek invasion?"

"Kerek? Kerek? I've heard that word somewhere. . . ."

"An alien race who are making war on mankind!" Rachad supplied, amazed to see the unconcern on the duke's face. "A race who may well end up enslaving the whole of humanity!"

"Enslave? Not I, not I. . . . This invasion you speak of will wash over the Aegis but never break it. . . . Never will man or alien dictate to me. . . ."

They walked on, deeper and deeper into the Aegis. And as its atmosphere engulfed him, Rachad found himself less and less able to speak of outside events. . . .

In fifty years the Aegis had become an inward-looking world of stunning artistic perfection. It was an art gallery, a museum, a sybarite's palace, all rolled into one.

In his short tour Rachad saw only a fraction of the vast and mysterious building. But it was enough to give him the flavor of the duke's aesthetic experiments—for he soon realized that though many men of genius had been at work here, they were all influenced by the peculiar private tastes the duke had inherited from his father. Everywhere there was quiet music, sometimes from the drifting melody mist, sometimes from indefinable distant sources, much of it strange and jarring to the ear—developed, Rachad imagined, from the odd dissonances and mind-twisting themes, lacking key or regular rhythm, that the melody mist generated. And often there were eerie cries, bellows, prolonged and unintelligible monologues, and frighteningly strange singing—though whether all of this emanated from madmen or from some form of drama that was being performed, Rachad did not inquire.

Yet despite all these sounds, an unnerving air of silence prevailed in the Aegis. Every noise, every cry, every note of music, seemed to be surrounded by this silence, seemed to be separated from every other sound by long gulfs of silence. It was a heavy, blank silence that to a newcomer was depressing. It might, Rachad thought, result from the surrounding walls of deadening adamant—yet somehow it seemed to him to be the endless silence of a long and continuing decadence.

The duke took him through a series of suites, each drenched in a particular color: the blue suite, of a rich luminous blue; the saffron suite, the magenta suite, and so on. "By lingering in these," the duke told him, "one's mind becomes saturated with a single color. Given long enough, I believe a human being would become incapable of perceiving any other color—anything but blue, for instance."

"Has the experiment been carried out?" Rachad asked.

"Yes, by a second cousin of mine," the duke replied. "He stayed for one year in the magenta suite. But he never emerged to put our thesis to the test. One day he accidentally opened an artery with his scarlet razor. Being unable to distinguish his flowing blood from the crimson satins, he quickly bled to death without realizing it."

Wordlessly they left the monochrome rooms. Rachad found himself in a small picture gallery hung with a charming set of largish paintings. They all showed similar scenes: graceful men and women in long robes, conversing and relaxing in Arcadian settings, in shady groves, amid fluted columns and spacious colonnades. Their intelligent, serene faces, their ease of gesture, showed them to be a highly cultivated people. Rachad could imagine them to be the philosophers of ancient times, discoursing on the nature of the world.

"These are by Giacourt," the duke announced evenly. "In my view, the greatest painter Maralia has ever produced. He spent his last twenty years with us."

He conducted Rachad through the opposite door. Beyond was an identical gallery, hung with what at first seemed to be identical paintings. It took only moments, however, to realize the difference. In expression and stance, the figures had been subtly altered. They looked at one another now in a sly, speculative way, as if seized by new thoughts and feelings they could not subdue.

Beyond that was yet a third gallery, also identical. Here, using the same figures and the same settings, the artist had carried his sequence to a nauseating conclusion—an orgy of perversion, rape and hideous butchery that left Rachad sick and trembling with horror.

"Giacourt had no illusions concerning human nature," the duke murmured. "You find such visions disturbing, perhaps? No matter . . . here in the Aegis you may enjoy whatever pleasures you choose. Come, and I will show you something that is the answer to all life's strivings."

They walked through a seemingly endless garden of multicolored orchids of enormous size which threw off clouds of heavy, sleepy scents. Purple and pink humming birds darted hither and thither, dipping their beaks into the giant bells and emerging dusted in golden powder. The garden was lit not by ceiling lights but by pulsing globes mounted on four-foot-high pedestals, so that a jungle of flaring shadows seemed to be added to the scene.

Finally they descended some steps and came to a sunken part of the garden. Here, in a low grotto, was what appeared to be a tiled circular mud bath, in which a dozen or so people sprawled with eyes closed, as if in sleep.

"This we call dream-slime," the duke said, his distant, drifting voice adopting a caressing tone. "The recipe for the concoction was discovered by my father's personal apothecary, after much trial and error . . . and considerable mental derangement of the patients he used as subjects."

Stooping, he scooped up a handful of the mud, then took Rachad by the wrist and daubed a gob of it on the back of his hand. Immediately Rachad felt a warm, tingling sensation in the flesh of his hand. From it, a feeling of pleasure began to seep into him, a piercing, near-orgasmic pleasure, with an as-yet-undefined sense of expectancy. . . .

He stared at the slime. On closer inspection the claycolored stuff was actually composed of millions of motes, each a different color so that they all merged into the same muddy brown.

The pleasure intensified. With sudden panic he slopped the slime from him, letting it fall to the tiles, and wiped his hand on his breeches.

The duke laughed softly. "That was merely a foretaste. The real meaning of the slime is in the dreams it brings— waking dreams that take the place of current reality, or sleeping dreams, as you will."

"It sounds . . . unhealthy," Rachad muttered.

"Oh, no . . . the slime creates no fantasy world. It gives one nothing false or invented . . . it can create no new experience. What it does is cause one to live over again the pleasurable events one has already experienced —but to experience them intensified and heightened to exquisite, almost unbearable levels. Have you ever felt that life's pleasures are a disappointment? How often, young man, have you desired a maid, only to find, when eventually you enjoy her, that it is less of a delight than you imagined it would be? Then what you need is the dreamslime. In it you can experience the highlights of life over again, but with an intensity that would make you faint away were you awake."

Rachad stared bemused at the slumberers in the slime bath, for the first time noticing that they were all naked. "You will appreciate by now," the duke said in a nearwhisper, as though he barely possessed the energy to speak, "that we in the Aegis live a life of the utmost debauchery of the senses, indeed of all the faculties. And if our senses become jaded by abuse, if our bodies can no longer be stimulated to respond, why, it makes no difference. Dream-slime will add all that is missing, and more."

Wordlessly Rachad followed his guide out of the orchid garden. His mind was scarcely on the other wonders that the duke showed to him, such as the waterfall of drugged wine that tumbled for seven of the Aegis's levels, splashing onto rocks to form sparkling pools in which one could bathe and become sated. Indeed by this time his own capacity for new sights was itself sated, so much so that he merely felt bewildered when the duke showed him one of the most impressive of the Aegis's artistic accomplishments: a number of salons and apartments based on illusion, which by means of clever lighting tricks, oddly shaped rooms and ingenious screens that moved unseen by the observer, left the occupant disorientated and unable to make normal perceptual judgments. He was then receptive to new perversions of the senses that were then introduced. Here were boudoirs where, by moving from one part of the room to another, one became either a midget or a giant in relation to one's sexual partner. Here were private bordellos where women seemed to flit in and out of the walls, the floor, the air, attacking their client in endless streams and enmeshing him in an inescapable web of lechery. Here were painted picturamas so cunningly devised that Rachad could not believe that he would not be able to step into the incredible scenes they depicted.

Shortly he was to receive more evidence that the duke richly deserved his reputation for insanely wanton sensuality. Perceiving that his charge was by now surfeited with new impressions, the haughty aesthete observed that the Aegis's day was well advanced, and that it was time to repair to the regular evening banquet.

While the meal progressed he turned the pages of *The Root of Transformations*, commenting lengthily on the text and pointing out significances in the illustrations, even in fine details, which were entirely novel to Rachad, and which he suspected would have been so even to Gebeth. Closing the book, the duke continued, in the vague and faltering voice that clearly belied a keen intellect, to talk of alchemical principles in general. He spoke of the fusion of positive and negative, of the alchemical marriage which must always take place within a sealed vessel, of the joust of the red and black knights, and so on. Going on from that, he gave Rachad the first clear account he had ever heard of the three primordial forces of sulphur, quicksilver and salt.

To this one-sided discourse Rachad added little, firstly because he knew little, but also because the duke's table habits left him stupefied. His own food was familiar and appetizing, but to the duke there was served dish after dish of different foods altogether—unrecognizable stuffs which gave off bizarre aromas. The flavors, it seemed, were equally strange, a combination of the delicious and nauseous so overpowering that several times the duke lost control and turned to vomit into an urn placed near his chair.

Nor were his table pleasures limited to this stretching of the range of the palate. Rachad's eyes bulged as, at intervals, young women, youths, even children, came forward from the sides of the hall and, in full view of everyone present, performed lascivious and perverted acts upon the duke's person. In mid-sentence the duke would pause to grunt and moan, turning up his eyes in ecstasy. Then, giving Rachad a friendly leer, he would continue the talk where he had left off.

Finally he pushed away the latest offering, a plate of odious-smelling pale fruit, and gestured to the retainer to indicate that he was satisfied. Rachad looked around the hall. The other diners, who talked little, and came and went as they pleased, had noticed nothing unusual. The denizens of the Aegis were individualistic, little given to formality, and mostly pursued private interests.

The duke leaned close. "One thing is plain, young man —you know little of alchemy. Do not prevaricate, now."

Rachad grimaced ruefully. "I am only an apprentice," he admitted. "My hope is to become Master Amschel's assistant in the completion of the work. Then I will return to my own master and impart to him the method of the preparation of the stone."

The duke pursed his lips, adjusting his dress and brushing away the fondling hand of a maiden who bent over him.

"I shall speak to Amschel of your desire," he murmured.

A silence descended, the same dead, stifling silence that Rachad had noted before. He realized that the duke was a classic case of self-obsession. He was trapped within his own consciousness, encased to a point that in the outside world would have been regarded as insanity, but that here passed without comment. Indeed, the whole Aegis was a hymn to solipsism, to the rejection of any outward involvement, to the creation of a world that sprang solely from one's own desires.

"And when shall I meet Master Amschel?" Rachad asked.

"Tomorrow. But enough—the hour is late, and my strength flags."

The duke rose and sauntered toward the wall, turning just before he reached it. "And so to my bed of slime. I bid you goodnight."

A section of wall slid aside. Within, Rachad saw a small chamber containing a sort of bath or coffin rimmed with ornate gilt and filled with the same muddy concoction he had seen in the orchid garden.

The duke entered. Before the wall closed again an attendant helped him strip. He lowered his bony body into the bath. His eyes closed, the slime enclosing him and leaving only his face showing.

A footman approached Rachad. "Allow me to show you

to suitable apartments," he said quietly. "Any reasonable service you require is available. You may, if you wish, partake of a slime-bed. But I warn you, once you have sampled it you will not willingly leave the Aegis again."

"Thank you—all I need is a place where I can sleep normally."

The footman led him away, and Rachad's mind became busy. He could not dislike the duke, but there was the awful extent of his degeneracy. This was not the healthy, robust world Rachad knew.

Up until now he had not been sure whether he would in fact attempt to carry out the mission Baron Matello had set him. But now he found it easy to rationalize such treachery. He was, he told himself, furthering not only his own ambitions but also helping mankind to defend itself against the Kerek.

At the earliest opportunity he would endeavor to open up the Aegis.

Chapter ELEVEN

After a long sleep between linen sheets, Rachad was awakened by a maid-servant who brought him a breakfast of fruit and crumbly flavored bread. Shortly, when he had washed and dressed himself, a footman arrived and escorted him to a part of the Aegis he had not seen before. The sumptuous luxury with which the walls were normally draped gave way once more to gray adamant, bare and metallic.

The Duke of Koss, clasping the lead-bound pages of *The Root of Transformations,* waited for him at the entrance to a featureless corridor. He smiled, and seemed refreshed.

"Good morning, young Caban. You slept well, I trust?"

"Yes, Your Grace," Rachad answered, addressing the duke as etiquette would elsewhere have required, though in the Aegis it scarcely seemed necessary.

"I, too. Our evening meal was delightful, when experienced for the second time."

The duke pointed into the corridor. "At the heart of the Aegis there lies a second stronghold, protected by an adamant maze of great intricacy and cunning. It is, almost, an aegis within an aegis—there is machinery by which its structure can be rearranged, so that even if an intruder knows his way through the person it protects can render this knowledge useless. If the maze shifted around him in mid-journey, in fact, he would be trapped."

He tightened his robe about him. "I installed Amschel's laboratory there, to save him from meddlesome curiosity-seekers. We will go to him now."

"*We* can get through safely, I take it?" Rachad asked, staring down the corridor.

"Oh, indeed. One needs but to memorize a certain sequence of numbers, which I have done by means of a mnemonic system." Again the duke smiled, sardonically this time. "Of course, if Master Amschel takes it into his head to alter the maze, we will be lost."

They set forth, walking side by side. "What's the reason for this inner fortress?" Rachad asked as they went. "Is it in case the Aegis itself is breached?"

The duke shook his head. "No—such a possibility was never admitted by the alien beast who constructed the Aegis, which is specified to be invulnerable. Ostensibly he included it so as to offer a place of shelter should warfare break out within the Aegis."

Rachad kept silence as the duke threaded his way through the maze, muttering to himself and hesitating only occasionally. The maze was, as he had said, extremely complicated. They moved not only through a labyrinth of corridors but also up and down winding ramps and steep staircases. Their route twisted and turned at such a rate that it was impossible to estimate the size of the maze in terms of space, and Rachad lost all sense of direction.

Always there seemed to be at least half a dozen possible directions to take. Once the duke stopped, and gestured to Rachad, pointing to a passage ahead of them.

"Walk down there," he ordered.

Rachad attempted to obey, but came up against an invisible wall of what felt like glass.

The duke laughed softly. "You have just walked into a mirror."

"But *I* am not reflected in it!" Rachad protested. "And neither are you!" Bewildered, he glanced behind him. "In fact it doesn't reflect our surroundings at all."

"True—it's a trick mirror. The image is conveyed from elsewhere by means of lenses and visual conduits. Just one more means to confuse the wanderer in the maze. He never knows whether what he sees is real or not."

Rachad thought of the viewscreen aboard the *Bucentaur*. They passed on, and presently came to what he took to be the maze's indwelling secret, emerging into a small wood of stunted trees, the uneven floor being carpeted with moss. The overhead glow-globes were dim; the wood seemed to be cast in dusk.

Sitting in a hillock was a small, round-shouldered old man with silky hair which fell to his shoulders, and who turned at the sound of their footsteps. His age, Rachad guessed, was close to Gebeth's, or he could have been even older. At first glance his face was monkey-like and melancholy, but this impression faded quickly. The brown eyes did, indeed, seem more introspective than was usual, but their steadfastness, and the general air of collectedness that surrounded him, dispelled any resemblance to a dodderer. One hand on his knee, he watched as the two visitors approached.

The duke bowed respectfully. "Master Amschel, I bring what was promised—the missing sections of the book. In addition, may I introduce its bearer, Master Rachad Caban, also an aspirant in the Great Work."

Rachad felt Amschel inspecting him without visible change of expression. "Master Caban has named a price for his donation of the text," the duke continued. "He wishes to join you in the preparation of the stone. I find," he added, in a sterner tone which showed he expected no opposition, "the request to be a reasonable one."

"Indeed," the artifex replied in a mild voice. He reached out and accepted the tome. Opening its lead covers, he spent what seemed like a long time poring over the pages.

Then he looked up at Rachad. "And what stage have *you* reached in the preparation of the stone?"

Rachad faltered, and swallowed. "No stage at all," he admitted timidly, intimidated by the alchemist's air of self-assurance. "I am here on behalf of my own teacher, Master Gebeth of the planet Earth, who has spent a lifetime striving for success."

The brown eyes lingered on him.

"Are the chapters all they should be, Master Alchemist?" asked the duke eagerly.

"They appear to be authentic. The book is complete. We may resume work."

"And how long before the stone is ours?"

Amschel rose to his feet. He barely reached up to Rachad's shoulder.

"If we use the lightning method, the operation itself is almost instantaneous. But the preparation of the *primus agens* may take a good deal of time, as will the construction of the necessary apparatus."

"Then I will bid you good day, and I wish you success," the duke said distantly. Without another word he strolled off the way he had come, leaving Rachad alone with Amschel.

The alchemist beckoned to him. Together they walked through the silent wood, between gnarled, twisted trees, until an adamant wall loomed up ahead of them.

A square portal slid open. Amschel led Rachad through it. Behind his back the door closed with a loud, decisive clang.

"This," said Amschel, "is my laboratory."

The air was charged with pungent, penetrating smells. Rachad recognized the bite of acids, the stink of heated metals, and the acerbic odor of the energy known as infusoration.

He could not immediately see how extensive the laboratory was. It resembled a crypt, consisting of vault-ceilinged chambers connected by arched openings, and these seemed to go on and on. But already the variety and scope of the apparatus bewildered him, used as he was to Gebeth's back room. He could see not only the usual array of furnaces, descensories, sublimatories, crucibles and flasks, but also devices whose purpose he could not remotely guess at, tended by up to a dozen white-smocked workers.

Amschel, however, directed Rachad to a chair, and sat opposite him, knee to knee, *The Root of Transformations* on his lap.

"So, let's find out about you. Ask me a question."

"What?"

"It's to discover your level of knowledge. Ask me something you, or your master, would like to know but haven't been able to find out. Something specific."

Rachad thought for a moment or two, then nodded. "There *is* something," he said. "What is the correct sulphur-mercury ratio for gold? We know that all metals are composed of sulphur and mercury, and can be converted into one another by altering the ratio between the two. But Gebeth could never discover what the various ratios are."

"Well, that tells me roughly your level of competence," Amschel said wryly. "The sulphur-mercury theory of metals is wrong, and any efforts made in that direction are a waste of time. Never mind. Tell me more about your master."

Nonplussed to learn that his ignorance was even deeper than he had believed, Rachad began, haltingly at first, to speak of Gebeth, describing what he could of his methods. But he dissembled when it came to relating how he had left Earth, implying that Gebeth himself had given him his part of the book, and making no mention of

Baron Matello. Amschel, however, gave no sign that he suspected duplicity and only asked where Gebeth had obtained the book. Rachad said that it had come from the last surving priest of an ancient temple, at which he seemed satisfied.

Finally Amschel leaned back with a sigh, eyeing Rachad. "It strikes me you are a rash and impulsive young man," he said. "Such qualities can be useful, even in the Work, in which caution is a handicap. Of greater use, however, are patience and the capacity for long, careful thought— these I believe you lack. Nevertheless you may join my staff and I will teach you what I can. Does that suit you?"

Rachad nodded. "I have one further question, Master Amschel," he said.

"What is that?"

Rachad hesitated. "On Earth, where I come from, gold is precious. But here in Maralia it is common. Why, then, do men such as yourself still wish to manufacture it? It seems to me that the aim of the art is redundant."

Amschel smiled. He, too, hesitated. Then he seemed to make up his mind to speak.

"We are in a secret place," he said. "The Aegis is secret, and this, the center of the inner maze, is a secret within a secret. So now I will tell you a secret within a secret within a secret—the making of gold is *not* the object of the Hermetic Art. That was a screen, erected for the gullible in the distant past—though to be sure, it has often happened that men who in the beginning were motivated by greed for gold have found in the end that the Art has worked an inner alchemy upon them, and their greed is transmuted into desire for knowledge, for its own sake."

"I don't understand, Master Amschel," Rachad said, bewildered. "If not gold—then what?"

"The goal is the creation of the Philosopher's Stone, also known as the Tincture, or the Elixir, an ultimate state of matter which can accomplish much more than the mere transmuting of lead into gold—though if need be, it can achieve that too. For that reason the making of gold is a symbol, or by-product, of the alchemical goal. But we will speak of the Stone later."

Amschel rose. "For today I will show you some of our simpler apparatus. The more difficult equipment can wait until you have a better appreciation of our work."

Laying aside the book, he stepped through the nearest

opening. In the adjoining chamber Rachad saw a huge brick structure that reached almost from floor to ceiling.

"This furnace can deliver three hundred and eighty different temperatures at one and the same time," Amschel said. "I designed it myself. It greatly reduces the time that need be spent on routine operations."

In another chamber stood ten smaller furnaces. These were cylindrical and high-necked, and smoked slightly. "These sublimatories supply a variety of unusual substances," Amschel explained. "They are in constant use."

"What happens to the fumes?" Rachad asked.

"They are carried out of the Aegis by a system of flues. We can also admit starlight by opening other small shafts. The light of certain stars can exert a subtle influence on some specially delicate operations, as can planetary configurations."

They moved on. "I have taken a particular interest in etheric compounds," the artifex said. "Prominent among these, as you may know, is light. Here is something intriguing."

They had come to a bench neatly laid out with labeled bottles and sample boxes. From a felt-lined tray Amschel picked up a stony blue pellet, or possibly a semiprecious gemstone. "These are found on the planet Aggryxa. Watch."

Fixing the stone in a nearby bracket, he gestured to the assistant who had been following them, and who took from a cupboard a peculiar-looking lamp which was backed by a concave mirror, presumably to focus its light in one direction.

The attendant lit the wick, and directed the ensuing flame's bright glow onto the stone. For nearly a minute nothing happened, and Rachad began to grow impatient. Then, without warning, a dazzling shaft of blue light shot from the pellet and struck the adamant wall opposite, scattering in all directions in a coruscating display.

In seconds the emission ceased. The assistant blew out the lamp and put it back in the cupboard.

"The light projected by this gem has special properties," Amschel informed Rachad. "A beam of it will travel endlessly without spreading. If focused through a lens, it is able to slice even diamond. I believe the material of the gem achieves this by storing and modifying the light of the lamp in some way. I have tried to duplicate the effect artificially, and have manufactured an inferior variety of Aggryxa gems by impregnating ruby with metallic sublimates."

Rachad's eyes smarted from the explosion of blueness. "Can anything else be achieved with it?" he asked.

"Very little, owing to its fleetness," Amschel said. "As you probably know, visible light combines ether and fire, with ether predominating. There are other radiations composed of ether and air, but these are just as fleet and also are invisible, since the sense of sight responds to fire alone. For practical work I prefer compounds in which ether plays a lesser role, and which are therefore slower and more manipulatable. In infusoration, for instance, ether and fire are nearly equally balanced and mingled with about one-twentieth part water. Do you know it? Some call it galvanism, others the electric fluid. It will flow easily through solid iron or copper."

"Master Gebeth has an infusorator using zinc, lead, copper and acids."

"He would be interested to see my own facilities, which I boast are unexampled in the entire galaxy. I have developed new types of infusorator capable of delivering the substance with unprecedented intensity. And yet—it is still not enough." His voice fell to a mutter. "Still not enough."

Speaking in a low tone, he unscrewed the gemstone and replaced it in its box. "For fifty years I have studied and worked. But one lifetime is not enough. Given another fifty years, perhaps I could solve all remaining problems and produce the Stone unaided."

"Have you always worked in the Aegis?"

"For many years I traveled extensively and worked with other adepts, including non-human philosophers. Ten years ago the Duke of Koss sent word that he had a part of *The Root of Transformations* in his possession, a book thought lost forever. He promised to search for the rest of the text and offered me unlimited resources. So I came into the Aegis."

"It amazes me that the secret is so inaccessible," Rachad remarked. "Does *no one* know it?"

"You would not be amazed if you knew what is entailed," Amschel replied. "It is the most difficult of all works, the greatest of all treasures."

"*Someone* must know," Rachad fretted. He brightened.

"What about the alien creature who built the Aegis? He must know all about the transformations of matter. He can make adamant."

"Oh, I too can make adamant, in small quantities," Amschel chuckled. "Still, I am glad to see that you have a lively mind. Let me explain adamant to you. It is simply elemental earth, purged of all trace of other elements. Being so purged, and pure, it is impervious to all assaults—impervious even to the alkahest."

Rachad listened with interest to this new information. "That's what I don't understand. Isn't the alkahest a solvent for *everything?*"

"It will dissolve all naturally occurring substances," Amschel corrected. "But that is because the alkahest is simply water—elemental water, purged and pure, as adamant is, and just as difficult to obtain as adamant is. You see, any natural substance contains all five elements to some extent, though only the major constituents are generally taken into account and the rest are present in negligible quantity. The alkahest, however, will immediately find and blend with whatever water is present, however negligible. It will flood into the substance, overpower it and disperse the other elements. For this reason elemental water is said to carry the qualities of universal dissolution and of like finding like. But it cannot enter adamant, because adamant is the only solid body to contain not the slightest trace of water."

"I wonder what pure air would be like?" Rachad wondered. "Or pure fire?"

"That I cannot tell you. But perhaps you would like to handle pure earth." Amschel turned and spoke to the assistant, who then moved to a cupboard, opened it and drew out a small trolley, which he wheeled forward with an effort disproportionate to its size.

The interior of the trolley was yet another felt-lined sample case. In it, Rachad saw a glistening gray brick or slab about four inches by three.

"Flammarion's secret is that he knows how to make adamant in vast quantities," Amschel said. "Here is a sample I prepared myself. Pick it up."

Rachad bent and took the tiny slab in his fingers, but it seemed to be stuck. He pulled harder, then, squatting on his haunches and using both hands, he managed to raise it an inch or two by using the strength of his legs.

Panting, he dropped the brick, then stood up. "How could *anything* be so heavy?" he asked.

"Ultimate hardness, ultimate rigidity, and extreme weight—those are the qualities of earth, when unmodified by combination."

"Hmm." Rachad pondered, then laughed lightly. "I suppose this answers the old riddle of what kind of vessel one would keep the universal solvent in."

"That's right. The alkahest must be kept in a vessel made of adamant. Any other vessel it will dissolve." Amschel pointed to an arched opening. "Come, I will show you to your sleeping quarters. Then we will see how you may best be fitted into our work."

Chapter TWELVE

For the next month Rachad saw little of Amschel, who withdrew into his study with the new knowledge Rachad had brought him. Instead, he began a period of training in the laboratory, at first learning to tend the sublimatories and other furnaces, and later going on to the operations of distillation, congelation and projection—at which Amschel's assistants were incomparably more learned than Gebeth, even though most of them were but borrowed liegemen of the duke's.

Every day Amschel would issue fresh orders for the preparation of some strange-sounding substance or other. Even without such instructions there was plenty of work for the laboratory, for there were a number of long-standing operations to attend to—operations which, Rachad was assured, had been in progress for a number of years.

There was, for instance, an hermetically sealed crystal vessel which had been subjected to the gradually increasing heat of an athanor for over five years, and whose contents were inspected daily for the expected color changes. In a complicated pelican, a type of double-reflux alembic, a substance had undergone cohobation—repeatedly recycled distillation—for even longer. And there were other operations, less easy to understand, all pursuant to the alchemical theory that new properties would evolve in a material if a process were continued for long enough.

In this way he learned a great deal he had not known before of practical alchemy. He also had access to the library, where he found hundreds of books and manuscripts, ranging from very ancient tracts such as *The Sophic Hydrolith* and *The Visions of Zosimos*—as well, of course, as the *Asch Mezareph*—to somewhat later works, among them *The Secret Art of Plasmas* and *The Etheric Chariot*. Of their texts he could grasp little, but he found great pleasure in poring over their numinous illustrations, especially those which depicted the interior of a flask as a little world, sometimes complete with landscape, in which strange, beguiling acts were taking place.

But eventually Rachad's interest waned, as had happened under Gebeth's tutelage on Earth, and he began to think how he might carry out his secret mission.

Luckily his movements were not restricted. He had been taught the number code which enabled him to find his way through the maze, and he had the freedom of the Aegis. Flammarion had also given him a rough idea of its layout, and he had little trouble in reconnoitering the approaches both to the main gate and the smaller side entrance.

In addition Flammarion had taken care to explain how the main gate was opened. It soon became evident to Rachad, however, just how difficult this would be. Both entrances were guarded round the clock by companies of pikemen. He also learned, from conversations with others, that extra locks had been put on the mechanisms—locks too large to be operated by one man. And as if that was not enough, the locks were protected by timber encasements which first had to be broken open with axes.

It seemed that Flammarion's scheme had foundered. Rachad returned in frustration to the laboratory, where he continued to wrestle with the problem.

Amschel was more to be seen in the laboratory after the first few weeks. He resumed what was apparently his practice of lecturing to his assistants—partly to make them better helpers but also, Rachad guessed, to impart genuine knowledge to those who were interested.

His talks were often rambling, sometimes fascinating, sometimes, to Rachad, dull. Sometimes, however, they were masterpieces of conciseness, especially when on the subject of technical operations. Amschel had a surprising knack of relating experimental processes to profoundly symbolic lore. In a way that offered a thrilling insight into the workings of the macrocosm, he spoke of the Worm Ouroborous, representing the creative powers of nature. He spoke also of "the Coiled Dragon," or "the Sleeping Sulphur," as it was alternatively called, which, he said, referred to the spiral of the galaxy which was coiled up like a spring. This spring was held in dynamic balance by secret forces of such power that should they be released they would destroy everything within the limits of visibility.

In another of his talks Amschel gave forth on the primitive philosophical ideas of ancient times. The ancients, it seemed, had been ignorant of the five elements and so had also failed to understand the principle of blending or "commingling." They had hypothesized that matter was composed of "atoms," microscopic particles which were supposed to be indivisible and indestructible, and which stuck crudely together in innumerable combinations.

"The theory is amusingly quaint," Amschel remarked, "but unsound in the logical sense, and also it is hopelessly complicated. To account even at that time for all the qualities found in the world it was necessary to hypothesize more than a hundred different types of atom—and to reckon with all the substances known to present-day alchemy, no doubt another hundred would have to be added.

"The same spirit of naive speculation governed astronomical ideas. At that period in history humanity was still restricted to one world, and there was no clear knowledge of the macrocosm generally. Ridiculous though it may seem to us, it was presumed that the home planet—which some say was called Earth—was the center of the macrocosm and that the whole of the heavens revolved around it. The other planets of the home system moved across the sky in ways that did not fit easily with this idea, of course, and a complicated, rather unwieldy system of wheels within wheels had to be devised on their behalf. These 'epicycles,' as they were known, may remind us of the equally artificial doctrine of 'indivisible atoms.'

"The philosophers who tried to explain nature on the basis of these speculations can have known little of the Hermetic art or of its goals. Even in that arid time, however, there were true alchemists, working in secret and possessing knowledge handed down since the time of Hermes Trismegistus."

Amschel pointed to Rachad. "Young man, you tell me you come from a planet called Earth. Is this the same that is reputed to be the birthplace of mankind?"

Rachad gave the same answer that Zhorga had once

given to Baron Matello: that had Earth truly been man's original home, lack of ether silk would have kept him there.

Then, one day, Amschel took Rachad aside and began to speak to him privately.

"It is time," he said, "to explain the Stone to you, and to show you the stage we have reached in our work."

Still in his work smock, Rachad seated himself and listened attentively, but Amschel did not come immediately to the promised business. Instead, he launched into a discourse on how the five elements combined to produce everything that existed—all worlds, all life, all minerals; everything that was fluid, aerial or energetic, everything that imparted motion. He explained the relation of the elements to space, a subject scarcely touched upon before. There was no such thing, Amschel informed, as empty space; space was but one of the properties of matter—its extensibility—and space that appeared empty was better described as ether. Hence matter and space were identical and continuous, to the discredit of the ancient atomic theory, in which they were deemed to be separate entities.

There were, Amschel proceeded to say, a number of ways in which the elements could combine. First and most important there was "blending," in which elements coalesced in various ratios, and the substances formed in this way were the true compounds. But there were also "mixes," in which elements, or blends of elements, compiled and interpenetrated in laminations, platelets, rods and slivers, crystals, raveled tendrils, simple coagulations and so forth, all on the microscopic level. The diversity and complexity of structures so obtained was limitless, accounting for the endless range of properties to be found in the macrocosm. This, Amschel explained, was also the reason why arcane substances were often named after living organisms or man-made constructions, their inner structures sometimes being almost as elaborate.

"In this way the five elements give rise to the world of multitudinous phenomena," Amschel said. "But they are not the end of the story, for they themselves were derived, countless ages ago at the beginning of existence, from *prima materia*, which alone can be called the primal substance. The elements are, so to speak, corruptions of it. Ether was the first derivation; then there followed, in quick succession, fire, air, water and earth. In the *prima materia* itself there is no differentiation. It is unconditioned, single and absolute, and in it all opposites merge as one. You may have heard it spoken of by other names—*hyle*, the primordial chaos, and so forth."

"This I already understand to some degree," Rachad said. "What bearing does it have on the Stone?"

"The Stone is made of the *prima materia*," Amschel answered. "Or rather, the *prima materia* forms the basis of its substance. The first stage in the production of the Stone is to destroy the elements and reduce them to the primal state. As *hylic* matter, however, the subject could not be handled, perhaps not even seen—*hyle* is formless, appearing as a void according to some authorities, as an inchoate black mass according to others. It would soon decay into elements again, and so a second process is needed. This impresses form upon it, fixing its qualities—whereupon it becomes the Stone: the ultimate state of matter!"

"And can this Stone turn lead into gold?" Rachad asked innocently.

Amschel chuckled, his eyes twinkling. "Oh, that is the least of its powers! The possessor of the Stone can work marvels. He can rotate the elements. He can project his will into the macrocosm. By mingling parings of the Stone with elemental substances, he can prepare a whole new range of efficacious agents—for the Tincture is the perfect medicine, the cure for all bodily ills, and the means to prolong life. If desired, the agents known as the white lion and the red can transmute base metals into silver and gold."

While Rachad pondered this, Amschel rose to his feet. "These operations I have described—reduction to *prima materia*, and then fashioning this into the Stone—are difficult in the extreme. Let me show you how I have attempted to achieve them."

He led the way to a section of the vaults Rachad had not visited previously. He lifted the latch of a massive door, made not of adamant but of timber, and pushed it open.

The space within was dominated by cucurbits and retorts of unfamiliar shapes and sizes. Most striking were those that were spherical. These were enormous, the largest of them a monstrous piece of glassware ten feet in diameter. Many of the vessels contained complicated structures of metal, finely wrought into sheets and wires, and their sealed delivery spouts—some cucurbits had as many as half a dozen—were connected not to glass pipes but to infusoratory cables which snaked across the floor.

Two white-smocked assistants bowed as the master alchemist entered. Rachad quickly realized that this was a special laboratory devoted to the use of infusoration. The smell of galvanism was in the air, plus an unmistakable sense of tension which was added to by angry buzzing noises leaking from the metal conductors.

His eye was caught by a bulbous, fairly small cucurbit that seemed to be inwardly alive. It flashed, writhed and bubbled with frenzied light which washed against its walls in waves.

"The mercuric compound within this vessel has experienced a continuous discharge of infusoration for the past three years," Amschel supplied, noticing his interest. "Shortly I will end the experiment and see what change has come about."

"Where are the actual infusorators?" Rachad asked. "I see none."

"They are very bulky, and are kept in adjoining chambers," Amschel said. With a wave of his hand he indicated all the apparatus by which they were surrounded. "To understand what I have been doing here, you must recall the ages-old belief that the Great Work can be accomplished if only sufficient heat can be generated. To try to develop an unnaturally high temperature is one reason why alchemists heat the subject for long periods in an hermetically sealed crystal egg. For many years I, too, concentrated on trying to obtain more and more heat by means of fire. I worked with a man who believed he had found the answer in a heavy metal called *the second lead*—though the ancients named it after one of their gods, Uranus. This metal hides great quantities of fire in itself, which can be concentrated and extracted if it is refined in a certain way."

Amschel's voice fell. "The experiment was disastrous. The temperatures obtained were enormous, but the fire of the second lead is no ordinary fire. It proved so penetrating and dangerous that it overcame the metal itself and came bubbling out of the pit we had prepared for it. I was the only survivor, and even I have suffered ever since from a weakness of the blood."

He paused before continuing. "Eventually I concluded that fire alone will never be sufficient. I decided to switch my attention to *etheric heat,* using infusoration to create tenuous, rarefied forms of air and fire known as plasmas. To make a plasma, the vessel is first emptied of atmospheric air, and the subject to be transformed is then injected and infusoration is applied in immense quantities. Temperatures so obtained can rival those in the center of a star.

"That, at least, is the bare principle. In practice, lifetimes could be spent researching plasmas. Note one of our first efforts."

Amschel directed Rachad's attention to possibly the weirdest device in the laboratory: a large glass tube in the form of a six-foot ring, collared at intervals with thick coils of wire. "Meet our Ouroborous—our attempt to construct the Great Worm in physical form."

Amschel pulled down a lever. The air crackled and snapped. A hazy ribbon of light sprang into being throughout the length of the circular tube, pulsing along the center of the channel. Brighter and brighter it grew, and for a second seemed stable. But suddenly it writhed, jerked, and abruptly vanished, leaving black scorch marks on the inside of the glass.

"Try as we might, we could never get it to maintain itself," Amschel said. "Not for nothing is the Worm described as the Impossible Stability."

The alchemist moved to the great cucurbit that occupied the center of the chamber: globular, ten feet in diameter, plates and coils arrayed within its walls. "Later, however, we were more successful," he said. "I have been able to confirm that infusoration, if intense enough, can produce such torsions and tensions as to bring matter close to the threshold to *prima materia,* though we have not, as yet, produced complete breakdown. We will demonstrate."

He gestured to his assistants, issuing clipped orders. The helpers dragged heavy cables across the floor, clipping them into big junction boxes.

Finally everyone stood back as power was applied through five different delivery spouts. The very air Rachad breathed seemed to sizzle; sparks flew from the junction boxes. He became aware of a hum that seemed to set his eardrums shaking just below the level of audibility.

Inside the cucurbit, the metal plates glowed fiercely. A spot of light appeared in the center of the globe, expanding, writhing, then coalescing into definite form.

Rachad gaped at what he saw. Hovering in the globe was the shape of a man, draped in a purple robe, staring toward them through the thick glass.

As quickly as it had come, the vision vanished, to be succeeded by an inhuman, brass-colored figure mounted on a horse-like beast that apparently was galloping onward. Then it, too, was replaced—by a gorgeous flowering orchid as tall as a man.

Faster and faster the phantoms came: people, animals, plants. Amschel, aware of Rachad's bewilderment, leaned close to him.

"These creatures are not mere apparitions: they are real, though transient. The field of stress causes them to stream spontaneously out of the threshold to *prima materia*."

Suddenly there was a deafening *bang*. One of the cables had parted at a solder joint, spitting out a shower of sparks. In the cucurbit, the visions died.

"But this is magic!" Rachad exclaimed.

"Not magic, but art. Thus was the world created; thus did all things proceed from the One. *Hyle* contains all forms in potential."

Amschel moved across the chamber and opened one of his ubiquitous sample cases. Returning, he showed Rachad a number of small objects he held in the palm of his hand: honey-colored pills about half an inch in diameter.

"Although the creatures that stream from the threshold are momentary only, there is a way to trap and fix the life-denoting virtue within the field. These seeds, if placed in water in which certain mineral salts are dissolved, will bring living forms to fruition."

"Homunculi," Rachad breathed.

"Yes, homunculi. The minor goal of the alchemist's art."

"It still seems like magic to me," Rachad said.

"But think: is not nature's work also alchemy? Every planet is a cucurbit, in which chemicals are mixed. Every sun is an athanor, which heats planets; and so life arises. By compressing the work of eons into a small span of time, the hermetic art is achieved."

"But the Philosopher's Stone doesn't occur naturally at all."

"No," Amschel said. "The Stone is solely the work of man."

Chapter THIRTEEN

Dressed all in purple and black stripe and wearing his insignia of rank, Baron Matello was waiting in the courtyard of his castle when King Lutheron's golden coach came clattering through the gate, its windows shrouded. The carriage came to rest; a footman hastened down from the rear to open the door, with its elaborate coat of arms.

The monarch stepped to the ground, looking all around him with melancholy gray eyes. Matello fell to his knees, and put his lips to the back of a limply proffered hand.

"What is your will, my liege-lord?" he asked solicitously as he rose. "Rest, or refreshment?"

"I require neither for the present, Sir Goth," the king said, his tone business-like. "I must talk with you—in private."

Lutheron the Third was tall and thin, barely older than Matello but seeming much older, his austere face lined and grayish. His visit to Castarpos had come as a sudden surprise to Matello, who had received less than one day's notice of it, and he was nervous as to what its object could be, especially as he had been instructed to arrange no pomp and to make no public announcement of the king's presence. He had, however, moved the *Bucentaur* into orbit so as to make way for the royal barge.

Leaving his majordomo to attend to the rest of the party, he conducted his monarch to his private office and sent for the best of his wines. Dismissing the manservant who arrived with it, he decanted it with his own hand and filled the king a goblet. Lutheron merely sipped the ancient vintage, and waved the standing Matello to be seated.

"Is this an inspection tour, liege-lord?" Matello enquired.

"I am afraid it is somewhat more than that," King Lutheron said, smiling sadly. "The Kerek threat is developing more swiftly than ever anticipated, making it imperative for me to muster my forces. I have lately received intelligence that a major invasion is imminent."

Matello suddenly became as stiff as wood and he

clenched his hands. "By the gods, I've heard nothing of this! Where could the Kerek have built up their forces?"

"In the shoals and reefs bordering your end of the realm, where they have managed to amass unobserved, it seems, by using asteroids for natural cover."

"*Agh!*—I should have guessed it!" muttered Matello after a pause, remembering the attack upon the *Bucentaur*. "That's too close to home for comfort."

"It is indeed, and it is essential that a fleet is raised immediately to meet the attack, or to strike first if that is possible. What can you supply by way of men and ships?"

Matello paused, then answered crisply. "I have five thousand men-at-arms. But I haven't the ships to carry them all at once. Besides the *Bucentaur*, my personal ship, I have three battle-galleons, third class, and assorted smaller craft which will need to be carried by mother ship. I can manage most of those, I think."

The king twisted a jeweled ring on his finger. "We will take everything," he announced. "Get your men on board somehow. Any you can't take can come aboard my own barge—later we'll attend to their redistribution."

"These measures will strip my domain of all troops, liege-lord," Matello pointed out doubtfully. "I don't like to leave my people without protection."

"It is from the Kerek that they need protecting most," the king answered with a sigh. "If we do not beat back the impending wave, then Maralia will be lost, just as other realms have been lost."

Matello brooded.

"Luckily we do not stand alone," the king went on. "The king of Wenchlas is sending help, as are the republics of Capalm and Venichea."

"*Wenchlas?*" spluttered Matello. "Our sworn enemy, liege-lord!"

King Lutheron's smile was weary. "At the present juncture of events we are natural allies. King Causus knows that if we fall, Wenchlas will be next. Indeed, were we able to rally all the human nations in a common defense, perhaps the Kerek could be contained. So far, this has proved beyond any man's diplomacy. Now: how long before you will be ready to move?"

"To recall my troops from the Marsh worlds will take six days at least."

"Hmm. Too long. We will leave the day after tomorrow. Your Marsh Worlds forces can make their way later."

The main business dealt with, the king relaxed and took a deep draught of the baron's excellent wine. "It is a great trial to me that I am able to count on so little from the dukedom of Koss," he remarked. "You were the only man to presume to assume responsibility there, I recall. I see that you are not installed in the Aegis, however."

"I have a plan at work," Matello rumbled. "But I am still waiting for it to come to fruition."

"Indeed?" The king leaned forward. "What is this plan?"

Matello hesitated, not liking to disclose his scheme. "I have succeeded in getting a man inside the Aegis," he said.

"And you are hoping he will open it up for you?"

"Yes, liege-lord."

"Not a perfect plan of operations," the king commented after a moment's thought. "Though getting a man inside at all is an achievement of sorts, I suppose."

"The young man I am using is resourceful. I believe he will find a way eventually."

"And how long has he been in there now?"

"Several months," Matello admitted.

The king laughed, to Matello's discomfiture. "Evidently, then, your plot has come unstuck. Either your conspirator has been discovered or he prefers the Duke of Koss's service to yours. Tell me: is it true that you have the builder of the Aegis as your guest?"

"It is, liege-lord. You know the story of how he was cheated by the old duke, I suppose?"

"Yes. Quite an amusing tale. I would like to meet this beast."

"Certainly, liege-lord. We will go to him directly."

The king nodded, drained his goblet, and stood up. Matello rose after him, and guided him through the castle's passages to the underground hall where Flammarion rested. "The creature's life here is rather a dull one," he said as they walked. "Most of his time he spends in a tank which keeps him fairly comfortable. It must be a peculiar world he comes from. . . . I give him the freedom of the castle, too, and he sometimes roams around it. No amount of tedium or discomfort seems to bother him, I might say. He'll wait it out for centuries to get what he regards as his due."

"A most persistent creditor."

"It's the nature of his race."

They entered the underground hall, where Matello ushered his royal guest toward the open iron tank at the far end. "Flammarion!" he called out. "Present yourself to our great king, Lutheron the Third, monarch of all Maralia!"

After a moment or two a shape rose up from the tank, showering fine yellow powder in all directions. The king watched while the alien flowed over the side of the trough and came closer, its flat cape-like body warping over the floor in waving motions. Finally it halted, raised its front end and managed a grotesque bow.

"Your Majesty. . . ."

The king turned to Matello. "What an odd odor he has."

"That's mainly from the powder. . . . It's made up to his own recipe."

Matello fetched a chair for the king. Lutheron sank into it, spreading his light cloak. He gazed at Flammarion with interest.

"Does that tail of yours have a sting?"

Flammarion flexed the pointed tail a little. "No, Your Majesty, it is vestigial, though the primitive forebear of my species did have a sting."

"Strange how a life form seems to lose its natural weapons when it acquires a thinking brain. Well, so it was you who built the Duke of Koss his Aegis, eh?"

"Yes, Your Majesty."

"And I understand you did it alone?"

"That is so."

"It seems a mighty labor for one small individual. How did you manage it, without a work force?"

"I have my methods, Your Majesty. These, of course, are my secrets. I employ one method to create adamant. I use another method to shape it as it forms. For this I use a device which I first build with my own tentacles, and it is this device which makes possible the erection of so large a structure."

"And how long did this enterprise take you?"

"Building the Aegis for the Duke of Koss entailed three years of continuous effort on my part. Alas, I wait and wait to receive my due reward."

"No one's plans can be guaranteed to go right," said

the king absently. He reflected, then said: "I am glad finally to have met you. Maralia could use more of these constructions, provided they remain in the right hands. I will commission you to build one for me."

Flammarion's tone became doleful. "Oh, I will build no more for humans. Never, never again!"

The king bristled angrily at this. "You dare to refuse me, alien? I can torture cooperation out of you! What do you say now?"

"You cannot torture me," Flammarion responded, still in his aggrieved voice. "I am incapable of feeling physical pain. I suffer emotionally only. I suffer when I am cheated, gulled, or made to labor in vain. Therefore, never again will I work for humans."

"Hmph." The king fell back in his chair, disgruntled but convinced. "This creature interests me, Sir Goth," he said. "Allow me to take him off your hands. No doubt he will find my own court a more amusing place than this draughty castle."

"Liege-lord. . . ." Matello frowned and bit his lip, not liking this turn of events at all.

"My single interest is to enter the Aegis!" Flammarion protested. "I must remain near it!"

Matello nodded in agreement. "Quite so, liege-lord. I in turn need his knowledge and talents if I am to succeed in toppling Koss."

"But your progress is slow, Sir Goth," King Lutheron murmured. "At home I have men of great wit and perspicacity, who in conjunction with Flammarion may perhaps hit on the answer. But don't worry—I won't forget the part you've played in the affair so far. When it comes to choosing a new Duke of Koss, I shall bear you in mind.

"Transfer the creature and his effects to my barge. I shall take him with me when we leave."

Matello swallowed and fumed inwardly. "Certainly, liege-lord, if it is your will."

"It is contrary to *my* will!" Flammarion interjected.

The king shrugged. "We are not all as despicable as Koss, my friend. You will serve your own interests by cooperating with me."

He paused. "Have you ever seen a space battle, by the way?"

"Hitherto the nature of the *primus agens* has been the most obscure of all alchemical secrets," Amschel said as they entered the laboratory one morning. "The text you provided confirmed what I have long suspected, that the first principle is mercury—not common mercury, but *azoth,* the mercury of the philosophers. Now, at long last, its preparation may be possible."

While he spoke Amschel was opening the door of an athanor. A blast of heat billowed out; he and Rachad bent to inspect a cucurbit nestling in the ash bath.

"If the subject is to be reduced to *prima materia,* it must incorporate all five elements in exact and equal balance. This is the chief and unique virtue of *azoth:* it is the great absorber, receiving all elements in a perfect blend, which may therefore be adjusted accordingly."

In the cucurbit, there was a continuous seething. Then Amschel frowned. He had discerned a greenish tinge in the pearly fluid.

Suddenly a livid green, shot through with bilious yellow, seized the whole mass. Amschel huffed with exasperation, his face becoming sad.

"We shall have to begin again," he announced. "The divine water should seethe until it is pure and shining. Green signifies that the operation has misfired."

He beckoned an assistant, who removed the cucurbit from the ash pan with a pair of tongs, suspending it in a fripod where it was left to cool. The subject, emerald in color now, began to solidify almost immediately, surging slightly as if alive.

"Three months we have spent already on this part of the work, without success," Amschel muttered. "Still, Nicholas Flamel himself described the preparation of the *primus agens* as extremely difficult, even when one understands it. It is true that only an experienced and learned adept could divine the process from the book at all, even though its instructions are fairly explicit."

He turned, a small and stooped figure. Rachad, however, failed to find any real dejection in his face.

"More study is needed," the artifex decided. "I have misunderstood some small point, perhaps."

He wandered off. Rachad, guessing that there would be no more work today, also took his leave, back to the living quarters beneath the laboratory. The accommodation, like the laboratory itself, was rambling and many-chambered, but afforded some privacy. Rachad was able to close a door and be alone in his tidy, if spartan, room.

He was glad of this, for the tediousness of lengthy alchemical research bored him to tears, and the laboratory dwellers, Amschel especially, spoke of little else. The Aegis, too, had become depressing to him, with its cloying atmosphere and degenerate way of life. He longed to see the sun—any sun.

Only one aspect of Amschel's work really fascinated him. On a low table against the wall, opposite Rachad's bed, were four large glass jars, filled with water.

The homunculi he was growing were now perfectly formed.

Amschel, who it seemed regarded the growing of homunculi as no more than a childish experiment, like growing crystal flowers, had agreed readily to Rachad's request to do so. He had shown Rachad how to prepare the simple mineral solution required, and had given him leave to take seeds from the drawer where they were kept.

The seeds, he had explained at the same time, contained non-differentiated life—they would grow anything, the end product being determined by the power of thought, by whatever mental image was projected onto the organism by the experimenter.

There was an amusing tradition connected with this, which Amschel had invited Rachad to try. He had given Rachad a group of four playing cards: the King, the Queen, the Priest, and the Knight. One of these placed on top of each jar, he had explained, would automatically focus the mental energy of the experimenter on the growing seed, even if only given a passing glance now and then.

Rachad had followed this procedure, leaning the cards against the wall so that they stood upright over the jars, and he was delighted to see how effective it was. The jars now contained miniature human beings, twelve-inch figures which, though frail-looking, were easily recognizable as corresponding to the crude caricatures painted on the cards above them, mainly because of the regalia which had also grown onto them. The King and Queen were crowned, and wore flowing purple apparel. The Priest, in an orphreyed cope, carried a holy circle, and the Knight, wearing the lightest of armor, was armed with a battle-axe which he held upright before him, after the manner of the playing card overhead.

Since the day before, the creatures had also awakened to consciousness—or whatever passed for consciousness in homunculi; Rachad was vague in his mind on that score. They gazed sadly from their glass jars, as if pathetically aware of their fleeting hold on life.

Amschel had offered two more fascinating facts. The first was that homunculi were telepathically obedient to the will of their creator (giving Rachad a fresh insight into the deployment of space dragons). The other concerned an intriguing piece of behavior resulting from the playing-card technique. It seemed that the King invariably sought to escape from his jar in a vain attempt to join the Queen—a consequence, it was thought, of the alchemical marriage which the pair weakly symbolized.

The King was already enacting this inborn urge as Rachad came into the room, pressing his hands to the lid of the jar and feebly attempting to push it off. When he became aware of Rachad watching him, however, he left off his efforts as though discovered at something clandestine. He stood stiffly in the jar, his paper-like face staring haughtily ahead, his purple cloak waving in the currents his movements had stirred up in the liquid.

A thought came to Rachad. He reached out and unscrewed the lid, leaving it in place but loose on the top of the jar. Then, crossing the room, he lay on his bed and closed his eyes.

He had intended merely to sleep and to spy on the King surreptitiously, but instead found that he must have dozed off for a few minutes. He awoke with a start, to see that the King had succeeded in climbing out of the jar and, dripping water onto the tabletop, had made his way to where the Queen was imprisoned at the other end of the line, separated from him by the Priest and the Knight. Now the homunculus was frantically trying to shin up the smooth glass surface, while the Queen, her hands pressed against the inside of the jar, watched him intently, her pretty face wide-eyed with alarm and expectancy.

Already the King was beginning to flag. Rachad recalled that an homunculus could not live long once removed from its nurturing solution. He continued to watch for a while, until the King fell to the tabletop in exhaustion, his arms clasped pathetically around the jar.

Then it occurred to Rachad to try a second experiment. In his thoughts, he ordered the King to rise, to return to his own place. At first nothing happened. Propping himself on one elbow, Rachad tried again, imagining his thoughts as a mental force that was reaching out to the dying homunculus, silently commanding his obedience. Now the King responded. He raised his head, clambered slowly to his feet, and with stooped, dragging steps plodded doggedly back the way he had come.

Thrilled, Rachad followed every inch of his progress, never letting up the mental effort. Halfway home, however, the King's strength gave out, and he collapsed in a bedraggled heap.

Rachad sprang from the bed, not wanting to lose one of his living toys, and picked up the homunculus. It felt cold and soft in his hand, and wriggled feebly. He plopped it back into the empty jar and screwed on the cap.

The King sank to the bottom, where he squatted with his head between his upthrust knees, hiding his face with his arms.

The incident seemed to have disturbed the other homunculi. The Knight was impotently swinging his axe against the wall of his glass prison. The Priest, too, banged indignantly against the inside of his own jar, silently mouthing.

Rachad returned to his bed, much entertained by the entire episode.

He grinned to himself. Next time he would arrange for the King actually to succeed in reaching the Queen. It would be fun to see what the two of them got up to, when ensconced in the same jar together.

But in a way, he thought wryly, his own situation was not unlike theirs. They were encased in their glass jars, he in the Aegis. By now he had all but despaired of ever finding a way to open the gate. He was so wearied of his life here that, were he not afraid of what Matello might do to him, he would have considered abandoning his mission altogether and asking the duke to let him go —if that could have been done without arousing his suspicions.

Refreshed by his immersion in the mineral water, the King was coming to his feet again to adopt the formally upright pose which was characteristic of all the homunculi. At least, Rachad reflected, he could now find some diversion in using his mental power on them, using them as living dolls.

He lay down and was about to drift into sleep again, when he suddenly sat bolt upright. The idea that had come to him had illuminated his thoughts like a flash of lightning.

What fool he had been! How obvious it was!

He stared at the homunculi. The way to open the Aegis was right there in front of his eyes!

Chapter FOURTEEN

Desperately Baron Matello hacked with his long-bladed broadsword at the Kerek officer that was trying to dismember him with one of its curiously curved sickle-weapons. Skittering back and forth on its four legs, the creature swung the sickle to and fro in clever, deceptive thrusts. Matello swiped the weapon aside hastily and, wielding his sword with both hands, renewed the attack.

Vapor puffed as the edge of his blade bit into the alien's nacreous neck armor. He chopped again, and cut the giraffe-like neck right through. Decapitated, gouting greenish blood, the Kerek collapsed.

Then a human Kerek-warrior rushed at Matello from across the deck of the *Bucentaur*. So swift and furious was the onslaught that the baron reeled back, receiving a confused impression of honey-colored armor and a deadly, flickering scythe-sword.

Wildly he sought to defend himself. Suddenly the golden-armored figure bent at the waist and tipped forward, a crossbow bolt protruding from his chest, falling on Matello.

The baron pushed the corpse aside and raised his sword in thanks to the archer who had probably saved his life.

He had never known such a shambles. Though his men had practically cleared the *Bucentaur*'s deck of Kerek now, the galley that had rammed her was solidly enmeshed in her superstructure. But the fact was that so far Matello's ship had come off lightly. Not far away floated the gutted hulk of the royal barge, still glowing with sticky fire, and attached to the *Bucentaur* by a long flexible trunk through which the king and his retinue had escaped as the flames spread.

Matello leaned wearily on his sword, thinking that there might have been a chance of victory if only everything could have been gotten ready in time. As it was, the Kerek had emerged from the shoals and attacked Lutheron's gathering fleet with a huge horde, catching it by surprise.

The two fleets were now battling as they traveled together at super-light velocity. And that battle, invisible from where Matello stood for the most part, was ending in the total destruction of Maralian power.

Peering into space, he saw something that chilled him. He saw glints of blue in the distance, quickly resolving into a score of galleys bearing remorselessly down on the *Bucentaur*. And these new, larger galleys the Kerek were deploying now, Matello knew, were equipped with catapults and spring cannon. He glared around him, aware that the *Bucentaur* had already lost a good part of her armament—as well as her smaller craft—in earlier encounters.

Then a gladsome sight glided into view to cut off the attacking squadron. It was the *Amanda*, a giant Maralian galleon, almost as large as the *Bucentaur* but every inch a fighting ship. She bristled with huge weapons and besides that was undamaged, being part of the small reserve that had but recently added itself to the battle.

Even as he watched she let loose a drenching salvo of sticky fire, the combustible that burned under any conditions, that stuck to its target and spread until it had consumed it. Matello watched for a few moments, then turned and dodged through one of the hooded doorways. Sheathing his green-dripping sword, he loped through the long passageways, a tall figure in his tight-fitting purple spacesuit which was ribbed with steel bands for armor. Soon he came to the control room. Sliding back his faceplate, he entered.

King Lutheron was present, his face pale, his features gaunt. He was staring at the big viewscreen where the huge galleon was beating off the Kerek ships.

The captain rose as Matello appeared. "The *Amanda* is screening us from further attacks while she can, my lord. She signals us to withdraw, to save the king while we may." He glanced at Lutheron with a troubled expression.

"I agree," Matello rumbled. "Without doubt that is what we should do."

King Lutheron tore his gaze with difficulty from the glass screen. His voice was reedy with grief. "A king without a country?" he said. "Maralia is about to be overrun."

"To lose the battle is bad enough," Matello argued, "but if Your Majesty falls too. . . . While Your Majesty lives there is still hope. But when a king falls in battle, often his nation disappears under the heel of the conquerer forever."

King Lutheron dropped his eyelids, seeing the force of this. "But where can we escape to? Already the Kerek horde will be spreading out. They will pursue us, perhaps head us off. We will not get far." He sighed. "Aghh. . . . Better, perhaps, to go down fighting."

Matello was silent. "I know a hiding place," he said after a moment. "We are not far from where the Duke of Koss has his Aegis. There I have a secret underground camp. We can hide there, covering the *Bucentaur* or else destroying her, or setting her to sail crewless in space." He hesitated. "Likely even the Duke of Koss will give his monarch shelter in these circumstances. Once in the Aegis we would be safe for all time."

Briefly and without humor, King Lutheron laughed. "Koss? I think not! But for him, we might not even be in this mess."

They all flinched as a sudden white glare lit up the circular glass screen. A fire-dart had found its mark on one of the Amanda's weapons turrets. The Kerek galleys had got close in to her, too, like jackals worrying a larger prey, and already fighting was taking place on her decks.

"We must decide *now*, liege-lord," Matello urged. "Another few minutes and it may be too late."

King Lutheron was despondent. "Very well," he conceded wearily, "we shall slip away like cowards. Attend to it, Sir Goth."

Pulling his cloak around him, he strode from the room. When he had gone, Matello rounded jerkily on the ship's captain.

"All right!" he barked. "You heard him! Let's get out of here!"

As had been the practice of the supply ships that visited the secret camp from time to time, the *Bucentaur* landed well beyond the Aegis's visible horizon, putting down near to the screened tunnel entrance.

From the grounded ship streamed a procession of men and stores. Like ants, they vanished underground, following the miles-long tunnel to the subterranean barracks. It was going to be crowded, Matello admitted. Over a thousand people would be compressed into a space meant to accommodate a couple of hundred. But the access tunnel could be used, and if that was not enough, well then some people would just have to shift for themselves in the open for a while, until more excavations could be arranged.

King Lutheron paused a few yards inside the down-sloping passage to examine the circular walls. The rock and soil was held back by a framework of what at first he took to be metal. He reached out and touched it.

"Adamant," Matello explained briefly. "Flammarion himself took a hand in constructing this place. I don't think we could have done it unnoticed but for his help."

"Why didn't he line the walls with adamant altogether? Then we would have been invulnerable here."

"That would make it a miniature aegis. Flammarion refuses to build aegises gratuitously—something to do with the guild he belongs to."

They stood aside to allow the procession of refugees to stream past. Flammarion's tank rolled past them on wheels, drawn by serfs, the alien invisible beneath the yellow powder.

Matello turned to the bearded officer who accompanied them. It was Captain Zhorga, the former Earthman who had made himself so useful lately.

"Take His Majesty to the camp and see that he is shown suitable quarters," he instructed. "I have to see to the disposal of the *Bucentaur*. With your leave, liege-lord? . . ."

The king nodded. Matello bowed and left, making his way back up the tunnel into the open.

The planet's blazing sun was low in the sky. The ship's entire company had left her now, and he saw her captain, the last to disembark, stepping through a side portal.

There was nothing for Matello to do, but he felt an urge to watch his prize possession's last few minutes of life under human direction. The ropes that were to trigger her departure had already been laid. While he watched, teams of men hauled on them, releasing the spring bollards that snapped out lengths of silk on the enormous yards.

It was a pity to waste her, Matello thought, but it was best to eradicate as many traces of their presence as possible.

Landing on uneven terrain had damaged her still further, but even so the huge vessel was more than equal to the last demand made on her. Her sails darkened the place where Matello stood as she first lumbered, then soared into the air, rapidly gaining height. Her direction had been set; she would make it into space with ease. With any luck she would also reach the destination intended for her, and fall into the raging, multicolored sun.

The great glass jar in the corner of Rachad's room was over six feet tall. It was in fact a giant cucurbit he had taken from the laboratory with the help of one of Amschel's assistants. It curved gracefully, the lamplight gleaming off its surface.

On the table, the four small jars still stood, but the four homunculi they had contained had reached the end of their natural life span now. The tiny corpses slumped against the glass bottoms, degenerating into slime which was clouding the water. In time, Amschel had assured Rachad, the water would become clear again, a simple mineral solution as before.

Filling the big cucurbit with a similar solution had taken him several hours. But that had been weeks ago. Rachad now sat on a chair in front of the vessel, thinking hard. Every evening at about this time he spent an hour at the exercise, holding an image in his mind and attempting to project it into the burgeoning mass. The work exhausted him, for he had never found it easy to think in a sustained way.

The huge homunculus was almost fully formed now, but the features were still indistinct. The next few days would tell if his efforts were to be rewarded with success or failure—would tell if, in the end, his creation would step forth and speak in a faint, drifting voice....

Rachad was beginning to daydream again. It always happened after a few minutes. He pulled his mind back on the job, focusing his mind's eye on the necessary picture, thinking, thinking....

"And how close are they, would you say?" Baron Matello asked, his brow furrowed in a frown.

"No more than fifty miles, my lord!" the kneeling messenger answered unhesitatingly.

Matello grunted dourly. The news was bad.

With the Kerek's famous knack of tracking human ships, he had been afraid that something like this would happen. The enemy, it seemed, had come upon this uninviting world only days after the landing of the *Bucentaur*. The serf kneeling before Matello and King Lutheron had ridden from the nearest mining town, which was in panic after hearing of the Kerek's doings in other such towns around the planet.

It would not take the Kerek long to spot the Aegis. They would then attempt to besiege it, and the situation of those in the underground camp was therefore unenviable.

King Lutheron, sitting in a plush chair with what in the circumstances was a luxurious amount of space around him, spoke up. "Perhaps it is time we should seek Koss's hospitality after all."

"Perhaps," Matello admitted grudgingly. Although he had been the first to offer this possibility to the King, the truth was that he hated the idea of going begging to the hated duke. He would rather have perished.

"Leave it for a while," he said. "The Kerek have not discovered us yet. I still hope to be able to take the Aegis without our demeaning ourselves."

He ignored the incredulous looks of the officers around him, the camp commander included, who until the interruption had been idly occupying themselves with all there was to do in such a place—cleaning and sharpening their weapons.

"Yes, my liege-lord," he repeated in a murmur, "I suggest we leave it for a while . . ."

Caban, what the hell has happened to you? he thought furiously to himself.

The homunculus had been growing for about ten weeks. Rachad came into his room one night and stared at it, biting his lower lip.

As far as he could judge the creature was fully matured. The facial features had taken final form several days previously, and a haughty, austere visage stared back at him through the side of the jar, the head, with its long bony nose, tilted ever so slightly on one side.

It was a marvel to Rachad how faithfully the development of the homunculus had followed the direction of his thoughts—the likeness to the original was uncanny. Yet still he had hung back, wanting to be sure. He would only get one chance.

Suddenly he made up his mind. The time for hesitation had to end sooner or later. It was do or die. And the present moment—the Aegis's nighttime, its activity subdued, and when the laboratory staff had all retired—was most propitious for his purpose.

He stepped to his bed, bent, and drew from beneath it a large hammer. Standing again before the oversized cucurbit, he braced himself and swung the hammer with both hands.

The first blow starred the glass with cracks. The second shattered it and the cucurbit fell to pieces. A gush of water flowed forth, swilling around Rachad's legs and flooding the floor of the small room.

And following the flood there stepped forth the man-sized homunculus. The fluid seemed to fall away from him to leave him perfectly dry, even dropping out of the fabric of his voluminous purple robe. He stepped hesitantly, looking frail, gazing around him with glazed eyes.

Rachad focused his thoughts. *Say to me: I can speak, young Rachad.*

The voice that came was distant, breathless, vague. "I can speak, young Rachad."

A perfect imitation!

Rachad walked the creature up and down the room, still under thought control. To look at, it was hard to believe it was not a genuine human being.

He would have to move quickly. It was odds-on whether they would get to their destination before the homunculus collapsed.

"Come with me," he ordered.

Stealthily they left the sleeping quarters, making for the entrance to the inner maze.

Low ceilings of soil and rock confined the noise of bustle as, in the underground tunnels, men readied themselves for a last stand.

Outside, Kerek ships were dropping from the sky like autumn leaves. Baron Matello closed his ears to the bitter arguments going on around him, getting Captain Zhorga to help him strap on his armor. He lifted up his two-handed sword, his favorite weapon, and ran the lamplight up and down it before sheathing it in its enormous scabbard.

Nearby, visible through the open door of the commandant's section, a squad of men-at-arms were checking their bell-muzzled muskets. It was so cramped and crowded here. It would almost be good to get into the open once again, even though it was to face certain death. Sourly Matello glanced at the periscope at the far end of the chamber. The man who sat peering into it was one of a round-the-clock watch of six, and the presence of the niggling, useless duty had begun to grate on Matello's nerves.

Suddenly the argument broke off and King Lutheron turned to Matello. "What do you say, Sir Goth? The Commandant here is trying to persuade me that now is the time to seek refuge with the Duke of Koss. It was you, I remember, who first raised the possibility."

"There are too many of us, liege-lord," Matello rumbled. "Koss would never let us in—even unarmed, we are enough to take over the Aegis, and he will let nothing interfere with his private wretchedness." He paused to pull tight a large buckle, moving his arms to test his freedom of movement and grunting with satisfaction. "In a way I brought about this state of affairs, liege-lord—but I never thought the Kerek would descend on us like this. Rather, I thought they'd pass this star by—but there's the Kerek for you, they seem able to sniff anything out, and it will only be a short time before they find us and dig us out of our hidey-hole. I say, make a sally against them while they are unprepared, then retreat back here and kill them by the droves as they try to reach us through the access tunnel. We'll make a good, hard fight of it before they get us all."

"That I agree with," the camp commandant said, his face turning red with something like anger. "But the Duke of Koss might admit the King at least, if not the rest of us!"

"We would have to reveal the presence of our camp, which will put the duke in a strange frame of mind. Still, it is up to His Majesty to make that decision."

"Give me a sword," King Lutheron said. "I will fight with the rest of you."

Matello nodded. "Come along, Zhorga, let's inspect the men."

At that moment a yell went up from the man at the periscope. *"Commandant!* Come quickly!"

The officer lumbered to the instrument, bent and put

his eyes to it. After only a second he straightened and turned to address the room in astonishment.

"The gates are opening!"

Matello blinked. He rushed to the periscope, nearly shouldering the commandant aside in his haste. What he saw through the eyepiece made him gasp.

The eyepiece communicated with a lens that, hidden in the shadow of a rock, kept watch on the Aegis. Two great doors were now edging slowly outward, giving a glimpse of geared machinery within.

"He's done it!" he gasped hoarsely, turning back to the others. "The Aegis is open!"

Like him, everyone was paralyzed for a moment. Then Matello began to bellow wildly.

"Get moving, you curs! This is what we've been waiting for!" With his clenched fist he gestured at the commandant, his eyes bulging. "Drop the ramp! Sound the advance!"

The commandant snapped out an order, then strode to the two big levers that were set in grooves at the side of the chamber. As a trumpet began to sound he took them one by one in both hands and pulled them hard over.

The result was dramatic. The roof fell in, a section of ground overhead folding inward to form a ramp which showered dirt and dust directly into the post. Matello was first to leap up that ramp, his great sword in his hand, closely followed by Zhorga and others who had already arrived in answer to the trumpet's summons.

He emerged scant yards from the Aegis gate. Matello raced for the widening gap. His broadsword flashed briefly in the fierce sun. Then he was inside, looking for young Caban.

But it was not Caban who had opened the Aegis. Matello found himself facing a large, nearly empty plaza, illuminated by soft ceiling lights. A line of pikemen, in the peculiar pied livery of Koss, stood behind a mass of timber that looked as if it had been newly chopped to pieces. A large adamant box-shield lay on top of the pile. Matello could easily guess that this had protected the wheeled mechanism which was now being worked by two more pikemen as the foot-thick doors continued to swing open.

The line of guards were standing stiffly at attention, the ends of their weapons planted firmly on the floor, and were making no response to Matello's entrance. Then Matello saw Rachad, standing beside a gaunt, pale figure in a long purple robe.

He knew at once that this was the Duke of Koss. Though the figure looked ill and consumptive, he recognized him from a painting he had once seen of the former duke. Yes, this was the detested Koss's son for sure.

Zhorga drew abreast of Matello. The two of them stared in puzzlement at the unexpected scene. Suddenly the duke swayed, his head drooped, and he fell in a graceful swoon to the floor.

"Your Grace!" The captain of the guard rushed to the limp form, taking the lolling head in his hand. "Two of you over here, on the double!"

Rachad sidled hastily over to Matello, his face feverish. "Round them all up—quick!" he hissed. "Before they realize they've been tricked!"

"Tricked?"

"They think the duke ordered them to open the Aegis —but that's not the duke at all! It's an homunculus I made!"

"Eh?" Matello growled, not fully understanding what Rachad was talking about. But his earnest advice was good enough. He glanced round at his men who were still streaming after him through the doorway.

He thrust out his sword, and roared: *"Kill them all!"*

The ensuing fight was brief and bloody. The pikemen were totally bewildered. Only when actually attacked did they move, in sudden panic, to defend themselves, wielding their long pikes with skill, so that several of Matello's liegelings were stretched out on the floor before full possession was taken of the plaza.

While men continued to pour through the gateway, Matello wiped his sword on a pied tunic and returned to stare thoughtfully at the body of Rachad's homunculus. Already it was beginning to shrivel up. The purple cloak, also organic in nature, had become like a huge withered leaf.

"How did you manage it?" he asked. "I had almost given you up."

"It wasn't possible to open the Aegis straight away," Rachad explained eagerly. "It was too well guarded. I've been working with Master Amschel, in his laboratory. That was where I got the idea of making an homunculus replica of the duke, under my mental control. And it worked!"

Rachad was bursting to tell the whole story. Surreptitiously he had guided the rapidly weakening homunculus through the Aegis. For the last stages of the journey he had been obliged to support the ephemeral creature by letting it lean on his shoulder. Then, at the gateway, there was the stunned astonishment on the part of the guards, as they heard the reedy voice of their duke order them to open up. At first they had reacted with inbred reluctance. Three times the homunculus had pressed his command, and only the actual presence—so they thought—of their master had prodded them out of their stupor, making them perform the incredible act, something they had been sure they would never see in their lifetimes.

But when he tried to launch into his tale Matello shut him up with an impatient wave of his hand. "Later," he said, but nevertheless he clapped Rachad fondly on the shoulder. "It was a brilliant piece of work, my boy. You've saved all our lives, though you don't know it, and I'll remember that."

Straightening, he began to bark orders. "Commandant, see to it that everybody gets in here without delay, before the Kerek find out what's happening. Then close up these doors again, and we'll organize a general takeover of this place. There might still be a bit of fighting to do."

"With odds in our favor, this time," Zhorga added. He grinned at Rachad. "You've done well, shipmate. I'm proud of you."

They went through the Aegis like a storm.

The impact of hardened fighting men, drawn both from Matello's forces and King Lutheron's, on the sybarite's paradise was like that of a barbarian horde on a soft, decadent culture—which, in exaggerated form, was exactly what the interior of the Aegis represented. There was practically no resistance and Matello, sensing his followers' relief at having escaped imminent death at the hands of the Kerek, allowed them a brief catharsis of rape and ransack. Artworks were smashed, sumptuous drapes torn down in acres of billowing finery to reveal the bare adamant beneath, and for a while the omnipresent haunting music was mingled with coarse bellows of triumph.

Flammarion, moving with surprising agility by means of his warping wings, attached himself to the party led by Baron Matello and proved as eager as any. But his search had only one object—the Duke of Koss himself, the man who had spent a lifetime as his creditor.

They eventually found the defeated duke deep down in the fortress. He lay limply on a samite couch, a servant girl dabbing at his brow with scented water. He seemed to be in a state of collapse.

He stirred feebly when Matello and his men burst into the chamber. His face was fully as pale and deathlike as the face of the homunculus that had recently impersonated him. "Who are these strangers who disturb my peace?" he murmured, his voice so faint as to be barely audible. "Vandals, despoilers, desecrators of my pleasure. . . ."

"We are here because *you* failed to do your duty, Koss!" Baron Matello stormed.

From behind him Flammarion came forward. He reared up over the supine noble like a threatening cobra. "Now is the time to remind you of our contract, Your Grace!" he exclaimed, his voice vibrant with passion.

"What strange beast is this?" the duke queried breathlessly. "Ah yes, the builder of my retreat, of my cosmos."

"My fee! I am here to collect my fee, unpaid for all these years!"

"But the Aegis was not invulnerable, master builder," the duke replied in a pained whisper. "No payment is due."

"*Not* invulnerable?" Matello demanded incredulously.

"Why, no . . . as is attested by your presence here. . . ." The duke smiled faintly. Then he uttered a sigh.

His head suddenly lolled.

"He took poison," the girl told them. "It takes a few minutes to work."

Matello grabbed the duke's head by the hair and turned it so as to lift an eyelid with his thumb. Then, with a grunt, he let it drop.

"Well that's that. Don't worry, Flammarion, there's plenty of stuff here. I'll see you get your reward."

Flammarion's response was dolorous and labored. "But the logic of his argument is inescapable," he droned. "To collect payment, I must first force access to the Aegis; yet once that is done the terms of the contract are broken. How completely the old duke tricked me! I can accept no fee."

"What are you worried about? Take what you want anyway."

"No. The ethic of my craft will not permit sharp practice. What an ill day it was when I ventured into Maralia! I have labored in vain!"

"Well, it probably won't make any difference," Baron Matello muttered to the others as Flammarion shuffled despondently away. "The way things look, we'll all have to spend the rest of our lives here."

Chapter FIFTEEN

As the months passed, the atmosphere within the Aegis sank into gloom. Outside, the Kerek were encamped in force. A constant barrage of ballista missiles, cannon balls and sticky fire was hurled against the sloping walls of the fortress. Galleys sailed overhead and dropped immense stones from great heights. None of this was felt or even heard within the adamant casing, however. Once the original exultation of victory and escape was over, the Aegis's all-pervading reservoir of silence, of cloying degeneracy, took over.

King Lutheron made some effort to prevent this. He tried to keep his own people apart from the Duke of Koss's followers as much as possible and forbade most of the pleasures the fortress offered, tearing apart the intricate bordellos, destroying extensive apartments whose weird artistic purpose offended him, and spoiling the dream-slime by mixing acid in it. But nothing, not even the regular military drill he insisted on, seemed able to halt the slow, steady slide into listlessness.

It could not even be said that the whole of the Aegis had fallen into his possession. When Rachad attempted to lead a party through the inner maze, it was to find that he no longer knew the way. Amschel had rearranged the labyrinth, rendering his number code useless and prompting him to retreat hastily, afraid of becoming lost or possibly trapped. He had refused to venture into it again despite Matello's gibes.

When he could be avoided Matello who, nominally Duke of Koss now, had taken to prowling the Aegis in a fury of pent-up energy, lashing out angrily with his tongue, and sometimes his fists, at anyone he met. Rachad, who himself was utterly appalled by the way events had turned out, did not see how the baron would be able to endure his imprisonment, even in so capacious a refuge as the Aegis. He feared that he would do something foolish, such as open up the Aegis again so as to go down in a blaze of glory.

He had spoken to Zhorga about the dismal prospects for them all. The former merchant airman had stuck out his lower lip glumly.

"We've got two choices: either to stay here or take our chances with the Kerek," he had said. "They'll be crawling all over Maralia by now—and I reckon it won't be long either before they get to Earth."

One night, as Rachad lay in his private room, restlessly trying to sleep, the door opened slowly, and someone entered.

Rachad quit his bed and raised the wick of the night lamp. The intruder closed the door behind him and stared solemnly at Rachad.

"Wolo!" Rachad exclaimed in surprise. It was one of Amschel's assistants, clad in a plain blue robe. Wolo nodded his head in greeting.

"The master has sent me to take you to him," he said calmly. "Kindly get dressed, and come with me."

Rachad felt an acute embarrassment. "Why does he want me? He knows? . . ."

"That you opened the Aegis to the duke's enemies? Yes . . . but the fastness of the Aegis is not, after all, Master Amschel's concern. His work nears culmination. He reminds you of his promise."

"Promise?"

"He made a bargain with you."

"Oh. Yes." A note of suspicious belligerency entered Rachad's voice. "Well, what if I refuse to come with you?"

Wolo lowered his head, as if understanding something. "I see. . . . Then I will bid you good night, Master Rachad. I will inform the master that you have no interest in the Stone of the Philosophers."

"Wait!" Rachad said as the other turned to go. "I'll come."

Quickly he dressed. Having come this far in pursuit of Gebeth's goal, he might as well see the business through, he thought. At least it would provide a temporary diversion in what promised to be a lifetime of tedium.

Wolo led him calmly and confidently toward the maze. The Aegis seemed to be sleeping. Once they heard the sound of carousing, as some of Matello's troops, in defiance of King Lutheron's orders, disported with the Duke of Koss's former courtesans. Then they were in the maze, and a distracted look came over Wolo as he repeated the sequence of numbers he had learned, guiding Rachad through into the dim wood.

In the laboratory, Amschel was waiting, wearing a colorful smock on which were woven patterns of star clusters. He sat at a table on which lay *The Root of Transformations*, the two halves bound together now in lead covers. Beside it was a thick pile of loose papers.

"Good evening, Rachad," he greeted genially. "Your intrusion into our lives was not, it seems, entirely from honest motives."

Rachad reddened, and felt sufficiently stung to retort angrily. "What I said was true—I *did* come to Maralia to obtain the secret of the Stone, though originally I had expected to look no farther than Mars. As for the other thing—yes, I admit it. Baron Matello sent me in here, to open the Aegis and unseat the duke. And for good reason!" Rachad's voice became more heated. "Don't you know what's going on outside? Humanity is being invaded! Koss's estates could have helped in the war—but now it's too late!"

"Oh, I am aware of what is happening," Amschel said quietly. "Did I not tell you that I am a much-traveled man? At a time when Matello and his ilk took cognizance only of their own private quarrels, I already knew how scant mankind's chances were of prevailing against the Kerek."

"And so you hid yourself in here and studied philosophy!" Rachad accused. "Why didn't you invent new alchemical weapons to fight the Kerek, instead? That's all alchemy is good for anyway, Baron Matello says."

"Weapons alone will not prevail. The Kerek are too numerous, too ferocious, too resourceful. They will swallow Maralia, then Wenchlas, as they have swallowed others. As they go their numbers increase by reason of their control over captured populations. A large part of the galaxy, if not all the galaxy, may one day comprise the Kerek empire."

"How readily you seem to accept it," Rachad muttered.

"I fight the Kerek in my own way," Amschel told him. "At last I have made *azoth*. I have impregnated it with all five elements in equal measure. Now only the last two operations remain to be performed: reduction to *prima materia*, and the creation from that of the Stone. I believe I now have sufficient information to carry these operations through to completion." He gestured to the book and file on the table. "There is *The Root of Transformations*, together with a set of my explanatory notes. Together they form an extremely valuable *corpus* of knowledge. You may take them, in fulfillment of my promise."

"Why are you giving them to me now? Why not *after* you have made the Stone?"

"Immense energies are involved in the final operation," Amschel explained. "The process could go wrong, the laboratory could be destroyed. Then this knowledge would also be destroyed."

"I see. . . . But how will the Stone help you fight the Kerek? Is it some sort of weapon, then?"

Amschel smiled. "No, the Stone is not a weapon. The true secret of Kerek strength is not, in fact, in their fighting ability but in the factor known as the Kerek Power. I have visited a Kerek planet, and I have seen how this power works. It is a mental force that takes command of cogitation. When under the Kerek Power a man's thoughts are not his own—they are given him by the Power, and he is unable to generate thoughts from his own consciousness. This force is such that the human mind is unable to withstand it, and that is why the galaxy may, in time, be dominated by a single mentality, a single thought."

He paused before continuing. "But a man who possesses the Philosopher's Stone is proof against the Kerek Power. His thoughts are his own, his consciousness is complete and invulnerable. He can rotate the elements, he can expand his consciousness into the macrocosm." Amschel shrugged, spreading his hands. "Perhaps, with Hermetic art, I could indeed do much to help combat the Kerek. I could create armies of semi-beings. Armed with the Stone, perhaps I could even turn Ouroborous, the great serpent of nature, against them. But still they might be victorious, and then we would have lost forever, with no man free of the Kerek Power. No, I must think centuries ahead. I shall be subtle. I shall train adepts. I shall formulate simpler paths to the Stone, paths requiring but rudimentary apparatus so that the great work may be carried out in secret. Only in this way can I ensure that others besides myself remain free of the Kerek Power—for it is a law that only he who himself prepares the Stone may possess it. A secret brotherhood of those not subject to mental slavery will come into being, albeit that the whole galaxy lies under the Kerek Power."

"Is *this* the reason for your work?" Rachad asked.

"I sought the Stone for its own sake. But to save mankind—that, certainly, has increased the urgency."

"And the duke—was it also his aim?" Rachad continued, thinking that perhaps he had wronged the haughty aesthete.

Amschel snorted softly. "The duke? No. His interests always began and ended in himself."

Again Amschel indicated the documents on the table. "Take these, then. Wolo will take you back through the maze and stay with you. After three days you may return."

Reluctantly Rachad picked up the volumes. "You talk of what you will do—yet none of us can even leave the Aegis!"

"As to that, we shall see."

Wolo beckoned him. Rachad followed, then turned back to Amschel. "If Master Gebeth were to study these, could *he* make the Stone?"

"I think not, from what you have told me. For one thing, he would not be able to duplicate my equipment."

"It saddens me to think that his search was hopeless from the start."

"Nothing is ever completely hopeless," Amschel said.

According to tradition there were three methods of attaining the Hermetic goal. The first was the slow method, in which the subject had to be enclosed in a sealed vessel and heated over a period of years. The second method, conducted in an open crucible, was quicker but more dangerous. And finally there was the instant or lightning method, about which tradition said very little except that the adept had first to master forces of a colossal order and that therefore it was the most dangerous of all.

The lightning method was the path Amschel had adopted. Once his assistants had helped him to make the final preparations he had sent them away for their own safety, through the inner maze to seek the protection of King Lutheron. He was now alone in the laboratory, ready to put the instructions embodied in *The Root of Transformations* to the test.

The infusorators, along with the accumulators and giant capacitors that accompanied them, had all been raised to their highest possible pitch; they could scarcely contain their pent-up energy. The great cucurbit Amschel had chosen to be the scene of the drama hummed loudly on low charge, the ten-foot globe's interior almost enmeshed in the iron and silver arrays that were designed to deliver precise patterns of etheric heat into the transmutation area.

The load of *azoth*, impregnated with all the elements it lacked as *primus agens* so that it was dominated by none, had already been introduced into the vessel. It floated in the globe's center, swirling slowly, suspended by magnetic emanations from the surrounding galvanic coils.

All that day Amschel had spent preparing himself for the ultimate moment, practicing meditation so as to clear his mind. He checked all connections for one last time, then pulled the master lever that, all at once, enlivened the apparatus within the cucurbit.

A haze of golden light filled the glass vessel. The floating ball of *azoth* seethed. It seemed to go through a multitude of color changes almost too fast for the eye to follow. Amschel put his hand to his eyes to shield them from the glare. Peering through his fingers, through the now white-hot grids and coils, he tried to watch what happened in the center of the cucurbit.

It took about a minute for the transformation to take place. And with every second of that passing minute, Amschel's joy and wonderment increased. How easy it all seemed, how flawless the art, when everything went according to exact knowledge! The most crucial secret, he now saw, was not in ever-increasing power, as he had once thought, but in the preparation—in *azoth*, that marvelous and unique substance, in exact and careful balancing, in the perfect measure with which the subject was slowly evolved, by process after process. No wonder lifetimes had been vainly spent attempting to perfect this subject!

Swirling, raving, boiling, the subject became a gas, a plasma, then solid, then liquid again, each of the five elements predominating in turn as the hypostatic principles governing them fought furiously, locked in a death battle destined to end with their disappearance in the merging of opposites. Again a procession of color changes, ending in *nigredo*—the blackest black.

So far everything was as predicted. And now the miracle happened. The subject became nebulous, seemed to expand and at the same time to sink in on itself, as though subsiding in a direction not contained within the cucurbit. The final sign appeared: and Amschel knew that the subject had reduced itself to *prima materia*.

This sign was described by the book in most curious language, but Amschel at once recognized it. At one moment the sample of *prima materia* seemed to be a roiling black cloud, at another a mass of obsidian, at yet another there seemed to be nothing there at all—just darkness. This, Amschel understood, was because *hyle* could not be seen by the eye. It was formless; it was primordial chaos—not the chaos of form in confusion, but the chaos that had existed before form ever was. It was the original substance of the world as it had been before separating into space, time, the elements, life—it was the One that had become many. It was *nigredo*, a black hole, an empty plenum.

If left alone it would dissolve and vanish into the *hylic* substratum that some said underlay the phenomenal world, or, if there were no such substratum (*The Root of Transformations* was vague on this point) it would degenerate back into a compound of elements. The final operation, to further transform this fused mass into the Stone, had therefore to be carried out without delay.

Amschel trembled as he pulled a series of levers. There was a loud sizzling and crackling as all the infusorators, including many he had kept standing by, poured their total energy into one vast capacitor he had erected in an adjoining chamber—filling nearly the whole of the chamber. When he knew from the quality of sound that there was not one trickle of infusoration left to be gained, he pulled the final lever.

In one colossal bang, the capacitor discharged its entire load, sending it flooding through the thick bars of solid iron laid across the floor and into the cucurbit, there to leap from an arrangement of sturdy black grids that had not been used hitherto. The resultant explosion flung Amschel across the laboratory. The flash blinded him.

The bang deafened him. He felt as though he were being burned alive.

He regained full possession of his senses to see that the chamber was wrecked. The bars of iron had fused and melted. Of the cucurbit, scarcely anything was left. There was a strong stench in the air, a stench he knew well from previous infusoratory disasters.

His clothing was charred. And when he tried to move, he discovered that the flesh beneath, too, was blistered and seared. Every inch of the front part of his head, limbs and body—the part that had faced the cucurbit—blazed with agony.

He knew that he was lucky to be alive. Ruefully he recalled the other precondition for attempting the lightning method—that the adept must have a nearly indestructible body. Even so, the damage was not so great that it could not be attributed solely to the release of electric fluid. The greater forces locked in the *prima materia* had evidently not gotten out of control.

He hobbled over to the shattered remnants of smoking metal and molten glass, stirring through the mess with his shoe and kicking aside fragments.

He was not long in finding it, even though it was coated lightly with a white ash which dropped away when he picked it up, leaving it clean and unmarked.

In color it was pale green, slightly translucent, like jade. Despite the intense heat it had undergone it was cool, smooth to the touch but with an odd smoothness so that the fingers were not quite sure they had touched anything.

Amschel was vibrant with anticipation as he carried the reward of his labors into the next chamber for evaluation. His injuries almost forgotten, he placed it on a table and sat down.

Through a magnifying glass he could detect no blemish on the perfectly spherical surface, or beneath it. Laying down the lens, he proceeded to the specified tests. He imagined the sphere to be a cube, and projected the thought. Instantly it was a cube, the sides perfect planes, the edges straight and square-set. Likewise he transformed it, by thought, into a double-ended cone, a tetrahedron, a torus, a statuette of the goddess Demeter.

He nodded, letting it revert back to a sphere. The test of amorphism was satisfied. The stone had no intrinsic shape. Next he took up a sharp saw-bladed knife and set himself to carve off a portion of it. Although of gem-like hardness in the hand, the stone offered little resistance to the blade, and he sliced off a piece of about an inch in thickness.

The severed portion hit the tabletop, but no longer as the jade-like substance of the stone. It had instantly decomposed into a scintillant red powder.

Amschel well understood this. Divorced from the fundamental unity of the stone, the fragment could not maintain itself and had begun to decay into merely normal states of matter. Already it was compound, partly elemental.

With this powder marvels could be performed. Compounded further, introduced into other substances, it would create a whole new range of efficacious agents.

More important, however, was that when pared the stone had immediately reconstituted itself. It was as if the knife had done no more than slice through water.

The test of wholeness and indivisibility was satisfied.

Amschel lifted the pale green ball and stared straight into its heart. This, then, was the Stone. This was the Tincture, the Most Excellent Medicine, the secret substance of the universe, wrenched out of the *hylic* realm by a blast of man-made lightning. Gazing upon this wonder, Amschel experienced a supreme joy and exultation. Now he *knew* that the Hermetic art was real, that the vision of Zosimos was true, that nature applied to nature transforms nature!

This much proved, it remained but to verify one more property of the stone—a little-known property conveyed cryptically, elliptically, in the alchemical code word V.I.T.R.I.O.L.: *Visita Interiora Terrae, Rectificando Invenies Occultum Lapidem*—"Visit the Interior of the Earth, Through Purification Thou Wilt Find the Hidden Stone."

Few indeed knew that this formula indicated how the adept may be transformed into a Magus of Power. The earth symbolized the adept's own body, the place where the Stone could be hidden away from the sight of ordinary man. Amschel moved the Stone. He pressed it to his forehead, between his eyes—and pushed. The Stone moved—inward, passing through skin and bone.

Into Amschel's brain

In the Philosopher's Stone was no differentiation of parts. The Stone was Ultimate Oneness. Immersed in the Stone, the tissues of Amschel's brain experienced transcendental unity, total access—to one another, and, eventually, to the macrocosm itself.

Amschel's consciousness was whipped away from the narrow laboratory where he sat. It expanded and expanded, until he seemed to be moving through an endless dark, a dark that was paradoxically filled with light.

The Black Light of the adepts, by which one saw without seeing. Vastness, vastness. And now Amschel perceived the macrocosm.

It was not a place, or region. It was the infinite world system seen from the point of view of totality, endless movement without destination, coming without arriving, going without departing. Man's reason, evolved in the microcosm, could not grasp the essence of the macrocosm. Even when super-conscious as Amschel's was, the mind could see it only in terms of entities, signs and symbols, the ancient eternal symbols of alchemy. The mighty Worm Ouroborous, appearing as a vast ring galaxy larger than milliards of galaxies put together, spinning at colossal speed, endlessly devouring and re-evolving itself—thus was the macrocosm maintained! The alchemical marriage of King and Queen, conjunction of opposites by which the eternal mystery of merging and separating was brought to pass.

These and other visions of macrocosmic processes blasted into Amschel's consciousness with such a sense of super-reality that the myriads of worlds flowing away from them seemed mere shadows. Then the direction of his gaze became more specific. He witnessed, as if it lay below him in some multidimensional region so that he saw it from countless vantage points at once—from north, south, east, west, nadir and zenith, externally and internally—the staggering spiral blaze of his own galaxy. He saw, slumbering coiled like a quiescent serpent within the spiraling star arms, the power known as the Sleeping Sulphur, and he saw that this power could, if one knew how, be prodded and disturbed, even, momentarily, awakened.

But he saw, too, that the struggle between man and Kerek, between self-determined consciousness and hypnotized slavery, was of no consequence to nature. It had no place in the macrocosm.

But Amschel did have a place. He was a Magus of Power. He could rotate the elements, converting one substance into another. He could rotate space and time, projecting himself to distant places. He was not governed by number: he could project himself into several different locations at once, unlimited by a single body.

He could, if he chose, disturb the Sleeping Sulphur.

With an effort, Amschel scaled his mind down from the Great World that was not available to him. He was back in the microcosm, sitting in his adamant-lined chamber, the burns on his body beginning to heal.

He had discounted the use of purely physical powers to achieve his long-term mission, but that did not preclude their deployment in a more limited sense, at this juncture, anyway. He must, he decided, arrange some means for his helpers to escape their adamant prison.

Also, he must cover his tracks.

Four days passed before Wolo could be prevailed upon to lead Rachad and Baron Matello back into the laboratory. The other assistants had come out two days before, but had said little.

As soon as the trio entered the dismal wood, a strong smell of burning reached their nostrils. When they passed through the door of the laboratory, it was to find a spectacle of devastation.

From the look of it a tremendous explosion had spread through the network of chambers, wrecking and charring everything that was not adamant. A penetrating stink, arising from numerous volatile substances, permeated the air; underfoot the floor was slippery with some foam-like stuff—the result, most likely, of the spilling of reactive chemicals.

Wolo moaned, then began to run, slipping and sliding in the mess. Pressing kerchiefs to their faces to ward off the acerbic vapors, Matello and Rachad followed, coming after a few minutes to the infusoratory laboratory where Amschel had sited the great cucurbit for the completion of the work.

Here, evidently the center of the explosion, the destruction was even more complete. With an expression of woe, Wolo looked on an almost empty chamber, practically its whole content being fused into one messy coagulation.

The baron looked about him sourly. "So Amschel's great experiment was very much a failure after all. Lucky for you he sent you away, or you'd have ended up as dead as he is."

"But where's the body?" Rachad said.

"Blown to shreds, and the shreds burned to smoke, I imagine. What's left of him will be soot, and you're treading that underfoot. Come along, let's get back. Later you can sort through all this and see if you can find anything useful."

"I can hardly believe it," Wolo intoned emptily. "Years of work—all for nothing!"

"Oh, an alchemist thrives on lost labor!" Matello retorted jovially. He strode from the chamber, Rachad and Wolo trailing reluctantly after him.

Rachad's heart was heavy as they retraced their steps through the maze. He had not expected this outcome, and it made him feel somber and shaken. In a way it seemed to dash any last vestige of hope—for the Hermetic goal, for the future of mankind, or indeed for his own future.

He no longer believed in the Stone, he told himself. It was all fantasy, and Amschel's exaggerated claims for it were the dodderings of an old fool. Matello had the right idea: he was a rude realist, unswayed by fanciful notions.

Back in his headquarters, news was waiting for Baron Matello that something unusual was happening outside on the plain. He hurried to the observation post and peered through the eyepiece that, by means of lenses and mirrors, brought a view seen from a narrow slit high in the adamant wall of the Aegis.

On the sloping ground before the Aegis, the Kerek were encamped in force. But now something was astir in the riotous sprawl of tall tents and grounded galleys.

The bombards and catapult guns were abandoned. Men and Kerek rushed to and fro in apparent panic, jostling together. Galleys were hastily taking off, both human and alien forms clinging to their sides and sometimes falling away as they ascended raggedly into the sky.

A ruddy, wavering light illuminated the scene. This in itself was not so unusual—the planet's sun burned sometimes white, sometimes red, sometimes both together in a fiery, whirling manner. The light was, however, much brighter than normally.

Was this what had caused the Kerek to take fright? Intrigued and excited, Matello continued to watch, until the glare increased so much that he snatched himself away from the eyepiece with a cry, holding his streaming eye.

A visible cone of light came from the lens. Curtly Matello gave the order for the observation slit to be closed up.

They all sat huddled blindly in the adamant shell, waiting and wondering.

The star which the Aegis circled had never been particularly stable, though human memory could not, of course, know that. Ever since mining had begun on the planet, the sun's temperature had never varied by more than a degree, and its unsteady appearance, the disk writhing and whirling like a flame, had generally been taken to betoken no more than an unusually mobile photosphere.

With the violent etheric storm that was now sweeping through the southern part of Maralia, however, the depths of the star became disturbed. The photosphere began to flash and boil, blasting out in fantastic storms as extra energy poured from the core. The amount of radiation it sent winging through the ether increased, erratically but substantially.

The effect on the small mining planet, the only one of three to be inhabited, was to scorch and bake it unmercifully. The atmosphere expanded, became unbreathably hot and thin. The landscape was pounded by furious red and white light, by great waves of searing heat. The mining towns burned like paper in a furnace, the Kerek camps burned, their ships burned as they vainly tried to claw through the sky. Only a few survived, those who were quick enough to seek refuge in the deepest mines.

For a week the solar storm continued. On the whole planet, one place was safe—the Aegis. Slits and flues tightly closed, the fortress remained cool, unaffected by the drenching energy that poured futilely onto its adamant exterior, for fire and ether could not penetrate those walls of pure earth. For several months the denizens skulked within, not daring even to open an observation slit for fear of what might come pouring through it.

Outside, meanwhile, the sun quieted and the planet

gradually cooled, like a ball of clay that was taken out of an oven. Eventually those within the Aegis peered out. More cautiously, they ventured out, finding a world even deader than it had been before.

Further empty months passed. And then a military starship bearing a Maralian standard sailed over the mountain range and set down before the Aegis. At first Matello and the king were suspicious. It had puzzled them when no Kerek arrived to replace their brothers annihilated by the wild sun, and they suspected trickery. But at length a party from the ship was admitted, led by the young Baron Rodrigeur, whom Matello had met briefly once and thought he recognized.

Rodrigeur, though barely above twenty years of age, was capable and self-confident, and already hardened by war. In the king's own quarters he told an incredible but heartening tale of a series of ether storms more violent and widespread than anything previously known, dashing the Kerek fleets to pieces before they could effect a proper occupation of their latest conquest. In the respite, Maralia had rallied. And though the struggle still went on, the cause was no longer regarded as completely hopeless.

Those present listened in amazement. "A miraculous delivery!" King Lutheron breathed.

Rodrigeur turned to him apologetically. "Your brother Murdon currently reigns in your place, Your Majesty," he said. "Everyone had thought you dead, until it was remembered that the Duke of Koss's Aegis lies close to where the first battle took place and it was suggested you might have taken refuge here. I was dispatched to investigate, as soon as could be managed."

"And where is the seat of government?" Lutheron asked sternly.

"At Myrmidia, liege-lord. All the western part of the kingdom lies in Kerek hands."

"But not for long!" Matello blazed. "We have half a chance of victory, you say? A quarter of a chance is good enough for me! Let's be away from here, liege-lord, and into the fray!"

"Steady, Sir Goth," King Lutheron murmured. "First, we travel to Myrmidia. It will be interesting to see how my brother takes the news of my continuing good health. . . ."

Chapter SIXTEEN

Captain Zebandar Zhorga, his armor clinking, scrambled down into the shallow dugout where the field surgeon had just finished stitching up the wounded trooper. The injured man lay on the bare dirt, heavily dosed with laudanum. His leather jerkin had been cut away and his tunic ripped open; bloodstained bandages were about his middle.

"How is he?" Zhorga demanded.

The surgeon shrugged as he packed away his instruments. He did not speak until he was able to turn away from the barely conscious soldier.

"What do you expect?" he muttered. "He'll be dead before sunrise."

Zhorga nodded, feeling very, very sad. The injured trooper was Rachad Caban.

He looked up over the rim of the dugout, at the drooping violet trees that perpetually dripped moisture into the marshes. It was this accursed world that did it. Elsewhere Rachad might have stood a good chance of recovering from his injuries. Here wounds turned septic almost immediately, producing a rotting gangrene and death within hours.

Previously the planet had been uninhabited, but the Kerek appreciated its strategic value and had moved in to begin converting its atmosphere. That could not be allowed, with the war swaying back and forth across Maralia the way it was, and King Murdon had sent in Baron Matello at the head of a large force—as punishment, perhaps, for his formerly stubborn allegiance to the disgraced and imprisoned Lutheron—to prevent it.

"Ah, Rachad, you've come a long way with me," Zhorga muttered, staring down at the pale, blank face with its enlarged pupils. "What a pity you have to turn in your ticket now."

It was one of those flying sickles that had sliced the young man open. Zhorga wondered if it might be kinder if he were to finish the job now. But instead he turned and clambered up the walls of soft red earth and made his way back to what he had been doing when he heard of the incident—supervising the placing of a great bombard to assail Kerek positions.

For about an hour Rachad drifted into a dreamless sleep. When he awoke, his whole body seemed to be burning.

Blurrily he saw someone come softly down into the dugout and lean over him. His vision cleared somewhat, and he gasped as he recognized a small, slightly monkey-like face, with quiet brown eyes and silky hair.

For a moment he could not speak. He stuttered.

"Master Amschel!"

The alchemist wore light leather armor and a brief, almost superfluous iron helmet. He ran his eyes over Rachad, as if inspecting him, then reached inside his leather hauberk, producing a small phial.

"You're supposed to be dead!" Rachad protested. "How did you escape from the laboratory—the explosion?"

Amschel ignored the question. "You are dying, my friend," he said in a dry tone. "Drink this excellent medicine, the true elixir. It will vivify your body, throwing off disease, hastening the healing of even the deepest wounds."

He must have fled the laboratory in advance of the explosion, Rachad reasoned hazily. He must have hidden somewhere, eventually contriving to leave the Aegis along with the rest of them. But what was he doing in Matello's army?

Amschel put the neck of the phial to his lips. A thick liquid poured out.

Rachad became immediately absorbed by a taste that was like a golden glow, so vivid he seemed almost to see it. The medicine trickled down his throat with a gentle burning, like the finest liqueur, and as it reached his stomach he felt golden drops of liquid radiance spreading through his body, giving him a feeling of lightness and vigor.

"That's.... wonderful," he whispered.

Amschel smiled. "It has even been known to revive men thought dead. But I see you have changed your occupation from that of laboratory assistant to that of soldier. Are you no longer seeking the Stone? What did you do with the book I gave you?"

"I left it in the Aegis, Master Amschel. After what happened I decided its information was too dangerous."

"I see." Amschel seemed to reflect. "The Stone can make you proof against the Kerek Power—have you not considered that? It could be important, in the times that lie ahead."

"But we are already holding our own against the Kerek!" Rachad boasted. "The tide has turned—Zhorga says we will have driven them out of Maralia altogether in a few years."

Amschel smiled. "Perhaps—but for how long? This is only one of the Kerek's present theaters of conquest. If they fail with Maralia they will simply, in a few years, transfer even greater forces from elsewhere."

"Perhaps *we* will have greater forces by then," Rachad said defiantly.

Amschel nodded. "Well, I must be on my way. Rest now. I think you may feel much better in a day or two."

"Wait!" called Rachad as he saw Amschel disappearing over the lip of the dugout. He struggled up and, holding his middle with one arm, crawled up after him—an exercise that only minutes before he would have found impossible.

Ahead, he saw the dismal landscape that covered most of the planet: great flat mist-covered marshes, interspersed with hillocks and ridges of firmer ground, out of which grew drooping violet trees.

Amschel's stooped figure was picking its way along one of these ridges. It was then that the Kerek sally came, as it did every hour or so. This time it was not a flock of flying sickles or disks, but a brief barrage of bombard shot. Rachad uttered a loud cry, the exertion tearing painfully at his stitches, as a ball exploded near the alchemist.

Even from where he lay, he could see that Amschel was practically ripped apart. Like a rag doll the alchemist's body, whether living or dead, was flung off the causeway-like ridge. Rachad crawled toward the spot, careless of any hurt to himself now, but already Amschel's remains were sinking into the wet bog, disappearing with a slurping, gurgling sound while Rachad looked on with horror.

He closed his eyes, overcome with nausea. War, he thought. This was what war meant.

Eventually he opened his eyes again and began to crawl back to his only shelter, the dugout. He had to admit that considering his injuries it was amazing how well he felt. The medicine Amschel had given him seemed to be glowing in every vein.

Was it really the true elixir, as Amschel had called it, or was that by way of being an apothecary's exaggeration?

Seeing Amschel again had put a different complexion on everything. Had what had seemed a dreadful accident in the infusoratory laboratory been misinterpreted? Had Amschel, in spite of such destruction—perhaps by means of such destruction—*actually produced the Stone?*

The question was already academic. The Stone, if indeed Amschel had possessed it, was at this moment accompanying him to the bottom of the marsh.

With a grunt and a sigh Rachad rolled into the dugout, where he fell once again into a deep sleep.

Olam was a quiet place these days. With the sea trade taking so much of commerce, with flying ships being grounded one by one for lack of silk, the time had come when the whine of ether whistle, or the billowing of blue sail over the rooftops, was unusual enough to make the townspeople stand and gaze nostalgically, knowing that before long such visions would be gone forever.

The Street of the Alchemists had also sunk into quietude as the town's fortunes declined, and fewer and fewer feet trod its sand-covered way. Master Gebeth was therefore surprised, late one winter evening, to hear a knock on his door. He opened it to see a small man, wearing a brown woollen cloak, and who addressed him by name in an accent he could not place.

The stranger introduced himself as a fellow practitioner, adding that he had been given Gebeth's address while living in foreign parts, and said that he would be glad to discuss the Spagyric art with one who had also sought the universal medicine. Gebeth, who had come to accept his loneliness along with his failure, nevertheless invited the fellow into his living room, and for an hour or so they conversed.

The visitor spoke with a strange confidence, as though the Hermetic goal were attained fact rather than something much sought after, and Gebeth, who knew all too well the difficulties involved, grew irritated with what he took to be a pretended knowledge. He asked his guest if he could tell him what was the *menstruum*, or solvent by which the mineral spirit could be extracted from metals. The other replied, with a smile, that it was a heavenly salt known only to the wise, an answer that Gebeth could as well have given himself.

Suddenly the despondency he had felt for so long surfaced, and he threw up his hands. "What's the use of talking?" he declared. "You are wasting your time here. I no longer believe in the transmutation of metals."

He lowered his head while the other stared at him with some seriousness. In a low voice he unburdened himself further. "A year ago I ceased all alchemical strivings. The Philosopher's Stone is but a figment. Only fools and charlatans speak of it."

There was silence for a while. Gebeth stared at the floor. It was not just the disappointment, the never-ended failure, that had brought on his despair. There was also guilt. He could not forget young Rachad Caban, whom years ago he had allowed to embark on a mad adventure. The *Wandering Queen* had not been heard of to this day. It was certain that she had come to grief in the trackless wastes of space.

The stranger's expression grew stern, and he spoke insistently, but softly. "You do not believe in the Stone of the Philosophers? In the Tincture that perfects metals, and that transforms man? Your experiences must have been disheartening indeed."

With careful movements he reached into his jerkin and pulled out a small box of carved ivory about the size of a snuffbox. From this he took out a yet smaller box folded from waxed paper, which he opened out and laid on the flat of his hand.

Gebeth bent to inspect its contents: a sparkling red powder. For long moments he stared at this powder, which was not like any substance he had seen before. It scintillated with a life of its own, as if light were ceaselessly emerging and dissolving within it. It defied the eyes; one seemed to be looking at the jostling lights of a distant gorgeous city.

"All I require," his guest said firmly, "is a crucible, a fire, and half a pound of lead."

Gebeth looked up into the face, with its steady brown

eyes and frame of silky hair, of his mysterious visitor. He blinked, not knowing what to say.

Then he nodded, rose, and led the way into his back room. It took but a little time to kindle a fire. Gebeth worked the bellows until the furnace roared, then set a crucible over the heat, putting a slab of lead into it as he was directed. Silently they waited, while the lead slowly melted, and at last was a gleaming pool.

His visitor produced a knife, and took up but a pinch of the powder on its tip, then scattered it over the molten mass.

The lead seethed and flashed with indescribable colors as the powder sank into it, while Amschel stirred it with an iron rod. "See now the victory of True Philosophy . . ." he murmured. He ceased to stir. Gebeth gasped, and his heart leaped. In the crucible the metal had stilled. Before his eyes it had all been converted into resplendent shining gold. . . .

Recommended for Star Warriors!

The Daedalus Novels of Brian M. Stableford

- [ ] **THE FLORIANS** (#UY1255—$1.25)
- [ ] **CRITICAL THRESHOLD** (#UY1282—$1.25)
- [ ] **WILDEBLOOD'S EMPIRE** (#UW1331—$1.50)
- [ ] **THE CITY OF THE SUN** (#UW1377—$1.50)

The Dorsai Novels of Gordon R. Dickson

- [ ] **DORSAI!** (#UE1342—$1.75)
- [ ] **SOLDIER, ASK NOT** (#UE1339—$1.75)
- [ ] **TACTICS OF MISTAKE** (#UW1279—$1.50)
- [ ] **NECROMANCER** (#UE1353—$1.75)

The Dumarest of Terra Novels of E.C. Tubb

- [ ] **JACK OF SWORDS** (#UY1239—$1.25)
- [ ] **SPECTRUM OF A FORGOTTEN SUN** (#UY1265—$1.25)
- [ ] **HAVEN OF DARKNESS** (#UY1299—$1.25)
- [ ] **PRISON OF NIGHT** (#UW1364—$1.50)

DAW BOOKS are represented by the publishers of Signet and Mentor Books, THE NEW AMERICAN LIBRARY, INC.

THE NEW AMERICAN LIBRARY, INC.,
P.O. Box 999, Bergenfield, New Jersey 07621

Please send me the DAW BOOKS I have checked above. I am enclosing
$_____(check or money order—no currency or C.O.D.'s).
Please include the list price plus 35¢ per copy to cover mailing costs.

Name_____

Address_____

City_____State_____Zip Code_____

Please allow at least 4 weeks for delivery